D0309635

Grandmother's Footsteps

By the same author

FICTION
Promises Past
Martha's Ark
My Sister, Victoria

NON-FICTION
George and Sam: Autism in the Family

FOR CHILDREN
Who Was Florence Nightingale?
Who Was Elizabeth I?
Who Was William the Conqueror?

Grandmother's Footsteps

CHARLOTTE MOORE

VIKING
an imprint of
PENGUIN BOOKS

MORAY COUNCIL LIBRARIES & INFO.SERVICES	
20 23 85 89	
Askews	
F	

VIKING

Published by the Penguin Group

Penguin Books Ltd, 80 Strand, London WC2R 0RL, England

Penguin Group (USA) Inc., 375 Hudson Street, New York, New York 10014, USA
Penguin Group (Canada), 90 Eglinton Avenue East, Suite 700, Toronto, Ontario, Canada M4P 2Y3
(a division of Pearson Penguin Canada Inc.)
Penguin Ireland, 25 St Stephen's Green, Dublin 2, Ireland
(a division of Penguin Books Ltd)
Penguin Group (Australia), 250 Camberwell Road, Camberwell, Victoria 3124, Australia
(a division of Pearson Australia Group Pty Ltd)
Penguin Books India Pvt Ltd, 11 Community Centre, Panchsheel Park, New Delhi – 110 017, India
Penguin Group (NZ), 67 Apollo Drive, Rosedale, North Shore 0632, New Zealand
(a division of Pearson New Zealand Ltd)
Penguin Books (South Africa) (Pty) Ltd, 24 Sturdee Avenue, Rosebank, Johannesburg 2196, South Africa

Penguin Books Ltd, Registered Offices: 80 Strand, London WC2R 0RL, England

www.penguin.com

Published in 2008

I

Copyright © Charlotte Moore, 2008

The moral right of the author has been asserted

All rights reserved
Without limiting the rights under copyright
reserved above, no part of this publication may be
reproduced, stored in or introduced into a retrieval system,
or transmitted, in any form or by any means (electronic, mechanical,
photocopying, recording or otherwise), without the prior
written permission of both the copyright owner and
the above publisher of this book

Set in 13.5/16pt Monotype Garamond
Typeset by Rowland Phototypesetting Ltd, Bury St Edmunds, Suffolk
Printed in Great Britain by Clays Ltd, St Ives plc

A CIP catalogue record for this book is available from the British Library

ISBN: 978–0–670–91706–8

www.greenpenguin.co.uk

Mixed Sources
Product group from well-managed
forests and other controlled sources
www.fsc.org Cert no. SA-COC-1592
© 1996 Forest Stewardship Council

FSC

Penguin Books is committed to a sustainable future
for our business, our readers and our planet.
The book in your hands is made from paper
certified by the Forest Stewardship Council.

For Simon

Prologue

The estate agent's brochure had arrived. How strange it made the house look, Verity thought. The wide-angled photographs turned the back lawn into a golf course, the orchard into an arboretum. And when the rooms were listed like that, the place sounded so large! Six beds, three recep., dining room, kitchen, two utility rooms – did they mean the scullery and pantry? Verity's mother had always described Knighton as an overgrown cottage. Evelyn had had a careless, dismissive tone about most things, but certainly when the house was built in the 1880s the impression aimed for was one of rustic simplicity. Everything made by craftsmen out of solid materials; and, yes, thought Verity, it has stood the test of time.

Would she be tempted by this brochure, if she were a buyer? She often ran this kind of conversation in her head, in the absence of anyone else with whom to have it. She leafed through the brochure again, and thought not. The estate agent's vulgarization had a deadening effect for her, but other people wouldn't notice that. Other people liked deadening, because it sanitized things. In this neighbourhood, down every lane, round every corner, there were rural retreats worth the best part of a million, double-fronted, double-glazed, double-garaged, all perfect for families with commuting husbands and more than double their share of this world's goods. And double lives for some of those husbands too, thought Verity. So many marriages were a kind of pact – the wife gets her tennis lessons and her four-wheel drive and her Caribbean holidays in exchange for turning a blind eye. It wouldn't take much tweaking to turn Knighton into just such another warm easy-to-clean playpen. A buyer wouldn't be long in coming.

She noticed that Mortlock Bell had concentrated on exterior shots. They had used only two pictures taken inside: one of the front hall, where the heavy oak staircase and glass boxes of stuffed birds shot by Verity's father created a misleading baronial gloom, the other of the largest bedroom, the one she and Simeon had used until his death, and even then the picture concentrated on the view of the garden and beyond. Mortlock Bell had cleverly avoided the 1970s wallpapers, the ill-fitted kitchen units, the forlorn emptiness of the underused bedrooms. Not that the house was in bad condition. Simeon would never have allowed that to happen. And of course they'd always had help, in the very solid form of Mrs Davidge, and they'd always had enough money. There would have been no excuse not to keep things in reasonable order.

Verity picked up a tray of vases filled with flowers – early pink rosebuds, mainly, their sweetness offset by the limey froth of lady's mantle. She took the tray from one room to another, placing a vase on a dressing table or windowsill in each of them. The rooms reminded her of old dogs. They looked at her with pleading eyes, saying love me, tend to me, even though we both know I'm not truly lovable any more. But, thought Verity, the task of loving is beyond me.

Once it had been her business to nurture the spirit of this place, but events had conspired against her, and she had failed. Now it was time for someone else to try, a new family, a family with a future. They would look at this brochure, glossy as an inflight magazine, and they would say, we could put in a swimming pool here, we could build a pool house where this old shed is, maybe a sauna, too, and they wouldn't know and wouldn't care that the old shed was where Verity's grandmother had housed her pony trap, and where old Apps had stored the apples in untouching rows on slatted shelves, to last the winter through. They would look at the orchard and say, it's an awful lot of upkeep, maybe we could get planning permission to turn it into a building plot and sell it off, and down would come the damsons, the medlars, the mulberries and the greengages; down would come the giant bergamot in the middle that in autumn drops its unusable fruit like rusty teardrops, and in spring sends up a fountain of blossom, foaming, greenish white. Oh well, thought Verity. These things have to happen. Life must go on, and I will resolve not to mind.

Verity had been born at Knighton. She had spent her childhood here, until she was sent to boarding school. In 1970 her mother had moved out, to the cottage in Ewes Green where she had spent the last decade of her life, and Verity had moved back in with Simeon and Hester. That was when they had put up these extraordinary wallpapers – the downstairs lavatory, for instance, was covered in turquoise-and-purple peacock-feather shapes. The wallpapers had been Simeon's choice. He'd grumbled about them, in later years, but somehow the impetus to replace them had never amounted to anything.

Verity had set out all her vases now but one. The last, and prettiest, she saved for Hester's room. Hester was her only child, forty, divorced, and childless. She hadn't consulted her about the sale, hadn't even told her yet. Verity had always shied away from anything revelatory or momentous. She tried to envisage Hester in her smart London flat: one bedroom, one living room, one balcony, and, significantly, no garden. Hester had an extremely good job in radio;

3

Verity could listen to her on air most days of the week, if she wanted to. She had listened to her earlier that day, and had been struck, as so often, by her daughter's quality of intelligent detachment. Her voice was smooth, forceful, yet understated; listening to her was scarcely different from listening to the voice of a stranger. Verity couldn't guess what effect the sale of the house would have on Hester. If she were a different kind of woman – married to a worthy commuting husband and with a brood of happy children – then perhaps the house would have made sense to her. But even then – well, one can have too much of the past.

Years ago, when Simeon had been a commuting husband, though hardly a worthy one, he had struck up an acquaintance with a man on the train. His name was Charles Prosser; he was a wine merchant, and he and his pleasant wife, Gail, had recently bought a cottage on the other side of the valley, where they lived with the Old English Sheepdogs they kept instead of children. The first time Simeon invited them in for drinks was on a summer's evening. They had sat on the terrace and watched the sun dip behind the great bank of lime trees, which were pouring their scent, like clearest honey, into the still air.

Hester sat on the parapet wall, her long brown legs pulled up so that her chin rested on her knees. She was wearing shorts that she'd made by cutting off the legs of jeans that she had outgrown. She had on a cream-coloured cheesecloth shirt, which she had knotted under her small new breasts. Her midriff and her long bony feet were bare.

'It's marvellous up here,' said Charles Prosser, rattling his ice. 'The House with the Golden Windows. That's what Gail and I call this house, because when you look across the valley from our place at this time of the evening it looks as if your windows are on fire.'

4

'Isn't that a fairy story?' asked Verity. '"The House with the Golden Windows"?'

Hester raised her chin from her knees. 'Yes,' she said in her clear voice, cool and unexpected, 'they thought the windows were made of real gold, but when they reached the house, they were disappointed.'

There was a tiny silence. 'The grass is always greener,' said Simeon, lighting one of his unwelcome cigars. 'That kind of story.'

'Well, we're far from disappointed,' put in kindly Gail Prosser. 'It's absolutely beautiful. I'd love to live here.'

Hester buried her chin again. Her straight fair hair fell in stripes over her face. 'Appearances can be deceptive,' she said. Or at least, that's what it sounded like. But it was a mutter, and a muffled mutter at that.

Verity set down the vase of flowers and retreated, closing the door of Hester's room. The house with the golden windows, she thought, remembering. Well, we all make mistakes.

I

1st January 1980

I've never been good at keeping New Year's resolutions. As a child, and a pious child, too, I drew up lists with enthusiasm, but I should think most of the projects had withered up and died by the end of the first week of January. I have no reason to suppose I will do much better now, but today is the first day of a new decade, and I am an old woman. I still have my health, and my mental powers are only a little moth-eaten in places, but I am beginning to feel like a wasp in autumn; the circles I make are shrinking, and I make them more slowly. I feel the need to set my thoughts in order, and there are some things that need to be told. I intend to keep a diary this year, and to use it as a fishing net to trawl the past for whatever still lurks, whether marvellous or monstrous.

Just as I've never kept resolutions, I've never kept to diary writing, beyond scribbled notes to remind me of times of appointments. Every so often I've attempted something more interesting, something that would preserve a moment in time for future contemplation, something that would exercise my writer's craft and explore the thoughts that flicker, flare and die in my mind every moment of every day, but somehow everything I wrote seemed false. Why had I selected that detail and not another? Why was I endeavouring to present myself in a good light to a non-existent reader? Was the reader, after all, non-existent, or was there a danger that my husband, my daughter, my servant, would break in and read things which could not then be gainsaid? And would I even know that such things had indeed been read, if the intruder did not choose to tell me? Their changed opinion of me could be leading them away from me down a path the very existence of which was unknown to me. Keeping a diary, which at first represented a kind of control, an ordering of experience, soon came to seem the very opposite.

My husband, Lionel Conway, kept a diary every day of his life. This record was impersonal to the point of eccentricity. Weather and wind directions were recorded daily, as were important political events, whether they interested him or not. His reaction to such events would be unguessable to the casual reader. He noted his own activities: 'A.M. Caught up with correspondence. P.M. To the Scott Polar Institute. Freckleton gave a talk on the navigation of the Bering Straits. Dined with McVeagh.' There was rarely more than that. The entry for 6th April 1930 reads: 'Evelyn walked with me to Firle Beacon, where she agreed to become my wife. Deo Gratias.' That 'Deo Gratias', the one glowing coal in all that ashy grey, could still have the power to move me to tears, were I to allow it.

It would be rational to assume that such diaries were evidence of a passionless man, a man obsessed with detail, a dry, reductive man who, in modern parlance, couldn't see the wood for the trees. Such assumptions would be quite wrong. Lionel had, at times, been so consumed by passions that he developed strategies for reining them in, or giving vent to them in indirect ways. He was a geologist, but since boyhood he had had a great love of things nautical, and he had had the good fortune to combine these interests in Polar exploration. He was thirty years my senior, and when

8

I met him his career as an explorer was over, though he was still advising younger teams and giving lectures about his experiences. He was a man of extremes, an elemental man, and his diaries reflect none of this. To an outsider the diaries would seem like an exercise in pointlessness, but to me, as to anyone who knew him well, the point of them is easily apparent. They are a system of self-restraint; self-restraint was all that stood between Lionel and mental collapse.

When I agreed to marry Lionel Conway, the Great Man, the hero of the frozen wastes, I took myself by surprise; I, who was thirty-five years old, I, who had made a vow after Jack's death – to myself, not to the God in whom I found I no longer believed – that I would never consider marrying anybody else. Lionel was a widower, and had been for ten years. His marriage had been childless and, I gathered from friends, fraught with difficulty. The great love of his young life had refused to marry him because of religious differences; he had turned to her cousin, who was, I learned, physically similar and spiritually more flexible. This turned out to be a mistake. Isabella Conway was faithless, and one of the lovers she took was a close family friend. Lionel's long absences, his difficult temperament, the lack of children, and the overarching memory of her cousin, Sylvia, the best-beloved, who died of typhoid soon after her final rejection of Lionel, go some way towards explaining Isabella's behaviour, but her choice of lover was unfortunate, exposing Lionel to humiliating gossip and the loss of one of his oldest friends. I hope I was not so tactless.

Lionel never spoke to me directly about any of this. He feared confession of any kind; he saw it as a letting-go. Letting go was dangerous. Metaphorically as well as literally, he ran a tight ship.

When I first met my husband I was, most untypically,

having an affair with a married man. He was a theatre manager with a dazzling wit and an even more dazzling smile. His name was Harry Bramante. I found him spellbinding, and I was not accustomed to being spellbound. Harry could dominate a room without crowding out anybody else. Never, before or since, have I met a man so at ease with his own body. Perhaps that was his Italian blood; certainly I've never come across a comparable quality in an Englishman. His long limbs seemed to glide under his clothes, his hooded eyes offered a world of possibilities. I jumped. His wife and four children hardly entered into it. I never saw them. It was an effort for me even to remember that they existed. This is not a chapter of my emotional history of which I am proud, and neither was it a short chapter. I was nearly thirty when I met Harry Bramante. My first volume of short stories had been published to modest but distinct critical acclaim, and I had nearly completed a novel, which made me feel that I was rather marvellous. I was feeling bold, and restless, and the social life I had established for myself in my twenties had begun to seem stale and tiresome. I was stout-hearted in my resolution never to marry, but I suppose it was unsurprising that, at that age, and in those days when one's chances of marrying would theoretically have been dwindling fast, I should reward myself for my resolve by indulging in an affair like that. The shameful thing is that I gave so little thought to his wife. I don't know if she knew of my existence. I just didn't use my imagination at all, and that's a crime. If Harry and I had been in love with one another . . . well, of course it would still have been wrong. But I wasn't interested in falling in love. I continued the affair for several years, because he charmed and excited me. He never knew me, nor I him.

No man could have borne less resemblance to Harry than

Lionel Conway. Harry was an urban creature, a lover of artifice; in his element among brittle theatrical people. I shouldn't be surprised if Lionel never set foot in a theatre in his life. He disliked large social gatherings, though he enjoyed the company of trusted friends; London he regarded as a necessary evil. He never met Harry, nor knew of his existence except in the vaguest possible terms. Lionel and I met at a dinner given by my publisher, who was one of Lionel's oldest friends and who was bringing out a book of his Polar reminiscences. I remember the sinking feeling I had when I found myself seated next to this mountainous man with his stiff white beard and fierce bright eyes. He was the guest of honour. It was a privilege to be placed beside him, but his dinner jacket was old and not especially clean, he ate his food in unnoticing snatches, and I dreaded that such a man would try to flirt with me. He did no such thing. Despite my sex and relative youth he talked to me on terms of the utmost equality, which I may say in the late 1920s was unusual. When the time came for the women to withdraw, I realized that he had not uttered one polite platitude, nor made one remark that was not direct and challenging and interesting. It intrigued me, too, that a man of his age should seem so uncomfortable with himself. I had not thought much about old age – and sixty and more seemed most certainly old, which is an opinion I no longer hold – but I had, I suppose, assumed that with age would come peace, and stability, and a rather dull kind of inner resolution. In Lionel Conway I saw none of these things. I found passionate intensity, perhaps even ferocity, and a questing spirit still looking for a place to cast anchor.

It seems that Lionel decided immediately that I could provide that place. He pursued me with all the impulsiveness of a boy of twenty, but none of the bashfulness. He had no sense of the proprieties of those times, so he invited me to dine with him or walk with him, to attend lectures, visit museums, go sailing with him on the Thames at Marlow. It was his single-mindedness that won me over. The energy of his pursuit made Harry Bramante seem frivolous, insubstantial. After six months of this courtship I felt I had no right to refuse. I didn't love him, not as I had once loved Jack, but my feelings were warm enough to allow me to say 'I love you' to him, though not as often as he said it to me. I was moved by him, and no man had moved me for a very long time. I wanted to protect him, to be the solace of his old age. I valued his opinion of me, and I worked hard at converting the feeling I had when I was with him in public, which was akin to embarrassment, into insouciant pride. As for my vow that I would never marry, I explained it away to myself. This was different. This was no ordinary marriage – my life with Lionel could in no way parallel, and therefore betray, the life I would have had with Jack. Lionel and I were offering each other a mutually beneficial bargain; for me, the freedom to write, the nurturing admiration of a great man, and – yes, certainly – money, which I could use to expand my world. For him there was honour and respect, intelligent companionship and – I believed – a haven in which to rest. I hardly know why, but I never considered children as a possibility. The subject was not mentioned during our courtship.

6th January 1980

The colour of autumn crocuses. That is the first colour in my mind when I think of Knighton, because the autumn crocuses were in flower when I first came there as a bride.

Three great spreads of them by the kitchen-garden wall, some bending over on their milky stalks like weary Degas dancers, some fanning their eager cups to the slanting sun. Pinky-purple, thin-veined, translucent. The most delicately genital of colours. Naked ladies. Meadow saffron. Autumn crocus. Lovely names, all of them.

I'd made several visits to Knighton before our marriage, but I'd always felt like an outsider. The house had been half shut up since Isabella's death. A housekeeper lived there, and she kept a couple of rooms ready for Lionel, who used it perhaps one week in four. His study was on the ground floor. It was the least welcoming room in the house, cold, north-facing, with a gloomy outlook over dark laurels and rhododendrons, a very Victorian patch of planting which I was often tempted to get rid of but somehow never did. The study was crammed from floor to ceiling, every shelf crowded with Lionel's diaries, notebooks, bound copies of lectures on nautical and Polar subjects. On the mantelshelf lay dusty treasures – a portion of a narwhal's tusk, a piece of scrimshaw, a pair of sealskin slippers made for a faraway Eskimo child. And in the middle of the desk was the skull of the polar bear Lionel and his crew had shot and eaten during that famous winter they spent ice-bound at the North Pole. The skull reared up, sinister as an iceberg, its malevolent majesty undiminished by Lionel's habit of filling the eye sockets with pencils, rubbers, and the feathers he collected on his walks.

On his own at Knighton, Lionel hardly moved out of the study, except for these enormous daily walks. Mrs Apps carried in meals on a tray, brought him the post and *The Times*, answered the rare telephone calls on the single receiver in the front hall. He slept in his dressing room on a put-you-up bed. I don't think the marital half-tester had been

13

slept in by anyone since Isabella died in it. I didn't ask, but I gathered the dressing room had been Lionel's sleeping place for quite a lot of their married life, too.

Most of the other rooms were shut up, the furniture veiled in dust sheets, the shutters barred. So when I came there as a bride in September 1930 and saw the autumn crocuses shining against the garden wall, it was as if I was seeing it all for the first time. Lionel had been energetic in setting things to rights for me. Apps was the gardener and handyman; for ten or twelve years he had done little more than keep the place orderly, but throughout that summer he and his boy Fred had laboured to perfect the garden, and when I arrived I found, rather to my private dismay, that there was hardly a blade of grass out of place. But I loved the sight of the fruit-pickers' ladders leaning against the orchard trees, the baskets at the foot of each tree lined with green leaves and piled with damsons, greengages, yellow plums and whiskery cobnuts; the September spiders had cast glinting silver lines with quick gaiety from one basket handle to the next. And in the house the dust sheets were gone, the shutters folded back, the windows clean and open. For the first time I could look properly at the furniture and pictures. Mrs Apps had set vases of throbbing, sombre asters on the tables; from the kitchen seeped the purple smell of her jam-making. Lionel wanted to fill the place with love for me; it was all there for me to take. I hope I was gracious in my acceptance.

Let me remember that time as the best of my marriage. That was the time I came closest to giving Lionel what he wanted, to keeping my side of the bargain. He opened up his beloved house for me, invested in me the power to regenerate, to dispel old ghosts. He offered me respect and love and trust. I knew it, and if I didn't repay in kind, I believe I came close.

I prefer to think of those rich autumn weeks at Knighton, rather than the wedding itself. I have no photographs of my wedding, which may be one reason why my memories of it are so patchy. In old age distant memory is said to grow clearer, but I can now recall no more of this day, which should have been so important, than I ever have. Both of us wanted the quietest of ceremonies. Lionel wanted a church, and I went along with that because it didn't much matter to me. The church was near his Kensington flat – ugly, Victorian, and almost empty. No guests, no family; just us and my great friend Peggy Coombs for me, and on his side Alfred Winterson, the publisher who had introduced us. Alfred was jovial, back-slapping. Peggy was matter-of-fact. I could tell she wasn't convinced about the wedding, though she had been pleased when Lionel, or the fact of Lionel, saw off Harry Bramante. Harry was a thoroughly bad idea in Peggy's opinion, and as usual she was absolutely right.

I wore brown; a golden-brown suit with a high-necked bouclé jacket and a softly pleated skirt. It was made for me, as were most of my clothes at that time, and I remember it more clearly than anything else about the wedding. It was an excellent suit, with beautiful whorled buttons. Lionel was perhaps disappointed that I had chosen something so unbridal. Well, I softened it with a bouquet, an unusual mixture of ferns and tight creamy rosebuds, and Turk's cap lilies. I can still see their rusty curls. After the ceremony I handed the bouquet to Peggy, rather awkwardly. She took it without enthusiasm.

What else? Nothing of the ceremony, no words, no vows – only the pools of coloured light like molten jewels on the stones of the church floor where September sun struck through the stained-glass windows. The wedding breakfast, afterwards, at an hotel, and I can't even be sure which one. A couple of dozen of our closest friends, an uneasy mixture of seafaring men and Lionel's scholarly scientists, and my political, Bohemian types. Alfred Winterson made a speech, of which I recall not a sentence, and Lionel made a brief reply, and I was horrified to see that he was choked with tears. I believe we cut a cake. I can see the sudden unfamiliarity of the ring on my finger as I lifted my glass of champagne, but the moment of putting on the ring – that's gone. Just a sense of Lionel, black and bulky, by my side.

The honeymoon was a week in Paris. Poor Lionel! Fifty years of wrestling with the moods and mysteries of the high seas, and he'd married a woman who was sick crossing the Channel. Why Paris? Lionel was not interested in cities. London he tolerated, because he knew it, and because it contained people and institutions which were useful to him, but the great capitals of Europe meant little. I suppose he chose Paris in clumsy homage to what he saw as my cultural sophistication, but it wasn't a good idea. He was baffled by my admiration of Monet's sheets of water lilies, irritated by Manet's bold Olympian stare. I remember him in a quayside restaurant, hungry, chafed with boredom, hauling reluctant oysters out of their shells. 'Barely a mouthful,' he grumbled. 'Give me a nice juicy polar bear any day,' I added, to tease, and he laughed, but only just. Paris frustrated him. Only in the shadowy spaces of Notre Dame did he seem at ease; a cathedral is, after all, something like a great ship.

So it was with relief that we returned to Knighton, where Lionel was sufficiently securely based to extend his very considerable generosity to me. What a sentence that is! Pompous and ugly. Why am I unable to write about Lionel without condescension? As a defence against guilt, a kind of padding to muffle the facts? He was the Great Man, I was the one who did him wrong. Let me state what Lionel was in single, simple words. He was brave, strong, just, pure, and kind. Huge passions surged through his life – anger, love, and grief. To these he never became accustomed. They crashed over him night and day, but they never eroded him; there was no crumbling into comfortableness. He sought repose in me, and I failed him. Perhaps for those first few months ... well, that's how I choose to remember. Autumn at Knighton, golden, blooming. Clots of mulberries, the red juice running down my wrist. Lionel behind me holding the basket, laughing as I crammed my mouth. 'Hey, hey, my girl! How will we face Mrs Apps with an empty basket?' I chose the best, the blackest, the sweetest, and held it out to him on the palm of my hand; the brush of his lips against my palm was – well, I could bear it. He held me, and my hands left ruby trails on his shirt front. Mulberries are only perfect when they're just touched with decay.

And now I'm old, far older than Lionel was then, or than he lived to be. Lionel didn't quite see out the Second World War, which was a pity. It's always a pity not to know how things turn out. He died in 1944, just before Christmas. We'd made the parlour into a bedroom for him because the stairs had become too difficult. He suffered terribly from gout, which seemed most unfair, because he'd always been an abstemious man. What with gout and petrol rationing the last few years of Lionel's life were limited, and he felt it. His spirit was restless. What I wanted most for him was to get him back on the sea in some form or another, but the war prevented it. I did, once, get him to Beachy Head, about a year before he died. I can't remember how we managed that. A train to Eastbourne – then what? Could there have been a taxi? A bus perhaps . . . my memory is full of holes. But I do remember Lionel standing on the clifftop, leaning on his sticks, shaking in the cold wind but gulping down, sucking in great lungfuls of the salty air. His eyes glittered, brimful of fierce memories.

The stairs will be too much for me before long, even in this tiny cottage. I'll be eighty-five this year, and I've no ambition to grow any older. I have my home help twice a week, and a young man in the garden; he's the great-grandson of old Apps and Mrs Apps, which is reassuring, or would be if I needed reassurance. I'm weary now, and I need to stop. I'll sit by the fire and drink tea, and doze. But one thing has become clear to me, and I'll write it down now, in case I lose it again. I know why I'm writing this. I'm writing it for Hester.

2

Though Hester Oakes had now lived alone for almost five years, every day she still experienced a little rise of pleasure when she returned to her flat and found it exactly as she had left it.

Hester had always been tidy, and she was getting tidier. Her flat, her hair, her briefcase – even her morning routine had been honed, streamlined. She woke at seven, drank grapefruit juice, puréed exotic fruits and ate them mixed with yoghurt rich in probiotics. She did her exercises, took a shower, applied minimal but expensive make-up. She erased recorded messages as soon as she had absorbed their purport. Hester liked to rub away the tracks as they formed behind her.

At half past eight she left for work. She took a bus; she'd always liked London buses, and besides, in her job she needed to keep a finger on the pulse of ordinary life. On the bus she pretended to be deep in a book, but although she didn't want to talk to anybody, she did want to listen. The radio programme she presented prided itself on covering issues that affected the man or woman in the street in an intelligent and thought-provoking way. Hester was widely admired, and cited as a rare example of a broadcaster who had refused to 'dumb down'. She was happy to be, in a minor way, a household name, but she refused all requests for interviews from magazines and television. Her voice she didn't mind sharing; her face she regarded as her own.

Hester shared a workspace with two researchers, Jean

and Penny. Jean, whose considerable intelligence was never softened by tact, had swollen ankles that lapped at the tops of her navy court shoes and steel-coloured hair cut like a Norman helmet. Hester knew nothing whatsoever about her private life. Penny, less rigorous, was more open-minded – younger, fresher, and without Jean's flavour of spinsterish bitterness. The two of them discussed all manner of things; today, Hester had not been long at her desk when she realized they were discussing her grandmother.

'Another bundle from Caraway Press,' said Jean. 'They seem to have it in for us.'

Penny reached across. 'Oh, I like Caraway Press. Let's have a look.' She shook three slim volumes out of the Jiffy bag – elegant paperbacks, aquamarine with a subtle pearly shimmer. Books that would look fetching on a thinking-woman's bedside table. Penny held one against her cheek. 'They are such lovely things. Sort of silky.'

Jean snorted. 'Silky's not much use on radio, is it? Are they any good?'

'Um ... I don't know. Novels. By E. M. Albery. Never heard of him. Look, nice wide margins. And I really like the way they've done the chapter headings.'

Hester looked round from her computer screen. 'Her,' she said.

'Sorry, Hester?'

'Her. E. M. Albery is female.'

'Of course,' said Jean. 'Caraway are only interested in females. Only dead females, at that.'

'Sorry,' said Penny, whose outbursts of enthusiasm were often checked by apology, 'I knew that, really. It's just that two initials like that, E. M., feel masculine to me. Was she one of those women who had to pretend to be a man? Oh, hang about. This one's not a novel – it's poetry.'

'Do you know anything about her?' Jean asked Hester.

'Well, yes, I do. She's my grandmother.'

Both women shrieked. 'Hester, you're a dark horse,' said Jean. 'But' – and she winked – 'is she any good?'

'Jean!'

Hester laughed. 'I read it all in my teens, and I thought it was pretty good. But she was still alive then, which made me feel as if she was peering over my shoulder. But, yes, I should think she is quite good. They're real period pieces, at any rate.'

Penny flicked through *The Shadow on the Lawn*, reading bits of the poems out loud. It annoyed Hester when people did that. 'What's "hyaline"?' Penny asked. 'What's "fantoche"?'

'I can't remember. I looked them up once. I looked up all the difficult words.'

'She seems to have liked difficult words, your grandma.'

'She did.'

'"Hepatica"? "Hierophant"?'

'Try the novels,' suggested Jean.

Penny opened *Dumb Woman's Lane*. Hester turned back to her screen. She needed to check the facts about the latest rail dispute, because she was to interview a captain of industry for a programme later that week. But she couldn't concentrate. Grandma Evelyn rose up between herself and the screen, and Hester could almost taste her own youth. She was fifteen, reading *Dumb Woman's Lane* curled in the parlour window seat behind the half-closed curtains. She didn't want her mother to know where she was or what she was doing. Her instinct for secrecy had always been strong.

'This looks rather fascinating,' pronounced Penny. 'It's a kind of ghost story. This woman stops speaking after some kind of trauma – a rape, I expect, it usually is. And then she's kind of directing the lives of the people who come to live in her cottage after she's dead. Something like that.'

'Yes, it was a rape,' said Hester, remembering. She didn't like Penny referring to Margery in *Dumb Woman's Lane* as 'this woman'. Sensitive, tormented Margery had been behind the curtains with her as she read. The curtains were still there – original William Morris, hung by Isabella Conway, Hester's grandfather's first wife. The afternoon sun released their dusty vegetable smell; the knobbliness of the weave grazed her bare shoulders.

'And this one,' said Penny, '*The Word Girl*. I like the title. Is it autobiographical?'

'It may be,' Hester said. 'I can't remember.' But she could remember – and she remembered asking the same question herself, squeezing up the courage to ask Grandma in the overflowing garden behind the cottage. A hot day. Her cheesecloth blouse, the green dye dark at the bottom, fading as it rose up through the fabric. Ombré; that's what that technique was called. Hester had been so privately pleased when the sophisticated mother of a school friend had noticed it. 'Oh, Hester,' she'd said, 'I do like your ombré top.'

The blouse had little wooden buttons, miniature toggles. Hester's skirt, long, patchwork, fanned out at the bottom like a mermaid's tail. Her feet and stomach were brown and bare. She broke a stem off the yellow-flowered plant that spurted from the brick wall of the outside lavatory. The stalk oozed beads of juice the colour of saffron. 'Greater celandine,' said her grandmother. 'No relation of the other celandine, the one everybody knows.' Hester squatted on the worn step, traced patterns along the ridges of her feet, using the celandine juice like henna. 'Poisonous,' said Grandma. 'But don't let it worry you.'

Hester carried on tracing. 'You know *The Word Girl*,' she said, her eyes on her feet, 'is it about – you?'

Grandma Evelyn had a short, barking laugh. Her lap was full of brown envelopes, containing seeds saved from last year's flowers. 'No more than any of the others,' she replied. 'They're all about me – and they're not. Fiction is an oblique art.' She tugged a tuft of groundsel from between the paving stones. 'But if you're asking, did I do what Helen did in *The Word Girl*, did I use story writing as a way of telling the secrets that I knew – well, no. I haven't done that yet.'

Hester stole a look at her. Strands of grey hair were escaping from her careless bun; her hanging cheeks were mottled from even the smallest exertion on this warm day.

'There's still time,' she continued, over Hester's head. 'It may be that I'll write it all down, one day. One ought to tell the truth one knows. Though it can be hard to sort out which part is the most truthful. "Are you the leaf, the blossom or the bole?"'

Hester thought about truth. She thought about Paul Castle, pressing up against her in the station car park on Saturday night, his cigarette ground under foot, rough granite against her back. Her mother thought she was watching television with her friend Jennifer.

'The bole's the trunk, isn't it?' she replied to the question she thought she'd been asked. 'I'd like to be the bole. But I suppose I have to be the blossom, because you're the bole, and Mum's the leaf.'

Evelyn laughed again, with bottomless affection. 'What a lovely answer. It's Yeats, Hester dear. "Among School Children". His best poem. Yeats was a terrible old fraud in some ways, but he had marvellous moments. '"What youthful mother, a shape upon her lap/Honey of generation had betrayed . . ."'

23

Hester was lost. The only Yeats she knew was 'The Lake Isle of Innisfree', which her father had once made her learn as a punishment. Just like him, thought her adult self, to turn poetry into a punishment.

'It's very good,' she said. '*The Word Girl*, I mean. I think it's your best.'

'Oh, darling,' said Grandma, 'bless you for using the present tense. Here, take these poppy seeds to your mother. I meant to give them to her ages ago. Rather late for planting now, but worth a try. One never knows what may come up.'

'I'd love to take these home,' said Penny. 'They do look interesting. How would you feel if we did something with them, Hester? Perhaps your grandmother's due for a revival.'

Hester thought for a moment. The memory of Paul Castle's cigarette still rasped her tongue.

'Fine,' she said. 'I'd be happy with that. But – do you mind if I do the research? It's just that it's something I've always meant to do. And now I must get back to the shortcomings of Railtrack.'

The others fell silent. Penny wandered off to make coffee. Hester knew she had a way of closing subjects. She didn't particularly mean to. It just happened.

She usually returned home at half past six. She would take off her shoes, flex her long toes, and roam the flat, touching things with her fingertips, sniffing the stillness, even now, five years on, revelling in the absence of Guy. On this particular evening she drifted home on the warm June air. Her palate was already preparing for the glass of cold Chablis she had promised herself. Her solitude felt like a present, sumptuously wrapped.

She checked her emails. There was a long one from her friend Rosie, trying to persuade her to come to a college-reunion dinner. Devoted though Hester was to Rosie, not the wildest of horses would drag her to an event where the entertainment would principally consist of forty-year-old women showing each other photographs of their offspring and swapping details about violin lessons, grommets or amniocentesis, depending on which stage they'd got to. She fired off a quick reply. 'You'll go anyway. You don't need me. How about lunch, Sunday week?'

The reply flew back. 'I knew you'd say no, but it was worth a try. Yes, lunch. Come here, please. Your god-daughter needs some spiritual guidance.' Hester smiled. Contact with Rosie always made her smile. Nothing Rosie ever did or said could irritate Hester, which probably made her unique in her acquaintance.

There was one message on the answerphone, from Solly. He could see Hester tonight, if she wanted. That was all. Solly wasn't given to elaboration. She thought about him as she wandered through the flat, tidying things that were already tidy, putting others in a suitcase for her visit to her mother the next day. The more she thought about him, the more certain she was that she should see him that night. As she grew older she saw less and less point in deferring gratification. She had intended to spend the evening alone, composing herself for the ordeal of helping her mother sort through her late father's papers with the aid of some Chablis, some Brahms, and a small perfect salad – some grilled artichoke hearts, haloumi, and perhaps some toasted almonds. But the summer air drifted in through her open windows and stirred her, and she could find no reason not to succumb. It was the kind of balmy evening air, so rare and therefore so precious in England, that lifts you and floats the years off you, and allows you to become whoever you want to be. 'I shall have both,' Hester said aloud, which had rather been her motto ever since her divorce, and she rang Solly on his mobile, admiring as she did so her long forefinger and its pearly oval nail. Solly was still at work. Hester could hear the clang and roar of the garage behind his quick answering 'Yup?' It didn't matter that he was busy. She hadn't rung for a chat.

'Sol? It's me. Ten o'clock. All right?'

'No problem,' he said. 'Your place?'

'No, yours.' Hester didn't want to discompose her flat.

'My place, then. Got to go.'

Hester put down the telephone and checked the time. Just gone seven. Three hours to go. Three hours before Hester put aside the kind of orderly, civilized behaviour with which all her friends and listeners would have associated her, and replaced it with abandonment of a kind that not a living soul would expect. The thought pleased her immensely.

She finished packing – such a well-ordered suitcase, such sensible choices of clothes that would harmonize with each other and cater for her comfort whatever the changing weather or social circumstance. Then she poured some more wine and with the glass in one hand and a little green china bowl of black olives in the other she stepped out on to her balcony. The flat was on the third floor of a purpose-built block, very central, not far from the river. One large bed-room, one L-shaped living room, a small compact kitchen, and an even smaller bathroom – that was all. No garden – only a balcony just wide enough for a folding chair and table, and two tubs, which Hester had planted with herbs. Hester, in revolt against her mother and grandmother's mania for gardening, had deliberately chosen a flat without a garden, but she found she couldn't do without plants altogether. She liked to pinch the herbs and roll them between her fingers as she sipped her early-evening drink. Now, she snipped off a piece of rue with her long, hard fingernails. It entranced her; the fretted precision of its grey leaves, the deep and bitter smell, so subtle and so uncompromising.

Children's voices drifted up from the paved triangle of space that separated Hester's block from its almost identical neighbours. They were playing football round the base of the plane tree whose solid, speckled presence had become such a constant in Hester's life that she had come to think of it almost as a benign and uncomprehending landlord. Its top branches filled the windows now they were in the full rustle of their June dress. Hester had spent her later childhood surrounded by trees, flocks of trees, murmuring and sighing all about her, bare-twigged and evergreen, blossoming and fruit-bearing. Now she made do with one, but that was enough; even with one, its detail could almost overwhelm her.

On the plane-dappled balcony, the air was still warm, as warm as English evening air ever can be. Hester stretched out her legs and flexed her bare feet. People had often commented that Hester's excellent legs were wasted on radio. She admired their smooth muscularity as she sipped her Chablis and relished its cool flintiness, relished the way it chimed with her solitude. She hadn't always been alone. She'd been married to Guy for eight years, though now she could hardly believe it. Everything she now had – her job, her flat, her privacy, her freedom – had come in the last five years, since the divorce. She had everything, now. Except children.

Hester was quite good at choosing what she wanted to

think about, and she decided not to think about children. Instead, she pressed her toes against the sun-warmed railings of the balcony and concentrated on the hours of pure pleasure that lay ahead. Tomorrow would not be good. Tomorrow there would be the slow, hot journey through summer Saturday traffic to Knighton, where she would have to spend several days helping her mother prepare the house for sale. Hester had known Knighton all her life, first as her Grandma Evelyn's house, then as her own home. Now that it was to go, was she prepared to ask herself how much she would mind? Not tonight. Some disturbing processes might begin tomorrow, but tonight she was untouchable.

She ate her salad out on the balcony, then showered, and exchanged her lavender-colour linen shift dress for a pair of black jeans and a hooded top. She laced her bare feet into trainers and hung a leather pouch containing only a ten-pound note on a black thong round her neck. She set the answerphone, locked the balcony doors, pushed her keys deep into her jeans pocket, and took the lift down to street level. She checked her appearance in the mirror that had been installed in the lift, allegedly as a deterrent to vandals – Hester enjoyed the idea that vandals would be too busy preening themselves to do any vandalizing. Her straight, fine hair, blonde in childhood, now mouse with highlights, hung too smoothly in its neat bob. She ran her fingers through it, pulling strands down over her face.

There was no one else in the vestibule. Hester slipped out into the street. She often chose to walk to Solly's flat, along the embankment and across the slow thick river, into the directionless clutter of truncated terraces and tower blocks, scattered like children's toys not tidied away, that made up his patch of South London. She walked past high wire fences garlanded where waves of litter had broken against them, past scrubby half-parks where used condoms squatted, malevolent as fungi, past brave little bursts of gentrification – a third of a flat-fronted early Victorian terrace prettily painted and bejewelled with window boxes as if willing the surrounding squalor to melt away. Then she made her way into a dark estate that was like a hostile city on an alien planet. She rapped on the window of a ground-floor flat. It was uncurtained; she could see Solly inside, sitting at a table, the set of his shoulders, his dark outline, as if he was being interviewed on television and needed to stay anonymous. She knocked again. It was the window he rose to open, not the door. He stretched out his arms, thrust his big hands under her armpits, and without a word he hauled her in.

3

The table under the cherry tree was splotched with bird droppings. That just shows, thought Verity, how little I've used it this year. She considered scrubbing it before Hester arrived, but decided instead to cover it with a cloth – the blue gingham. She would set a jar of sweet peas in the centre of the cloth, to anchor it. Hester would enjoy the silky sweet-pea colours against the blue cloth.

In the pantry sat a salad, waiting to be dressed, and a quiche, bought from the bakery in Ewes Green High Street. It worried Verity a little that she hadn't made the quiche herself. She'd prepared a tray – glasses, plates, knives and forks, salt and pepper. A jug of water – only tap, she couldn't yet get used to the idea of buying water – and she'd pop some ice cubes into it at the last minute. No alcohol. She would offer sherry, but it was Saturday lunchtime; Hester was bound to refuse, just as she was bound to refuse a proper pudding, so Verity had filled a bowl with cherries, washed and patted dry on kitchen paper. This may all seem something of a palaver, Verity reasoned with herself, but Hester had a way of making one notice deficiencies. Her gaze was like a shaft of sunlight on dusty furniture, level and exposing. Stay calm, Verity reminded herself. Over the next few days she was going to have to confront her daughter with decisions more frightening than what to have for lunch.

As mother and daughter, they were not truly close. Verity had reflected on this a great deal. Hester was her only child. Throughout her childhood they were rarely apart. There was no question of boarding school, no nanny, despite Simeon's urging, no career for Verity that might have weakened the natural bonds. Until Hester went to Cambridge they had spent nearly every night under the same roof. There was the odd fortnight here and there – Hester holidaying with school friends in Scotland, or on a not terribly successful German exchange, or those occasions when Simeon insisted on taking Verity somewhere like Rome or New York – which always seemed to happen just when the garden was at its loveliest – and Hester would be left in Grandma Evelyn's care. Otherwise, mother and daughter had twenty years of such constant companionship that one would have expected a great affinity, a deep well of mutual understanding, thought Verity. But no, no such thing.

There had never been a grand falling-out, or even any real coolness. There were weekly telephone calls – Hester usually rang on a Sunday evening – and never any blight of hostility or indifference. But since Simeon died, Verity had been thinking about it – she'd done nothing else, since, just thinking and tidying up – and she'd come to realize that almost every decision her only child had ever made had taken her by surprise. Not so much because the decisions themselves had been particularly outrageous or eccentric, but just because whenever Hester had announced some important piece of news Verity had never had any inkling of anything being in the air. New jobs, new flats, travel plans, men, were all presented as faits accomplis, as complete and compact as letters on a doormat. There was never any room for discussion.

She had wondered whether Hester's divorce would change all that, and perhaps she had hoped it would. Perhaps, rather shamefully, she had looked forward to a little loosening up, a little confiding, and the opportunity for offering comfort. In truth, she would have liked to see her daughter cry. But no. Hester had arranged the divorce as swiftly and competently as she had organized the wedding, eight years before. Almost overnight, Simeon and Verity found themselves without a son-in-law. Verity had always told people that she was very fond of Guy; once he had gone, she was shocked to discover how far this was from being the case.

Verity mixed a dressing for the salad – sunflower oil, with just a dash of olive for the flavour. Hester, she knew, would have used nothing but olive, and a very expensive brand at that, but even after all these years of affluence Verity had never overcome her innate parsimony. She stirred in a pinch of dry mustard. Am I the only mother in the land, she wondered, who has no idea why her daughter has no children? She tasted the dressing. Perhaps it was a little bland. She would snip a few chives on to the salad. She'd grown chives in a wooden tub just outside the kitchen door every year since they'd arrived at Knighton, but today might be the last time she used them. She could take the tub with her when she moved, but she rather despised people who did that – unscrewed light bulbs and bath taps and so on. It was best not to be sentimental. If she allowed herself to be sentimental about the grandchildren issue, she'd be sunk. People used to ask her about that when Hester was married – people could be awfully direct these days – and she'd murmur something about her daughter's career. In retrospect she wished she'd hinted at some inadequacy of Guy's – since his departure she'd felt an unseemly urge to cut that handsome, careless man down to size – but that wasn't the kind of conversation she was very good at. What was she good at? Secrets – she was expert at those. She'd no right to resent Hester's reserve, when she considered her own history.

Did they need new potatoes, or would the quiche be sufficiently filling? She could cook the potatoes anyway, and they could always have potato salad for supper. Which would mean using the chives again – so, how pointless it was to indulge in wistful nevermoreish thoughts about chives, or anything else. Hester loved tiny new potatoes. Pulling them up had been one of her favourite tasks, when she was a child and they kept a proper vegetable garden. Verity bought them from Sainsbury's now, and they had a fancy name and a ridiculous price tag, but they were clean and easy – you just threw them in the water. Lazy, really.

It was twenty to one. If she put the potatoes on now, they'd be done just in time. Hester was never late. She didn't seem to suffer from punctures or traffic jams the way other people did. Sure enough, the ice cubes in the water jug had only just begun to separate themselves into cloudy middles and clear rims, and here was the swish of her Renault on the gravel, as if in an advertisement. Verity had had the gravel renewed for Simeon's funeral. Hester had forced her to. What a ridiculous expense. Though perhaps it had impressed potential buyers. The 'For Sale' board was by the gate now, sticking out like the sore thumb that is often mentioned but rarely seen. Thumbs, in Verity's experience, were not especially prone to soreness. She wondered whether Hester's heart had lurched at the sight of that board, as her own had so uncomfortably done.

If so, Hester's appearance gave no clue. She stepped out of her car looking composed and fresh, not at all as if she had just driven for a couple of hours in what was becoming a sullen June heat, not at all as if she cared that the home of her girlhood was on the market. Verity watched from the window as Hester smoothed the wrinkles out of her dove grey dress, removed her sunglasses and stowed them in her shoulder bag, unlocked the boot and took out a brown leather suitcase, properly strapped up, and a matching vanity case. Verity waited for one more item – there it was. A black attaché case, like a man's. That travelled in the front of the car. Externally, at least, Hester's luggage was always so predictable.

Verity opened the door and held out her hand, though whether for the luggage or for an embrace would not have been clear to an onlooker. Hester deftly interpreted the gesture as both, and transferred the lightest article into her mother's hand while giving her a half-hug and a peck in the air near her cheek. 'You're looking well,' she said, without appearing to look. 'Oh, and I brought you these.' She darted back to the car for a brown-paper cone of flowers, artily tied with orange raffia. 'Coals to Newcastle, I'm afraid, but . . .'

'Not at all. They're lovely.' And they were. Just lots and lots of blue scabious. Verity had always loved flowers that trembled. As well as being lovely, they were uncharacteristic of Hester, whose presents were usually more functional. Verity recognized them as an acknowledgement that matters of an emotional nature would need to be addressed, and felt encouraged. 'Come on in, darling. Lunch is ready. Is just water all right, or would you like a proper drink?'

Verity insisted on washing up alone, as she always did for the first meal after Hester's arrival, so when lunch was over Hester went upstairs to unpack. She liked to unpack properly, to colonize, wherever she went. It was a small but real pleasure to her to take possession of a hotel room, to hang her clothes in the wardrobe and set her make-up and moisturizer on the dressing table and lay a paperback at angles to the bedside light. Verity had prepared Hester's old bedroom for her; she still called it 'Hester's room' even though there was so little childhood left in it. She would have preserved it as an untouched shrine to her daughter's adolescence, had not Hester insisted on carrying everything away with her, even the curtains. Hester neither wanted nor needed those curtains, but she felt a prickly embarrassment at her mother's reverential attitude to the family life that in Hester's opinion had never quite happened. All that remained of that seventies girlhood were some pink-and-orange stickers of formalized daisies that refused to peel off the window, and a stain like a wiggly balloon on the varnished surface of the dressing table where Hester had knocked over a bottle of nail-polish remover the first time she tried to use it. And yet, Hester thought, though she'd taken away books and pictures and curtains, there were some things she couldn't change. The trick the wardrobe mirror had of making one's face look fatter than it really was. The habit tortoiseshell butterflies had of leaving their corpses on the windowsill, fragile and silky as ash. Verity, generally a tidy person, wouldn't sweep away something she thought beautiful, so the desiccated butterflies lingered on. Then there was the way one of the small leaded window panes, greener than the rest, perfectly framed the summer house at the end of the garden so it looked like one of those funny little buildings stuck like Fuzzy-Felt on the landscapes in early Renaissance paintings. That window – Hester knew every warp and bubble of its hand-blown glass. Such irregularities could not be cleared away.

She hung up her clothes, which were mostly made of pure linen and cotton in cool summer shades of mint and stone and lavender – no patterns, save the odd subtle stripe. She arranged her three pairs of shoes, complete with trees, in a row. A pair of flexible light brown loafers, some plain black courts with a one-and-a-half-inch heel in case her mother had any socializing in mind – sherry with neighbours was always a hazard of visits to Knighton – and her favourite, comfortable, chestnut leather ankle boots, in case the weather broke. These, of course, were in addition to the thonged sandals she was already wearing. Hester had to have the right footwear to go with her clothes. When she saw smart suits worn with trainers, or young girls in floaty skirts and clumpy boots – that kind of thing made her feel quite irritable. It was like seeing a hat on indoors.

There was no desk in the bedroom any more, but the dressing table was large and bare enough to serve as one. She laid out pens, writing paper, envelopes, her laptop and a pad of A4. For some time she had been toying with the idea of writing a book, or at least an article, about her grandmother, and the arrival of Evelyn's books at work the day before had spurred her into action. This week would be a good time to get going on it. It would be something to talk to her mother about, something to divert both of them from the leaden business of sorting out whatever it was her father had left behind him.

Hester had always considered that Evelyn Albery was a grandmother to be proud of. She was the daughter of a crusading East End clergyman, a scholarly man who laid aside his academic ambitions to fight for social justice. He was an associate of many of those involved in the formation of the Labour Party, including Keir Hardie, though as a clergyman he avoided too public an affiliation with any one political group. Evelyn, in youth, was herself a great espouser of causes. She had been a suffragette, a very young and fearless one; she had chained herself to the railings outside Number 10 Downing Street and had longed to get herself imprisoned and force-fed. She had failed in this ambition because of her extreme youth, but several times she had clashed with the police. The Great War pushed all that to one side. Evelyn, though a pacifist, had thrown herself into war work, and became a proficient nurse. Hester knew little about her grandmother's emotional history during this period. Was there some sweetheart lost on the fields of Flanders? Something gave her the impression there was, though neither she nor Verity knew any facts.

What they did know was that after the Armistice Evelyn took a flat in Golden Square and embarked on a writing career. She had a patron who edited a political journal and soon her articles were appearing regularly. She signed herself with her initials, E. M. Albery, presumably to keep the question of her gender lightly veiled. There was a story about the first time Evelyn met the editor in his office, and he hadn't realized that she was female, but Hester had only heard her mother's version of this, and Verity was not a great raconteur. Hester suspected that someone else could have made more of it. Hester enjoyed the thought of her grandmother at this time, young, energetic, full of intellectual zeal, independent in her flat which she shared with her great friend Peggy Coombs, surrounded by a growing number of political and literary friends. It seemed to Hester a kind of ideal. And in the aftermath of the war there must have been such a strong sense of progress, of rebuilding; so many things to put to rights.

Then, in 1930, at the age of thirty-five, Evelyn, to everyone's surprise, had married Lionel Conway, a Polar explorer nearly thirty years older than herself. She abandoned her London life for this corner of the Sussex Weald, and set up home at Knighton, an Arts and Crafts-inspired overgrown cottage that had been built for Lionel's parents in the 1880s. Here Evelyn had lived until 1970. Just when people were beginning to murmur that she could no longer manage, she announced that she would be removing herself to a two-bedroomed cottage in Ewes Green. From here she could walk to the railway station and the village shop. Simeon and Verity sold the Chelsea mews house which until then had been Hester's only home, and took over Knighton.

The drama of Evelyn's life subsided. Her brilliant, brittle, important friends died or moved abroad or otherwise fell away, and as she grew older she increasingly immersed herself in the minutiae of village life and in her garden. She died in 1980, her faculties not much impaired, her independence compromised only by a home help twice a week and a man to do the mowing and the digging. During Hester's childhood Grandma Evelyn had probably been her favourite person. It felt right, now, to honour her life with a proper historical investigation.

Hester opened the casement windows as far as they would go, and drank in the scent of the lime tree that was just coming into flower. What a strange, etiolated, unfruitful family she belonged to! Hardly a family at all, merely a line, a thread. Herself an only child, her mother likewise, born in 1936 as a late surprise, she imagined, to forty-one-year-old Evelyn and ferocious, white-bearded Lionel Conway, suddenly a father for the first and only time. Evelyn herself had been scarcely more than an only child. There had only been Walter, a crippled younger brother who had died in his teens. Evelyn's mother had died giving birth to this boy, whose photograph Evelyn had preserved to the last. The photograph, always on her grandmother's dressing table, had been an object of fascination to Hester's youthful self, though disappointingly only the head and shoulders were shown, so you couldn't see how crippled he was. Hester scanned the mild young face with its prominent misaligned teeth for signs of inner or outer torment, but in truth her imagination had to do the work for her.

The Reverend Eustace Albery, social crusader, never remarried. He remained devoted to the memory of his wife. And what about herself, Hester Oakes, briefly and without much conviction Hester Harrison? How agitated Guy had become when she suggested keeping her own name! A bad sign, with hindsight. And now here she was, forty years old, single, independent, more than solvent, and childless. There would be nothing left of her family to carry on into the twenty-first century, unless she decided to do something about it.

This is the last time I will have my daughter in this house with me, Verity thought. She knew that anything could happen with house sales, but there had been quite a lot of interest already. Twelve sets of people had been round, and there was one couple in particular who seemed very keen. They had put in an offer, a little below the asking price, but the estate agent was confident that they would increase it. The couple were in their early thirties; one small boy with a ridiculous name (could it have been Mungo?) and twins expected by Christmas. They would be in a hurry, surely, to settle in somewhere by the time the twins were born. The husband did something in the City – something of no interest to Verity, but he was clearly well paid. Pleasant people, but definitely the swimming-pool types. Well, one couldn't choose one's buyers. That sort of thing didn't matter. The house was not alive. Verity would try not to mind.

Verity had been born at Knighton in what was now the

39

best spare bedroom, over the porch, with wisteria round the window and a view of Knight's Wood. In spring, you could see the soft pastel smudge of bluebells between the trees. Evelyn had always said that Verity was lucky to have been born indoors at all. A private nursing home in Marylebone had been booked. A rich neighbour had offered to lend their comfortable and reliable Daimler, complete with chauffeur and rugs. But Verity had come early, and fast. Evelyn was picking plums in the orchard on the most blue-and-gold morning – 2 September, almost the best time of the year, Verity thought – and then there the baby nearly was. Mrs Apps delivered her; there was no time to call a midwife. Evelyn was always very matter-of-fact about it, though it might have been quite hazardous, especially given her age. Verity had liked hearing the story when she was a child, and would pester Mrs Apps to tell it to her often, but she wished she had let her be born in the orchard, with hens scratching in the long wet grass and wasps rolling in the golden hollows of fallen plums.

It wasn't a bit like that when Verity had Hester. She and Simeon were living in their dear little mews house just off the King's Road. One would probably have to be a pop star to live there now, Verity supposed, but in those days, forty years ago, it was just the sort of house where a middle-class couple could set up their first home. Verity loved living there. She knew several other young wives in the neighbour-hood and they were in and out of each other's houses all day. None of them dreamed of working. Most had had jobs, but had given them up without question or regret when they married. The cosy, chatty company she kept took her mind off Simeon, Verity thought, or rather it prevented her from noticing what he was really like. Which may or may not have been a good thing.

There had been no question of having the baby at home. Verity wouldn't have wanted to. The sunny little legend of her own arrival had provided scarcely anything in the way of hard information, and it never seemed to have occurred to her mother to enlarge upon the subject. And the conversations she had with her female friends, though they felt intimate, were vague in detail. 'Caroline's waters broke in Selfridges! Can you imagine!' they would exclaim to each other, feeling daring and close; but, no, Verity couldn't really imagine, because she wasn't sure what the 'waters' actually were, and didn't like to ask.

There were nurses, of course, who told her things; things to do with breathing. 'And remember, don't be afraid to ask for help,' Verity recalled one saying. She was the sternly kind type, with a daunting bosom, and Verity nodded obediently, but didn't really know what kind of help she could have asked for. In the event her blood pressure shot up, she developed eclampsia, and Hester was delivered by Caesarean section. Simeon congratulated himself on having insisted upon a private clinic, despite Verity's pleas for economy, and she had to admit that she felt so desperately unwell that she was grateful. 'Whose baby is that?' she asked when they presented Hester to her once the anaesthetic had worn off. 'Is it Cynthia's?' Cynthia was one of the neighbours in the mews, due the same week. Verity couldn't think why they wanted her to look at Cynthia's baby when she felt so terrible.

After a day or two she began to feel something for Hester, but what she felt was interest, not love. She was still rather ashamed of this. Hester had a crest of spiky brown hair and long purple feet and tiny white spots all over her nose. Verity was fascinated to see her undressed, though it seemed almost unkind to look at her bent froggy legs and that awful

41

bit of umbilical cord that was like a slug sprinkled with salt. She wore a long white nightie with frilly cuffs and two ducklings embroidered on the chest. Verity remembered thinking how sensible it was for people to embroider pretty things on babies' clothes because it helped the mother join in the general pretence that the baby looked nice. She used to tuck the long hem of the nightie round Hester's feet when visitors came, to protect them from the sight of that flaky mottled skin, or to protect Hester from the reaction of disgust she assumed they would be unable to suppress. Protectiveness – that was the second emotion she felt for Hester. Fascination, then protectiveness, then – once she'd got her home and the nurse kept exclaiming about how fast she was gaining weight – pride. Love didn't happen for ages – at least two months. Then, one day, it just did.

She was bathing her in the nursery at Glendower Mews. The sun was pouring through the window, her little vest was airing on the fender, Verity's right arm, the sleeve pushed above the elbow, circled her under her shoulders, and with her left hand she trickled water on to her tummy from a tin mug. Verity's stitches had healed, her body was regaining some of its youthful elasticity – she was only twenty-four. Something made her slip – the mat she was kneeling on, most probably – and Hester dropped an inch or two lower in the water than she meant her to. The water covered her ears and lapped at her lower lip. Verity squealed – it shook her – and Hester's eyes turned into half-moons of delight, and she looked at her mother and smiled. She had smiled before – she had been smiling for a few weeks, and Verity had enjoyed her smiles, and so had Simeon. But this was different. This time she looked at Verity, and smiled as if they were in league, conspirators in some piece of safe, warm mischief. And Verity loved her.

She grew so fast. The brown spikes lay flat and turned to pale gold, her eyes lost their newborn thundercloud colour and settled to the cool grey-blue that they were to remain. Hester's eyes made everyone feel that she was intelligent – which, of course, she was. By her second birthday she was tall, long-limbed, careful in her movements, clear and fluent in her speech. And that's pretty much how she has been ever since, Verity thought.

Verity went on loving her. She had no difficulty about that, though she rarely recaptured the sense of complicity that had first kindled love in her. She was a little in awe of her small daughter, of her intelligence and self-sufficiency. Hester never had tantrums as a two-year-old. She didn't need to; she always seemed to get her own way without ruffling any feathers. Perhaps distance had lent enchantment to the view, but Verity's impression was that she had thoroughly enjoyed her daughter's infancy. Hester was a London child, a Chelsea child, with a little red cape and hat, pulling her wheeled dog along the pavement behind her on their way to play in the gardens of the Royal Hospital, or in the playground next to St Luke's Church. She was a familiar customer at the French baker's round the corner. Verity could lay the baguettes that Simeon loved across her lap as she sat up, bright-eyed, in her pram, and Madame behind the counter would give her a croissant to suck, in those days when a croissant was something rare in England. Later Verity remembered buttoning Hester's duffel coat over her ballet costume on her way to dance classes – she flatly refused to change when they got there, and, as far as Verity knew, she had a horror of communal changing rooms to this day. I can see her now, thought Verity, skipping along just ahead of me, her legs in their pale tights shimmering through the autumn evening. So many memories, most of them good. And me, a contented mother, conscientious, organized, young. Hester was not the reason I had no more children. Her difficult birth had nothing to do with it, either. I had no more children because I decided not to, for a specific reason. It is a reason that Hester will discover for herself, this afternoon, this evening, or whenever it is that the moment seems right for us to go through her dead father's things.

Hester had been ten when they moved to Knighton, when Evelyn had made the sudden and sensible decision that the house had become too much for her. To Verity's surprise, Simeon had seized on the move as the obvious thing. Such an urban creature, Verity had always thought, so very much more at ease with the works of Man than the works of God, or Nature. Verity herself had mixed feelings. She was a country child. She had always missed the garden, the animals, the orchard where she so nearly began, but she had enjoyed London. Chelsea had been an invigorating place to live for the last decade or so. But her friends were no longer the carefree and close-knit band they once had been. Some had moved out of town, one couple had emigrated to Australia, two were in the throes of divorce. Verity had worried about disrupting Hester's education, worried about spending more time alone with Simeon, worried about encroaching on her mother's domain. But Simeon had jumped at it. So here she was.

Hester had been very composed about the move. She gave no sign of missing her school friends. The house was almost home to her – she'd stayed there at least one weekend a month for her entire life. The only thing she seemed to mind about was that Grandma Evelyn would not be living there, too. 'But it's Grandma's house,' she objected, baffled and a little put out.

44

She started at The Turrets, a rather low-key private girls' school in Westbeech. Having boarded herself, Verity wanted Hester to be a day girl. Grandma Evelyn sniffed at The Turrets, thought it dull and pretentious. The eponymous turrets certainly were pretentious – two little Victorian stone roundels stuck on to the front of an otherwise unassuming brick box – but though the school was nothing special, Hester got on well there. She took the train from Ewes Green Halt, in the days when the trains still stopped there, before the station house became an antiques showroom – and got off two stations later. It was only for the first two mornings that she allowed her mother to come all the way with her. After that, Verity just waved her off at the Halt. She looked so brave, with her satchel and her trombone case and her squashy brown felt hat. The school's crest was stitched to the ribbon. This was thirty years ago, but it looked old-fashioned even then.

Verity met her off the train in the evenings. If it was fine they'd walk the mile or so home from the station. Verity enjoyed those walks. Hester didn't say much, but when the air was full of twisting yellow leaves and bonfire smoke, or when the banks of the lane were studded with rosettes of primroses, Verity could sense her delight. She asked the names of trees and flowers, deferring to her mother as the proper country person. Hester had always been good at giving credit where credit was due.

And then they'd be home, and that was a nice time, those two or three hours before Simeon's return. Verity would make her a cooked tea – very ordinary, beans on toast, cauliflower cheese, nothing much more than that. They'd talk over tea. Hester wasn't reticent; she'd tell her mother about school, what her geography project was, or how daring Sally Wallace had stuck an amusingly rude notice on the back of the biology mistress's cardigan. Nothing very personal, but plenty of information. Hester did her homework sitting on the kitchen stool with her books spread out on the table while Verity prepared Simeon's supper. She was disciplined about homework; there was rarely a fuss. When she'd finished, they would watch television together. Verity would watch whatever Hester chose, because she wanted to know what her daughter liked. They both enjoyed police dramas, *Softly Softly* or *Z Cars*. How solemnly the pair of them used to sit in front of *Top of the Pops*! If I could see myself now, thought Verity, I would laugh.

This companionable time would have been in their early days at Knighton, when Hester was eleven or twelve. As time went on, they spent less time together. They didn't fall out, but almost imperceptibly, Hester pushed her mother away. Hester started taking her homework up to her room. Verity got into the habit of listening to Radio 4 while she cooked. Hester had managed her own bath, hair wash and everything, from when she was about eight; she was thirteen when she started locking the door.

She came home from school later. There were clubs, or she'd go to a friend's house for tea. The routine of the evening meal started to slip – Hester would say she wasn't hungry, or she'd rather make her own – so Verity changed things, and encouraged her to wait and eat with her father. Simeon would talk to her, he'd argue with her, get her worked up about some issue or other, and she'd argue back, but if Verity tried to intercede they'd both round on her, as one. Hester seemed to be invigorated by arguments, but they worried Verity, who had never been very good at separating the political from the personal. Sometimes she would slip away while father and daughter were still sitting at the table. They didn't pay much attention. It wasn't long before Verity was going to bed earlier than Hester. In the morning she'd find that the remains of dinner had been more or less cleared away. That was Hester's doing – Simeon never lifted a finger. Hester had always been good like that.

She had friends, but she didn't bring them home very often. Perhaps she thought it was dull for them, with no brothers or sisters, and no pets, except for one cat, because Simeon didn't like animals. Verity used to worry that Hester didn't bring her friends back because of the atmosphere between her and Simeon, but that was probably a needless worry. He wasn't there so very much, and when he was they put up a good front – or so Verity liked to think. Hester never commented. One could not be sure what she noticed – perhaps nothing at all.

Other children did sometimes come. Verity would invite the children of her local friends, and that worked reasonably well. Verity wanted more stir, more noise about her; she would have loved a dog, but Simeon was adamant that there would be no dog. Eventually, as a great concession, they were allowed a slim, coal-black cat, but she wasn't very friendly because Simeon shut her out of the house every night. It was the last thing he did, his evening ritual. He used to make a hissing sound as he pushed her out of the kitchen door. Even the memory of that hiss stretched Verity's nerves.

Hester's best friend from school was called Jennifer Wentworth, and she was a thoroughly pleasant girl, in Verity's opinion. She came to tea from time to time, and occasionally stayed the night. Verity thought she was a surprising choice of friend, because she was rather ordinary and not very clever, but perhaps that was part of her appeal. Jennifer was the opposite of Hester in many ways – short, plump, with cropped, thick hair and rosy cheeks. Very chatty, very eager, not very imaginative. Their friendship lasted for years, and Verity was pleased about it. When Hester was with Jennifer, Verity always felt she was safe.

Hester didn't bring boys home. Guy Harrison was the first boyfriend she ever properly introduced to her parents. There were others – they'd ring up, or, later, deliver her to the door in their cars, but Hester didn't invite them in. Verity was obliged to sympathize with Hester's almost obsessive need for privacy, because she was the same herself. And the subject was a difficult one to broach. Other mothers of Verity's acquaintance would bemoan the difficulties of raising adolescent girls, the fights, the doors slammed over ear-piercings and not eating and unauthorized late nights, and she used to shrug and sigh along with them, but in truth their experiences bore little relation to her own. Was she blind? Perhaps – Verity's own mother knew very little about her during her adolescence, so why should it have been different with herself and Hester?

And now they had both come to the end of their association with this house. Verity had her eye on a detached cottage on the edge of Chiddingbourne, a village about eight miles away. It had the right amount of garden, and was within reach of shops, acquaintances, the rail link to London. These were all considerations. And Hester would visit her there, sometimes. Hester would never cut her out.

How dare I be so certain? thought Verity. I'm about to show Hester something that will change the way she sees me, sees her father, sees her childhood, herself . . . I'm about to break up the ground under her feet, so how can there be any more certainties? It's not only this house we will be leaving. A journey into the past lies before us, but I do not think we will be fellow travellers.

*

Hester fastened her emptied suitcase and stowed it in the bottom of the wardrobe. She took a notepad and pen and went out to sit in the garden. She would have liked to wander round, touching and smelling, saying goodbye to everything, but she knew her mother would be watching from the window for just such behaviour, and Hester had a dislike of being understood. So, she thought, I'll just sit in the shade looking cool and purposeful. When Verity had finished twittering about indoors she could come and fetch her, and they could start on the grand sort-out.

I do mind about this house, thought Hester, pen poised for bogus note-taking. She would mind, but it wouldn't hurt her or change her. Her childhood, she felt, was something she'd left behind her. It wasn't quite Larkin's 'half-forgotten boredom', but there were – well, gaps. She knew that it would be nice if she could show her mother that she minded, just a little, but she also knew that she couldn't do that. She didn't share.

In a funny way, the house had meant more to her before she came to live in it, in the days of the monthly visits to Grandma Evelyn – visits frequent enough to allow Hester to feel that she knew the place in every season, every weather. She had her own room, the one she carried on having when they moved there properly, the one she had so carefully denuded when she reckoned it was time to start her own life. The furniture in it had been the standard old-fashioned spare-bedroom furniture, but Grandma Evelyn had always put out something special for her, every visit. She remembered a fan spread out on the bed, black – could it have been real ebony? – with a view of a fantastical city painted across the struts, and a curled black feather glued to the end of each. Then there was a carved ivory ball, cats and rats scrambling over each other, and two of the

49

rats had red eyes. You had to turn it over and over until you found them. There was a lacquered box with a sliding lid that held mother-of-pearl fish, used as currency for games of vingt-et-un. There was Evelyn's own Noah's Ark, a survivor from that dark brown Edwardian childhood in the East London rectory where she and the crippled Walter sat by a small coal fire listening to their father read aloud from the *Pilgrim's Progress* on those fuggy Sunday afternoons. The Noah's Ark had been her Sunday toy, Evelyn explained to Hester. She arranged the animals in procession on the hearth-rug as her father read, but she enjoyed mixing up the pairs. The antelope escorted the leopard, the crocodile waddled by the side of the giraffe. By the time the Ark and its contents were laid out for Hester's benefit the zebra's stripes had all but worn away and many of the animals' thin wooden legs had snapped off and been replaced with pins. Verity was anxious – 'Do be careful with those pins, Hester. Really it's just for looking at, you shouldn't play with it.' But Hester was careful. Her mother should have known that.

Evelyn put out just one special thing for each visit, for Hester to concentrate on. There were other things in the room, though, that never changed. There was a row of books, pressed together by bookends carved like elephants. These were not children's books. Though Hester didn't read them, the titles fed her imagination. *Dreams* by Olive Schreiner. *Leaves of Grass* by Walt Whitman. *The Stones of Venice. The Goblin Market.* Chosen, presumably, to suit the tastes of a wide range of guests. Hester loved the muted colours of their bindings, blue that was almost green, red that was almost brown. She liked to run her forefinger over the gold lettering, the embossed twists of leaves and stalks that ornamented them regardless of their subject-matter. Each book was like a door to her, the kind of door you find in dreams; you go through it and glimpse or sense an atmosphere, something intangible and indescribable, and then it's gone. There was a small bookcase next to the bed with proper children's books in it, and those she did read. They were mostly from her mother's childhood – *Doctor Doolittle* and *Swallows and Amazons* and a marvellous book called *A Pony for Jean*. She read them with huge enjoyment, but they didn't have the almost mystical transforming quality of that row of faded spines.

In Grandma Evelyn's day everything seemed more distinct. Meals were odd, and not always very nice. One could strike lucky with a fruit pie, or some tiny new peas from the garden, but Hester did remember her father going on strike about bloaters. 'Really, Evelyn,' he said in his carrying voice with its faint Viennese clip, 'this is the last house in England in which one is expected to eat bloaters.' 'They're cheap,' retorted Evelyn, 'and nourishing.' 'They will fail to nourish me,' said Simeon, laying down his fork, 'because I will fail to eat them.' Evelyn laughed. She liked strong-minded people, and was slow to take offence. Verity's apologetic, conciliating tone irritated her far more than Simeon's rudeness.

Simeon didn't always come with them to Knighton. He was a barrister, later to become a judge, and he was always busy. A weekend in London without his wife and child was always an excellent opportunity for him to catch up on paperwork. Hester often heard her mother explaining that to people, again with a note of apology in her voice. But Hester liked the weekends when her father didn't come. She and her mother took the train – Verity was a timid driver. When school ended at about four, they'd take the Number 11 bus to Charing Cross. That had always been Hester's favourite London bus route, and her favourite seat was on the top deck at the front. You could see into all the King's Road shops and, more thrillingly, into the flats above the shops. One warm spring afternoon she saw a young man leaning out of a first-floor window, waving his arms and shouting. He had seen his girlfriend in the street. She looked up; he grabbed some flowers that must have been in a vase behind him and threw them down to her. She stood there, laughing, while the lipstick-coloured tulips scattered at her feet. Hester remembered it so clearly – her panda eyes, her small hooky nose, her short pinafore dress and baker-boy cap made out of the same brown checked material, her big pink mouth open and laughing. She wasn't pretty, not really pretty, but she was lit up by love. He ran down the stairs and through the boutique beneath the flat, he ran out into the street and grabbed her and twirled her round and round. Hester saw all this while the Number 11 bus waited at a traffic light. That was her sixties, her swinging sixties. That glimpse was enough.

The bus would trundle on to Victoria and down the grey wind tunnel that was Victoria Street, where there was nothing to look at except the Army & Navy Stores, on past Westminster Abbey and its Hawksmoor towers that looked like painted cut-outs against the sky, round Parliament Square and up Whitehall, where they were quite often held up by demonstrations, especially outside Downing Street. During one of these hold-ups Verity explained about suffragettes and Grandma Evelyn and pointed to the railings to which she had chained herself and Hester thought she would burst with pride and surprise. 'Grandma?' she kept asking, 'you mean, the real Grandma?' and her mother laughed, in a nice way.

The bus stopped outside Charing Cross Station. If they'd missed their train, which happened quite often, Verity would ring Grandma from a public telephone at the station. The youth of today, reflected Hester, can have no concept of how difficult it used to be to make a telephone call outside your own home – how rare telephone boxes were, how few kinds of coin they would accept, how many of them were vandalized, how long the queues to use them could be. After two or three goes of picking chewing gum out of the slot with a Biro or a key and banging the box to make the big brown pennies go in, Verity got through and arranged for Grandma to meet them an hour later, and then they'd go and buy a bag of seed to feed the pigeons from a man who sold it in Trafalgar Square, or they'd visit Uccello's five-legged horse in the National Gallery.

Hester liked the train journey – what child doesn't enjoy trains? She liked the feeling of ownership, of knowing the line – she would tell her mother which station was coming next and Verity would pretend not to know. 'Is it, darling?' she would say. 'Oh, you are clever.' Hester didn't realize, then, that she was pretending. Her mother must have known exactly where they were at any point, because the journey had been familiar to her since childhood, and because she was alert all the time. She carried worry with her like extra luggage. Hester always sensed, from her earliest years, that for Verity, responsibility was at least three quarters of motherhood.

Those journeys were good times for mother and daughter. In public places Verity's unobtrusiveness was something Hester appreciated, and the hour and a quarter the train took was the right length of time for harmonious companionship. And things were always better between them when Simeon wasn't there. Hester never fully formulated this to herself until years later. In the unlikely event that anyone had asked her, she would have declared that having one's two parents together was, of course, the ideal. But in practice, her father's presence diminished her mother. Verity became smaller, meaner, more colourless. At Knighton he laid down the law; his law did not overlap with Grandma Evelyn's and Verity slipped down the crack between them.

Going back home on Sunday evening was nice when Simeon hadn't come because he was always genial on their return. He met them at Charing Cross in his Jaguar – Simeon adored smart cars, whereas Verity didn't care at all as long as they got her from A to B – and then he'd drive them just a little too fast along the Embankment. Hester loved to watch the lights winking on in the purple dusk. Back at home, he'd have made them a special supper. Simeon always liked to make a fuss about food. In adult life, this kind of fuss made Hester crave something simple like Marmite on toast, but as a child she loved the palaver. He didn't really cook, but he assembled things. There might be strips of black bread with dollops of sour cream draped with a little apricot blanket of smoked salmon. Or sometimes he'd have boiled some eggs, scooped out the yolks, mashed them with cream cheese and paprika and piled the mixture back into the white boat of the half-egg. Hester enjoyed the colours, and she prided herself on being able to eat such food, as she knew most children wouldn't. She thought of it as princess food. It was a world away from her mother's weekday provision of mince and mashed potato and the obligatory green vegetable.

Her parents drank schnapps, or something similar, in small thick tumblers that looked opaque because Simeon had put them in the freezing compartment. Verity drank only a very little bit, just to please him. Hester asked to put her finger in it, but it made her cough. She drank orange juice, also out of a tiny cold tumbler. At the end of the meal Simeon would make thick sludgy coffee in a special aluminium pot that made only a thimbleful at a time – he put so much sugar into his that they joked that the spoon could stand up on its own. Then, with a flourish, he would produce Hester's treat. It was usually a cake, in a white box tied with round gold string, a millefeuille or a chocolate éclair, or a tart with three strawberries winking up out of their shiny glaze. Sometimes it was marzipan fruits on a plinth of darkest chocolate, and that was difficult, because though Hester thought the fruits extremely beautiful she didn't like marzipan. Her father never remembered that, and if he was reminded it seemed to make him cross, so she learned just to nibble the chocolate and tell him that she was saving the fruits for later, and that satisfied him because he knew how she liked to hoard and gloat over beautiful things. It certainly wasn't worth tarnishing the ruby glow of those Sunday evenings by voicing anything so trivial as a disappointment over marzipan. It was princess food, and it merited princess behaviour.

Those Sunday evenings saw her father at his best, and his best was good enough to tide them over the in-between bits. They were hugely preferable to the rare occasions when he'd been with them at Knighton and they drove back, late to avoid the traffic, with Simeon grumbling at them and cursing other drivers and Verity pleading with him to slow down. Those car journeys had a certain glamour for Hester, because she would be in her nightdress and slippers, with her coat over the top, bedded down on the back seat with a cushion and a rug. Her grandmother would give her a bag of barley sugar to suck in case she felt sick, which was particularly special as it was the only time she was allowed sweets after she'd brushed her teeth. She liked watching the inky trees wheel past, and the movement of the car easily lent itself to fantasies about travelling across a stormy sea or through the night sky on the back of a winged horse, but these fantasies needed to be worked extra hard to dissipate the sound of her parents bickering, and the effort would make her stomach feel tight. She was usually asleep before they reached London, though she would claim that she'd been awake all the way. She had a memory that bobbed to the surface, a memory that wouldn't dissolve, of a couple of sentences spoken by her parents, when they must have thought she was fast asleep. 'If it wasn't for her –' came Verity's voice, small and hard, and then Simeon cut across her with 'What makes you think you have the right to blackmail me?' In Hester's memory her father's voice was like a mastiff's growl.

Even though Hester was ten when Grandma Evelyn gave up Knighton, quite an old child, she was passive about the whole business. The decision to move from London was wholly a product of the adult world. Conscientious, fair-minded Verity did her best to talk it through – would Hester miss her school friends, would she be bored in the country? – but Hester seemed to be resistant to such conversations. They seemed to slide over her, as if she was covered in Vaseline. The thing that bothered her – though she didn't say so – was that Grandma would no longer live at Knighton. She was the permanence, more than the house itself.

They moved in the summer of 1970. Hester completed the term at her smart little London school, and then she had the whole of the six-week holiday to adjust to the change before she started at The Turrets. Everything was arranged with her well-being as the first consideration. It had been decided that she should take over the bedroom she'd always used, but her grandmother cleared it of almost everything – 'We don't want you to feel as if you're a visitor.' Hester didn't protest, and she liked the new curtains that were run up specially for her arrival; sprigs of forget-me-nots on a pale pink background, the same curtains she took with her, years later, to her London flat, where they didn't look right anywhere. But though she was pleased about the curtains, the thought of all the old spare-bedroom furniture separated and exiled in different parts of the house was melancholy. Together, the bed and the books, the chest of drawers and the dressing table, had made a little world, a stage for her early imaginings; separately they were nothing. Even that row of books, still wedged between the carved elephants but now moved to the landing windowsill, lost its resonance and became just another line of the great unread. The children's books went with Grandma to her cottage. 'For you to read when you come to visit me.' But Hester was just too old.

Hester was perfectly happy at Knighton, in the accepted meaning of the phrase; when people say 'perfectly happy' what they mean is 'mildly happy' or 'usually content', nothing to do with perfection at all. Her feeling for the place fell into different shapes that slotted into the different phases of the day. First there was the morning, which was a bright semicircle shape, like the rising sun. That part of the day was coloured brilliant blue and orange and it made her feel glad to be alive. She woke and relished the comfort of her bed, lay and gazed at the morning light seeping through the forget-me-not curtains, read a few pages, enjoyed the warm weight of the tabby cat coiled at her feet. It was an imaginary cat; her father didn't let her have a real one until she was fourteen, and then it was a thin black one, and not allowed on the beds. On a weekday her mother would come in at half past seven and chivvy her out of bed and into the school clothes that waited in a plump pile on her Lloyd

Loom chair, but on Saturdays and Sundays it would be her father who burst in. 'Move over,' he would command, and he'd fold his big frame up like a deckchair and cram into her bed. He wore expensive pyjamas. Hester had heard her mother complaining mildly to a friend about how expensive they were, and the friend had said, 'Well, he is a judge.' The pyjamas were pale blue with dark blue piping and a monogram on the pocket. His chest hair, like the hair on his head, lion-coloured and sprinkled with silver, curled out round the lapels. He had hair on his shoulders and in the small of his back, and the hair on his wrists was as thick and springy as a teddy bear's. He would have reading matter tucked under his arm, and he would read aloud to her – babyish things like *Struwel Peter*, or bits from the *Economist* or the *New Statesman*. The mixture appeared to be random. Hester leaned against his side and listened, and waited for the moment when he had had enough. She could feel it in his body like an electric charge. Simeon could never sit still for long – Hester did wonder how he managed his judging – and he never wanted to go on sleeping in the mornings. At this period, in the early 1970s, he was no longer a young man, but a young man's energy still spiralled through him. Ten, fifteen minutes of reading and he would throw aside the book or magazine, sometimes even in mid-sentence. 'Come on!' he would cry. 'Let's get going!' And seconds later he would be whistling and splashing in the shower. He had installed the shower when they moved in as an absolute priority. Grandma Evelyn would never have contemplated such a thing. Inside her old bath you could still see the traces of the line that had been painted on to ration bathwater during the war.

So that was the best bit of the day, the orange-and-blue bit, when everything seemed vigorous and bright and open.

The end of the school day was a quieter colour, a sort of pale fudge. Nice, in its own way, but quiet, and fudge-shaped, too, a sort of crumbly square. Hester liked the walk home from the station, the damp smell of the lanes in autumn, dead leaves mixed with a curl of bonfire smoke. She liked looking for the first spring flowers – her mother told her their names, and she associated them with her. There was one particular patch of celandines at the top of the lane that grew bigger every year. Hester thought they were heavenly, the way they shone, as if they had just been washed. Then in May there were such foamy waves of cow parsley, you couldn't believe there was so much. And then when it was over, you just forgot about it.

Back at home, that was the quiet, comfortable, fudgy bit. Tea, homework, television. Her mother an unobtrusive presence, moving about the kitchen, asking questions but not too many. The thing that irritated Hester was that Verity insisted on watching television with her. It was all right if it was *Z Cars* or the news or something, but during *Top of the Pops* her mother would tap her feet and hum, and comment on what Pan's People were wearing or not wearing, and Hester would be itching to be left alone, because she needed to absorb the important information that *Top of the Pops* gave her in concentrated silence. While Hester did her homework at the kitchen table, Verity chopped and peeled for the adult meal, and as she did so she would hand out slivers of carrot, curlicues of raw red cabbage, cubes of avocado like green butter, and sometimes the slices bore the pleasing taint of garlic or chilli if she'd been using the same knife. Some of the ingredients she used were quite exotic for those days, and quite expensive too. Left to her own devices, Verity would have been a safe plain cook, but Simeon insisted on bold food. He liked sabre slashes of flavour –

Hester associated him with a swirl of sour cream in a bowl of borscht, pickled gherkins like miniature crocodiles which he pulled out of their jar with wooden tongs, cubes of raw meat gasping for breath in the hot oil of a fondue. He couldn't bear stodge.

Verity was by nature abstemious, almost puritanical. She never picked at food as she cooked, despite encouraging Hester to do so; she never poured herself a glass of sherry before Simeon got home. She sat down with a cup of tea while Hester ate her meal, but that was all. On the days when Simeon didn't come home, which was about twice a week, she ate beans on toast with Hester and went to bed early. But when Simeon did return everything was ready, and perfect, or as perfect as she could make it, which in his opinion too often fell short.

Hester would be bathed and in her dressing gown by the time her father's Jaguar purred up the drive. He always rang the doorbell, never used his key, and when Hester heard his ring, that was when the final phase of the day began, the pointy black velvet time, jagged with crimson and purple. Her stomach would contract into a hard ball when she heard the door open. She was usually in her bedroom; she never ran down to greet him with cries of delight, as she might have done when younger. By the time she was eleven or twelve she no longer wanted to intercept the look on his face, because she could not be sure that it would be the look she wanted. So she waited for him to call her, and he didn't always do that. She listened; she could hear her mother hanging up his heavy coat, she could hear his voice, some-times irritable, sometimes genial, as without being asked he told her about his day. She could hear the clash of ice in his tumbler of whisky as he carried it from the kitchen to the small living room they called the parlour because that was what her grandmother had always called it. That was the moment when he would summon her, if at all. He would pause by the parlour door and shout, 'Hester! Here! Come and kiss me, Mouse!' Then she would go downstairs, not too fast, and sit on his lap in the armchair by the parlour fire, and pretend to steal his whisky, and he would pretend to scold her. He quizzed her about her day, much more vigorously than her mother ever did, and sometimes he sent her to fetch her homework so that he could inspect it. Every error or sloppiness would be challenged. He would want her to correct it straight away, but this was one area on which her mother held firm. 'Not now, Simeon. She's all ready for bed. She won't sleep if her mind's full of home-work. There's plenty of time in the morning.' 'All right,' said her father, setting her aside as he rose to make his way to the dining room, 'but remember, Hester, no child of mine takes shoddy work to school. Your mother will check it tomorrow.' It was at such moments that Hester felt most keenly that she was an only child. He sent her off to bed with a swipe across the backs of her thighs that was halfway between a pat and a slap. And she would lie in bed nursing her jangled nerves, because there was something about her father's evening self that could shake her almost to pieces.

Her mother never did check her homework the next morning, or at any other time. This was one of her mute defiances, as Hester knew perfectly well. But Hester checked it herself. Her father's censures were like fresh wounds; a night's sleep did not ease the smart. She did not forget the errors he pointed out. She made neat amendments, and received high marks.

There came a time – there always comes a time – when he no longer climbed into bed with her, when she no longer sat in his lap. One rarely knows, thought Hester, when the last time happens – the last supervised bath, the last tickle, the last story read aloud – but certainly by the age of fourteen she was staying up to dine with her parents and creating sufficient difficulties over displaying her homework to make him discard that aspect of parental responsibility. He was never a patient man. As her adolescence advanced, so her sense of separateness grew. Mentally, she lived apart from her parents, her life touching theirs only at certain designated moments. She had always liked to build walls between school life and home life, even when she was a young child in Chelsea, and in her teens this became almost an obsession. She invited few friends home. However well she got on with them at school, once she brought them home the feeling between them seemed to shrivel or wither. It was as if there wasn't enough emotional oxygen in the house to nourish a friendship. The one friend who was an exception to this rule was Jennifer Wentworth. Jennifer was so simple, so straightforward, that she remained unchanged in any context. At school she talked about ponies and teachers and how many children she was going to have (five) and what their names would be (Hester couldn't remember, except there were to be twin boys called Tim and Tom). At home – at Hester's home, or hers – she talked about exactly the same things.

She was a useful friend to have, because she was so entirely restful. Verity believed her to be Hester's best friend. Of course she wasn't. It wasn't possible to feel more strongly about Jennifer than one might feel about, say, a guinea pig – mildly affectionate and slightly responsible – but Hester was quite happy for her mother to misinterpret Jennifer's role in her life because it was such a convenient blind. When, at the age of fifteen, she started going out with boys, she tended to tell her mother that she was going to Jennifer's house. And she had never brought the boyfriends home with her, not once.

So Knighton House had been her base, but it had never been her life. Now that the whole thing was coming to an end, and her mother planned to move to a pleasant but unremarkable cottage on the edge of Chiddingbourne, the change was not going to affect Hester too much. She wasn't going to let it. She was forty years old, and by now she'd worked out how to stop things from affecting her when she didn't want them to. Everything, surely, was a matter of choice.

4

'When Simeon died, I was on the lavatory.' Verity often repeated this to herself. 'I was on the lavatory when Simeon died.' Which way round? Did one way of putting it make it sound better, or less bad, than the other? In any case, the statement might not be entirely accurate. Technically, life may have left Simeon just before or just after she sat down. It might have happened when she was pulling down her tights, or when she was washing her hands afterwards. Did his pulse flicker out as she pulled the chain, did his heart crumple in on itself as she turned on the tap? She had sat on the lavatory for quite a long time, because she wanted to finish an article about alliums in one of the Saturday papers, and she hadn't wanted Simeon to see her reading it. As time went on she disliked more and more that he should find out what she liked, or show an interest in anything that caught her attention. It gave her a small, hard pleasure to keep that kind of information from him. Of course he'd always known in broad terms that she liked gardening, loved flowers, but the specifics she needed to keep to herself. So she read about alliums behind a locked door, and when she had finished, Simeon was dead.

Most people were too polite to ask for details about a death, so she hadn't given many. She put it the same way of putting it to everybody – 'I left him in the parlour with his coffee, and when I came back he was – gone.' Nobody knew that she was on the lavatory. She didn't imagine that anybody ever would.

It was a heart attack, which was how they had both expected he would die, because he'd had a little heart trouble for years. His death was absolute. Verity knew, as soon as she opened the door of the parlour, even though she couldn't see much of him over the back of his chair. She hadn't gone in to see him. She went in to answer the telephone, prepared to be a little angry with him for not answering it first, but that was something that quite often happened. So she stood there, and Simeon was dead, and she just let the phone ring and ring, because what can you do if someone's just dead in front of your eyes? You can't answer and say, I'm awfully sorry, could I ring you back? She never did find out who was ringing. She just stood there, looking at him, counting the rings and thinking, he's just not there any more. What's in the chair is simply not him. Then the ringing stopped, and she picked up the telephone and dialled an ambulance, not because there was any chance that he might be alive, but to cover herself. That's what it was, if she was honest. To cover herself. 'Poor Verity did the right thing. What else could she have done?'

She could have touched him, for one thing. She had not touched him once after he was dead. She moved his coffee cup, which was full; she gathered up the newspaper which had slipped off his lap and lay scattered in sheets on the floor. But Simeon himself she failed to touch. That was another reason for calling the ambulance. The men could do it for her. When the boiler packed up, she called a man to dismantle it for her, of course. When wasps nested in the chimney, in came Mr Dallaway the pest controller in his overalls to deal with them. She was used to calling men to move things that she did not want to touch. And when she saw Simeon in his chair with his head to one side and his face a colour that it had never been before, a colour she

65

could not describe except to say that it was nothing to do with him, nothing to do with his real appearance, the thought went through her head straight away, *Simeon, I never have to touch you again*. That was another thing nobody else knew. Yet another.

Did she exult when Simeon died? Not exactly. She rested her hand on the piano lid and closed her eyes and allowed one wave of exultation to surge through her, like a heavenly scent, like lilac or gardenias. Then that was all, and she got on with things, including, later on, crying, and missing him, because as well as being thrilled by his death she was sad and bereft in quite a conventional widowish way, just as throughout their married life she'd felt affection for him or pleasure in his company as well as all the other feelings.

She couldn't ring Hester, who was in China. When he died his wife was on the lavatory, his daughter was in China! If only Simeon had known, he'd have made a ponderous joke about different sorts of china, she felt sure. Hester had left the address of the hotel, but not the number. By evening Verity had tracked her down, or rather her helpful friend Beryl had done it for her. Beryl Barber was the person Verity called upon to help, not because she was a particularly dear friend – she wasn't much more than a friendly neighbour – but because she was always in, and because it was the sort of thing she loved. Verity felt quite altruistic. She knew that she wouldn't be able to have all the proper soap-operatic reactions to this important event, and she didn't want the moment to go to waste, so she called in Beryl, and Beryl was marvellous. It was something about the three Bs in her name. Bustling Beryl Barber. She didn't have any option but to be marvellous. And one of the many extraordinary things she did over that weekend – he died on a Saturday – was to get through to the hotel in Beijing and leave a message for Hester.

When Hester rang back, bustling Beryl answered. Verity had been sent to her room to lie down. She lay flat on her back and felt all the energy run out of her. She reminded herself of an effigy on a tomb, cold, and calm. It wasn't an unpleasant feeling. When the telephone rang she knew it was Hester, and thought about picking it up, but her brain didn't seem to want to push the message all the way through to her hand, so she just lay there, inert.

Downstairs, Beryl was being very ert indeed. 'She's having a little sleep,' Verity heard her say, her voice vibrant with importance. So she didn't speak to Hester on the day it happened. By the time she arrived late on the Monday afternoon there'd been a shift. Simeon's body had long since gone, Beryl had reorganized the parlour furniture to take away that feeling of there being a great black hole where he had been, Verity was busy with arrangements, and the house had the usual sorting-out feeling, only more so, that Mondays always have, even when people are retired. Hester arrived and stepped straight into action. They said very little about the death itself. Hester was all for going through her father's belongings at once, throwing things out or bundling them up for Oxfam, but Verity wouldn't let her. She said it didn't feel right to do it before the funeral. So instead, Hester concentrated on making everything look perfect. She got in a team of cleaners who scoured the house from top to bottom and upset Mrs Davidge, who'd muddled through flicking dusters for twenty-three years. Hester got the gravel done, too. Verity did the flowers for the house, for when everyone came back after the funeral. She thought, that's one thing I can do for you, Simeon, without feeling complicated about it. She did the flowers to the high standard he would have expected of her, and he would have acknowledged that, though he would not have been able to see how truly beautiful they were, the hyacinths and the jonquils, the arching branches of cherry blossom, the coils of fern like bronze escutcheons, the scent of lilac just released from its dusky bud.

A lot of people came to the funeral, and most of them came back to the house afterwards, where Hester had organized caterers to hand round sherry and cups of tea and very small sandwiches. It was all quite impersonal, which may have made it easier to deal with, or may merely have delayed the onset of more difficult reactions. Most people told Verity how admirably calm she was, and how lovely the house was looking, and it was then that she decided to sell it. Only of course she didn't say so at the time.

This weekend, she'd got Hester down under false pretences. Hester thought they were going to sort through Simeon's things together because Verity hadn't been able to bring herself to do it, but that wasn't true. Verity had done it. Oh, not everything. She hadn't bothered about his socks and handkerchiefs and what have you – she'd leave all that to Hester, it was the sort of thing she would enjoy. A good chance to exercise her ruthless efficiency. But the papers, the letters, the locked drawers – Verity had done it all. She believed that she now knew everything she needed to know about her dead husband. And she had ordered and shaped it all so that Hester would find exactly what she wanted her to find. She believed that Hester knew very little. Verity had always found her incurious – unless that was just a front.

Verity would have to dissemble a little. She would have to put on an act. She'd already had to do some acting with Hester, and acting wasn't her strong suit. Keeping secrets, yes – her own and other people's. One could say that was her speciality. But keeping secrets and acting were not quite the same thing.

It was funny, thought Hester, that she had almost no memories of her father sitting in the garden where she now sat. It was one of the loveliest gardens she knew, and yet he had made very little use of it. He didn't do much sitting anywhere, not until the last couple of years when he had begun to feel his age. If he watched television he would switch on the chosen programme at exactly the right time, watch it intently, snap it off the moment the credits appeared. There was never any channel-hopping, no dozing in front of *Grandstand*. Nothing indiscriminate. The same went for reading. Sit down, read what you want to read, slam the book shut, get up, get going. Sitting over meals was the one time he would linger, but only if he had someone interesting to argue or flirt with.

Sitting about in the garden would have been, to Simeon, as much a waste of time as sitting about in the house, only more irritating because of getting too hot or too cold, or because of insects, or because of that tiresome habit the sun has of shifting so that the position of the shadows changes. He was proud of the garden, and generous in his praise of Verity and her labours in it, and visitors were always given a guided tour, but even that was something of a route march. Hester's father was essentially a city man. His own unmentionable, unimaginable childhood had happened in Vienna, and his professed admiration for the English countryside was somewhat theoretical. For him, crossing a muddy field was like wading through a giant's frying pan full of old black grease.

When Hester was told that he had died, she couldn't

think where to picture it. If it had been her mother, she thought, it would have been here, under this cherry tree, where she was sitting now. Hester could picture her lying, not sprawled, just lying, on the grass, a scatter of cut flowers all round her. She could see it now, even though it hadn't happened. But her father she couldn't see. Not in bed, not somewhere undignified like the bath. Not in the garden. At the wheel of his car, perhaps – yes, a heart attack at the wheel, a sudden swerve, the car up against a tree; smoke and flames. She needed to see – something. She had a strong urge to complete that mental image. But 'he went peacefully' was all she heard from bossy Beryl Barber. 'It was his heart.' Hester wanted to say, more, tell me more, but the line from China was poor, and she couldn't in any case have asked Beryl Barber many questions. She was the sort of person who would use your need to get a hold on you.

Hester gathered, in time, that he had, after all, been sitting. Sitting in his armchair in the parlour, coffee and newspapers to hand. An old man's death, comfortable, serene. 'Just how he would have wanted to go,' as more than one person had said to her over sherry after the funeral, and Hester smiled and said nothing but she couldn't have agreed less. Her father had been someone who wanted to make a difference. Easing out of life, slipping like the unread newspaper, cooling like the untasted coffee – that was not the end he would have chosen.

Her father in the house, though, and her mother in the garden – yes, that made sense. Separate – always separate – and yet not estranged. Moving and thinking, breathing and feeling within the same clearly defined parameters. He died, and she wasn't there, but she found out soon enough. She would have gone in, Hester imagined, to offer him a second cup of the powerful Italian coffee he liked to take after lunch. She could see her mother slipping off her garden shoes, easing the parlour door open in her aggravatingly considerate way, saying, 'Simeon? More coffee?' and then having to repeat it, stepping forward, speaking to him a little more sharply, and then – no, she couldn't envisage her mother's reaction to what she saw, which was probably because she didn't want to.

Verity had said very little about finding him. Now that Hester thought about it, she didn't even know that her mother had been in the garden. She may have assumed that because Verity said, 'It was a beautiful bright day, so warm for April.' No, Hester couldn't be sure where her mother had been, but she did know where she herself had been – in China, on a holiday that had been her fortieth birthday present to herself. She was asleep when the hotel buzzed her. She had that feeling that one has of being hauled out of deep, deep water, green and thick. The news didn't jolt her awake; rather, it in itself took on the quality of a dream. She remembered thinking, very calmly, it's all right. This is only something that happened to you a very long time ago.

After the funeral, people kept asking her how her mother was, and how did Hester think she'd taken it? 'Remarkably well,' was Hester's stock response, and then she added, in case she sounded too callous, 'I do think it helped that the end was so peaceful.' She didn't really know how she expected her mother to take it. They'd kept to fairly neutral topics in the days before the funeral, and the hovering presence of Beryl Barber had been useful as they'd been able to have a few quiet chuckles at her expense. At the funeral her mother shed tears, not noisily; up until then she'd seemed more or less her usual self, except dreamier, more remote. She was, as Hester would have expected, fairly limp about organizing anything. The only thing she really

71

concentrated on were the flowers for the post-funeral gathering. 'So therapeutic,' whispered Beryl, not quite out of earshot of Verity, who stood in the scullery twisting and stripping and snipping, plunging lilac stems into boiling water and forcing chicken wire into humps over blocks of Oasis. Beryl was probably right. Verity spent ages on the flowers, which she seemed to regard as some kind of personal mission. They looked, of course, magnificent.

The funeral was followed by a weekend, which was quite a satisfactory debriefing period, but only on one level. They put the house back to rights, and as they did so they discussed the people who'd turned up, how surprised they were to see X, how good it was of poor old Y to have made the effort, how much weight Z had put on. The vicar who conducted the service called; he knew both Hester's parents quite well. Her mother had been a quiet churchgoer for years, and since his retirement her father had rather surprisingly taken to joining her – to her dismay, Hester imagined. So the vicar's call was tactful, and welcome. They sat in the parlour drinking tea amidst the flowers, wreathed with the smells of woodsmoke and beeswax and narcissi, as if they'd been stage-managed, her mother hospitable and composed, the vicar solicitous and kind. He sat in the chair in which her father had died. Hester didn't know whether he knew. He may well have done. He would have sat in it, to exorcize it; he was a good vicar.

Verity's understandable and characteristic refusal to tackle Simeon's belongings that weekend had irked Hester, though she didn't say so. Hester wanted, quite badly, to finish everything off. At his graveside she'd been surprised by a sudden and powerful sense of satisfaction that fell on her like a thick blanket as the coffin was lowered into place. She would rather have had him cremated, but he'd left specific instructions. She liked it when the coffin was quite covered with earth. She'd been at funerals where people threw things into the grave – flowers, messages, even shells and stones – but nobody threw anything in with her father.

And now, over these next few days, all the sorting-out had to happen that should have happened after the funeral. Hester wanted to get on with it, yet she was reluctant to leave this sunny garden. Bees were trembling in the lavender, the lime tree leaves were whispering in the faintest of warm breezes, and she was held, suspended in a honey-coloured bubble that felt like the best of childhood. Would her mother call her in? Perhaps not. She needed to get up and seek her out, nerve herself to break the bubble and move inside to a much darker place.

From the window, Verity watched. I'll call her in, she thought. She won't expect it. She'll be thinking, I wish Mum would stop fiddling about in the kitchen so that we can get on with things. She looked so composed out there under the cherry tree, so cool in that dove-coloured linen despite the heat of the afternoon, but inside, Verity knew she would be itching with impatience. Any minute she'd get up and stretch, smooth the creases out of her dress, and come and find her. 'Well, Mum? Don't you think we ought to get on?'

So Verity would surprise her. She'd take control.

5

22nd April 1980

'If I live to be as old as you, Grandma,' said Hester, 'it'll be 2045.'

'That's a thought,' said Verity. 'A century since the end of the war.'

'For how much longer will the war be The War, I wonder?' I said. 'Not for a hundred years, I'm afraid. The Great War was meant to be the war to end all wars, and it wasn't.'

'Well,' said Hester, 'the next one will be the last, so my chances of living as long as you are virtually nil, because we'll all be nuked by the year 2000.'

'Not all of us,' said Verity. 'Some people always survive, don't you think?'

'Not a nuclear war. The whole world will be poisoned. And anyway, who'd want to survive? Not me. It's not even worth having children any more.'

Verity and I smiled at one another, but Verity's smile was anxious. 'I think most generations make that declaration,' I said. 'And then, somehow or other, they change their minds.'

This was the conversation we were having this afternoon, as we inched our way round the garden at Sissinghurst. I say inched, because my arthritic knee means that I have to shuffle along with a walking stick, one of those old ladies' sticks with a rubber foot, but Verity and I would want to go slowly in any case, because a passion for plants is something we share. Hester was impatient. She shows little sign of developing an enthusiasm for gardening, though what girl does at twenty? I'm sure I didn't know a geranium from a cabbage at that age. Little girls love planting things, candytuft and nasturtiums, being given their own special patch – I know Hester did. But then in the teens it all goes. I suppose human activity is so much more interesting than anything else at that stage. Then when they've got homes of their own they want the garden to look nice, but they want lots of colour and quick results, like wallpaper. It's not until after the childbearing's finished that they start to think about the essence of plants. Flowers become less important, leaves and buds and berries matter more. Now I'm old I love the garden almost as much in January as I do in June. The glint of silvery bark, a patch of bright moss in weak sunshine, black twigs shifting against a dun sky – these things accord with my old age. The interplay of permanence and renewal – this is what gardening is all about, but one cannot expect to find that of interest to a young woman. So poor Hester struggled to suppress her irritation as we crept through Sissinghurst on this my eighty-fifth birthday. No wonder she seemed quite buoyed up at the idea of the destruction of the human race.

'Mum, please don't do that,' she said to Verity, who had snapped off a sprig of daphne. Verity is good at growing things from cuttings. She cannot walk among plants of any kind without taking a couple of seed heads or a little shoot of something or other. It's a surprising trait, perhaps, in such a cautious character. It drives Hester to distraction.

'I'm sorry, darling. But I'm not doing any harm.'

'That's what boys who spray their initials all over bus shelters would say, but you would call them vandals.'

Verity was on the brink of reply, but thought better of it; it was my birthday outing, and her instinct is always to keep the peace. Hester's remark was hardly accurate. Disfiguring bus shelters doesn't bear comparison with removing a twig for the purpose of nurturing it into active life, but Hester has not yet grown out of the teenage belief that debate consists of throwing out more or less startling assertions, and perhaps where her parents are concerned she never will. Wise Verity stooped over a clump of particularly pretty auriculas, their centres almost black, the heart-shaped petals edged with cream in the precise manner of botanical illustrations. 'I wonder if they have any more of these for sale. Would you like some, Mother? It would hardly count as a present.'

I'd stipulated no presents – at eighty-five, I find it hard enough to do justice to everything already in my possession – but I could see that a little poking about in the nursery shop would be cheerful and, besides, I was rather taken by the auriculas. So we brought our garden tour to an end, and Verity bought the auriculas for me, and I bought a white dicentra for her, and Hester added a fleshy saxifrage for me because, she said, she liked the name. I like the name too – Dragon's Blood. Then Hester was the only person empty-handed, so I chose a potful of pheasant's-eye narcissus, just coming into flower. 'For you to take back to Cambridge,' I said.

'But I don't have a –'

'I know you don't. But you must have a windowsill. And when they've faded, give the bulbs to your mother.'

Verity suggested the tearooms, but I said, 'I think we ought to do our duty by Carol's cake.' Carol, my home help, brought in an iced cake for me this morning, together with a pot of yellow chrysanthemums about which I was polite, though I can't bear flowers out of season. So we drove back to Ewes Green through a misty drizzle that replaced the earlier sunshine, and made inroads into the cake. The youngest Appses – the great-grandchildren of my Mrs Apps – dropped in with their tributes: a basket of eggs, a box of Milk Tray and a very vivid birthday card signed by them all. I put it with the other cards I've received. They're standing in a row on top of the television and, combined with the chrysanthemums, they give the place the authentic air of an old-people's home. The young Appses disposed of more of the cake, and one of them – Trudy, the middle girl, the one with red hair – asked, 'What's the first birthday you can remember, Lady Conway?'

So I told her about my fifth birthday – a Victorian one, though only just. I told her about my visit to Regent's Park Zoo. I was taken there on the omnibus by my Uncle George, my late mother's brother, and his wife, my Aunt Clara. We rode on the top of the 'bus, uncovered, and that was the first time I remember feeling excited about London, about the colour and the activity and the endlessly interlocking lives. I told Trudy and the others about the brown bear accepting the bun that Aunt Clara held out to him on the end of her parasol, and how I declined to ride on an elephant, which I've always regretted, but accepted an ice cream, which was my first. And I'm thinking now about how impossible it would have been on that sunny April afternoon for any of us to imagine that eighty years on I would be sitting here on yet another birthday watching my big-knuckled, ridge-veined, brown-dappled hand moving across the page like some forgotten sea creature as I try to make sense of the life I've lived. This is the same hand that would have slipped, soft and small, into my uncle's grasp. I am the same person who had reservations about the elephant, smiled with delight at the brown bear. How hard it is to understand that, how ceaselessly I try to understand it!

Trudy, and her quieter sister Justine – the names they give these children! Still, I suppose I'm a fine one to talk – were full of questions, and their little brother Lee was full of cake. 'Didn't your mum come with you to the zoo, then?' Trudy asked, and I explained that I had no mother, and they looked stricken and respectful. I told them that I had a brother, whose name was Walter – Lee pulled a face, as if at an unfamiliar taste – but that Walter couldn't come to the zoo with us, because he was a cripple. As I spoke, it occurred to me that in these days a child like Walter would be taken to the zoo with his able-bodied sister as a matter of course. I certainly hope so. I remember – though I didn't say – that I was desperate that he should come, because I cared passionately about him, and I can recall the look that passed across my uncle's face as he said, 'No, Evelyn.' The look was not unkind, but it was unyielding. I think it was from that moment that I understood the extent to which Walter would be forced to spend his life in a kind of half-exile. Though my tears were dry by the time we boarded the omnibus, I never lost that small hard cyst of pain for my brother who, on my fifth birthday, could neither walk nor talk.

The pain is there still, and perhaps Hester noticed it flicker, because she said, 'Mum, Grandma's getting tired.' I protested, but not much, because I wanted to be left alone with my thoughts. I don't understand old people who complain of loneliness; I can't get enough of it. Fond though I am of all this afternoon's companions, and particularly fond as I am of Hester, I was more than ready to see them go. I stood at the window and watched Hester walk to the car. She was to drive; she needed the practice. Verity has put on L-plates. The sight of my long-legged, self-contained granddaughter is very gratifying to me. Hester is a force to be reckoned with. I think she's finding Cambridge life pretty satisfactory. She'd make a good lawyer, though law's not her subject. She's reading history. I can't see her becoming an historian, though; she's highly intelligent, but not a true academic. But whatever she chooses to do she'll do it excellently. So unlike poor Verity's vacillations at a similar age. Of course Verity fell into the clutches of a man who made all her decisions for her. I can't see Hester falling into that trap.

So off they went. It's been a pleasant day. I enjoyed Sissinghurst, because I'm still gripped by the quiet drama played out between the landscape and human lives, and I'm pleased with my auricula and my saxifrage, because I still can't resist plants, even though they'll probably outlive me. It was a civilized birthday outing, though as usual I find it a little awkward when I see Hester and Verity at the same time. I expect that's because I'd rather talk to Hester, and Verity knows it. Is it because I had no mother of my own, that I've been such a half-hearted mother to my only child? Or is it because Verity is not the baby I should have had – not Jack's? When I cradled Verity in my lap, when I rocked her and breathed words of love into her soft hair, there was always a ghost baby crying at the window. I've never told anybody that.

Now they've gone, and I'm writing about them. I think they'd be surprised. I want to write about my mother, because that seems to be the right person to write about on one's birthday, but I find I've little to say. I wonder if I can remember her? The only face I can summon is the one from her photograph, a thin-nosed young woman with a stern expression, but then most people in Victorian photographs have stern expressions. My father always said that the picture was not much like her. I could see that, like mine, her hair was dark and springy; at her throat I could see the cameo brooch that came into my possession. But I had no sense of connection between the face in the photograph and me. I do have a sense that I can't quite put into words, of what the house felt like before Walter. There's a presence that isn't my father's; it's almost a taste in the mouth. But if I try to grasp it, turn it into a memory, it slips out of reach.

My mother died giving birth to Walter. I was less than three years old. I imagine Walter's condition was caused by a lack of oxygen at birth, that whatever complication it was that pulled my mother away from us tried to drag the baby down with her. I never asked, and I don't remember being told anything about it. There would have been very little to tell. I'm sure my father asked few questions. In those days people were inclined to accept disasters, especially medical disasters, without inquiry. But that catastrophe, which had the effect of strengthening and somehow purifying my father's faith, made it impossible in the long run for me to sustain the beliefs of my childhood. Nothing is certain, nothing is just.

I can remember a lot about Walter, from very early on. I have a clear mental picture of him as a biggish baby, dressed all in white, and my father holding him up to the window to look at the moon. Walter was looking, he was reaching for the moon with his eyes, making gasping noises. I said, 'He's trying to say "moon",' and my father looked at me with sorrow and said, 'I don't think so, my darling. I don't think poor Walter will ever learn to talk.' But my father was wrong, and I was right. He did learn to talk, eventually, and to walk, too, though only on crutches. His legs were stiff and straight to his knees, then they stuck out at angles. He was put into callipers at various stages, but they didn't make much difference, except that they left painful, rubbed patches behind. He couldn't put his feet flat on the floor when he walked, but stumbled along with his toes curled under – his whole foot was like a big comma. His speech was hard to follow because he couldn't pronounce his consonants with any clarity, but there was nothing unclear about the way his mind worked. His intelligence was acute; ironically, his particular gift was for languages. My father started him off on Latin; he taught himself Greek. He loved French, too, and German, and just before he died he had started to learn Hebrew from Mr Abrahams, the old Jew who ran the bakery at the end of our road.

Walter died of pneumonia when he was sixteen. He was never strong. I think his passion for languages arose from the limitations of his life. In those days few cripples would have dreamed of travelling abroad, but through reading and translating Walter could travel in his imagination. He could travel in time, too. I remember him talking about the Athens of Socrates as if he'd actually been there. And his condition made him sensitive to other people's differences, physical, racial or cultural. He was attracted to the patient exile of Mr Abrahams, to the cheerful, pragmatic Rossi family who ran a small grocery and dreamed of opening an Italian restaurant in the West End, to the Polish watchmaker in Whitechapel who was full of mournful tales of his heroic homeland. Walter would sidle out on an errand, for a loaf of poppy-seed bread or a few slices of the Rossis' dried ham, his crutches wedged under his armpits and a canvas bag to hold his purchases hung round his neck. Then he would sit in one of these shops – chairs, or at least an old barrel, were provided for customers in those days – and talk, or listen to the talk. Walter never went to school, and he never would have gone to university. Our neighbourhood had to make up to him for all that, and it did. The neighbours loved him.

I've never been to a funeral as sad as Walter's, and few as well attended.

Given my father's passionate belief in equality, it's surprising that he was unable to approach his two children with any approximation of it. Our father was the Reverend Eustace Albery, a high-minded socialist who was as politically active as he deemed compatible with the duties of a parish priest. Shabby-suited intellectual philanthropists gathered in our house for discussion groups on Saturday evenings, and there was pressure on my father to stand for Parliament, but I think he only toyed with the idea. He was not without ambition, but he was able to consider most things objectively, and he always declared that he could do more to redress the evils of social injustice as an East End priest than as an almost certainly unsuccessful parliamentary candidate. He did have an ambition to write. He was always going to produce an analysis of the links between unemployment and crime, but he never had time to gather the information. He made it clear to me that I was to carry on his work, to fight the good fight. I was the pride of his life; he had absolute faith in me. He set aside a sum of money, which I believe originated from my mother's marriage portion, and this was put in trust for my twenty-first birthday. Its intention was to give me the freedom to devote myself to things that mattered rather than worrying about simple survival. A similar sum had been set aside for Walter, to pay, at least in part, for help for him in those days before the Welfare State, but then Walter died, and the money went to a charitable foundation, a school for crippled children, which was ironic given that my father had never considered Walter capable of a life outside our home.

My father's feelings about Walter were in all likelihood the most painful and complicated part of his life. It was so different with me. I was healthy, I was intelligent, I showed early signs of sharing Papa's moral and political sensibilities, though in my adult life I have perhaps moved further away from them than he would have liked. I was the beloved first child. I belonged to the early part of a marriage that was genuinely happy, and that, enshrined in memory after my mother's death, became something rare and sacred. Papa would never have considered remarriage. His loyalty was absolute. And Walter – well, Walter's birth killed my mother. I don't think my father could ever disassociate his son from that fact though he would have acknowledged the injustice of it. Papa tried to treat Walter kindly – he treated everyone kindly – but there was always a distance. I could see that he was repulsed by my brother's jerky movements, a frozen hesitation followed by a crab-like scuttle. Walter had some difficulty with swallowing; saliva swung from one corner of his mouth, leaving a sore red trail. From an early age it was my job to pat him dry, and to change the napkin I tied under his chin. I never once saw my father do it.

The Revd Eustace Albery, with his respect for the life of the mind, could not but admire Walter's gift for languages, and was relieved that the boy had such a talent for occupying himself, but he seemed to regard him as one might regard an especially prodigious parrot. I don't think he ever entertained the idea that Walter could earn his own living, or contribute in any way to the advancement of human learning or understanding. I did. My close involvement with Walter's physical care did nothing to diminish my belief in his intellectual superiority. And Walter was an achiever, though our father never saw it. If he wanted something, he kept going until he had reached his goal. I took Walter's abilities so much for granted that I had to remind myself that other people often had a very different reaction to him. When my father looked at me, he saw a standard-bearer, a brave, clever girl, handsome and strong, who would carry his dreams forward through the century of progress, the twentieth century. When he looked at Walter, he saw somebody who shouldn't have been there.

My father is physically as real to me now as he ever was. I was twenty-one years old when he died. If he could see me now, is there anything about me he could recognize? My hair, once thick and dark, now lies across my scalp in narrow grey stripes, my hazel eyes, no longer large or bright, have retreated behind pouches of flesh. They are almost lashless now, and rheumy as a tortoise's. My father thought vanity was a sin, and was largely indifferent to physical beauty, but I was his daughter – of course he rejoiced in the way I looked. He was so proud of my thick hair, my neat waist, my fine-boned wrists. My waist – where's that gone? A waist is more an idea than a real part of one's body. Certainly, I haven't had one for a couple of decades. And my pointed chin, my proud, inquisitive, suffragette chin! My father would run his finger along the line of it, sometimes. Jack, too. That's gone. I've a great wattle there now, like a turkey cock; a flapping curtain of molten flesh. Who'd want to touch my face with his fingers now?

My father looked as one would hope a clergyman would look – six feet tall, without an ounce of spare flesh on him. His hair, dark like mine, deserted him early; his bony skull would have been a phrenologist's delight. His nose was arched, his neck and fingers were long. He was sunken-cheeked and hollow-eyed, but without the appearance of ill health. The impression he gave was that his mind was on higher things, and he left his body to look after itself. This impression wasn't quite accurate. He did enjoy food, and had a special weakness for something called 'stuffed monkey', a

84

spicy fruit and pastry confection sold by Mr Abrahams, though it occurs to me as I write that this partiality may have been cultivated as a means of making contact with Mr Abrahams and his family. My father never tried to convert Mr Abrahams, or any other Jew. He had nothing of the missionary about him. What he did have was a limitless curiosity about and respect for other people, and if God chose to use him as a conduit by which to reach them, then that was something very marvellous. But it was entirely up to God.

It was through my father's influence that I became a suffragette. There couldn't have been many of us who could make that claim! It was his opinion that the world would be saved by women; the gloriousness of my mother's memory strengthened this belief.

Their marriage had been a union of equals. In her spinster days my mother spent several years teaching at a Froebel School in Westminster; it was run as a charity by a committee of women with progressive ideas. My father's sister, my Aunt Cicely, also taught there. She and my mother became friends, and that is how my parents met.

Aunt Cicely, who never married, spent a lot of time at our house, both before and after my mother's death. She would have hated the description, but she was something of a housekeeper for my father. It was Cicely who organized a rota of broad-armed women to cope in the early years with the washing, feeding and dressing of Walter. She was not naturally domestic, but she was a good organizer. She took her glint-eyed enthusiasm into the campaign for women's suffrage, and soon became prominent. I was only fourteen when my father urged her to take me to a rally. I became a regular attender – often the youngest there. My father expressed no concerns about my safety at public meetings; I suppose he put his trust in Aunt Cicely and her steel-tipped umbrella. Of course I had no fear myself – you don't, when you're young – and when the police detained my aunt overnight after a demonstration in Trafalgar Square I became determined to undergo a similar martyrdom. I was one of those who chained myself to the railings outside Number 10 Downing Street, and rejoiced when several of my companions were led away in handcuffs, but on this as on other similar occasions I was sent home with a caution. It was my youthfulness that was the problem. Even though I lied about my age, my sharp little face and narrow, boyish shape got in the way of my ambition to become a public enemy. My youth, and my address: The Rectory, St Walburga's Street, E1. Father's occupation? Clergyman. I detected at least one policeman in the act of suppressing a smile.

Then the war came, and redirected everything. I was nineteen in August 1914, and almost indifferent to the great rolling up of the map of Europe, because Walter's death in the February of that year had left me numb. I was meant to be studying for university entrance. My father was eager for me to go to Lady Margaret Hall; I was to read Greats, which had been his own subject, and he was my coach, though Walter was as much help, if not more. Walter read everything I read, and gurgled a commentary on it in that half-swallowed voice that no one could follow as well as I.

His fatal illness lasted less than a week. He'd been ill before, so many times. He'd even had pneumonia before. This wasn't meant to kill him. The doctor came; he persuaded my father that Walter would be better off in hospital. I was doing most of the nursing, which of course was what I wanted to do, but my father was worried that it was interfering with my university work and taxing my strength, so he gladly submitted to the yoke of 'doctor's orders'. Well, Walter died in hospital, and he was alone when he died, and I have never been able to shake off the feeling that . . . that things could have been different. Who knows? But I've never allowed myself to blame my father.

So August 1914 found me drifting in a limbo of purposelessness, which is not my natural state at all. It was Aunt Cicely who hauled me out of it, by insisting that I should train as a VAD. The campaign for suffrage, she said, together with university ambitions, would have to be suspended. The time was out of joint, and we were born to set it right. So I became a nurse, and in the rhythms of scrubbing and folding and bandaging I discovered the power of work to subdue unmanageable emotions, and this discovery has stood me in good stead ever since. My father died halfway through the war; he caught influenza in the winter of 1916. He was barely into his fifties. I had never known him pause for a day's illness. It was only six weeks after his funeral that I met Jack on the train.

My war was framed by three deaths – Walter, my father, Jack. I've lived a long, long time, and I've touched and been touched by many lives since then, but I'm afraid no human being has ever come close to meaning as much to me as those three. Not even my only child, though I have wished it could have been otherwise. I think I will tear out this page. What good could it do, for Verity to read that her mother's emotional life stalled eighteen years before she was born? But her name is Verity; perhaps the truth is something with which I should entrust her. It's late now. My eyes are weak, and I'm tired to the bone. I will decide, but not now.

6

Hester rarely entered her father's study. Of all the rooms at Knighton, it was the least familiar to her.

It was on the ground floor, opposite the parlour. It had a tall narrow window with a recessed seat, but it faced north, so there was no direct sunlight. The cool and steady north light was thought to be good for the storing of books, and, in her father's time, good for cool and steady thinking as appropriate for its function as a study, but for Hester that made it a place that didn't invite her in. Theoretically she should have liked the window seat, where she might have enjoyed curling up with a book and an apple in time-honoured fashion, but the window gave out on to the least appealing part of the garden, where there were banks of rhododendrons and laurels and, behind them, holly that looked almost black. In her early childhood Hester had associated that area with witches, and she was left with a feeling she could never quite shake off.

The walls were all but concealed by handsome bookcases which Evelyn had had purpose-built, but Simeon had stocked these with box files and folders full of correspondence. In his last years Simeon had been made quite unhappy by the technological revolution. He instantly grasped its importance, and bought a certain amount of equipment, but he never learned to make proper use of it. Nothing made him feel his mortality more acutely, thought Hester, than the idea of all this microchip magic galloping into the future and leaving him behind. So the files and folders and boxes stayed in the study, and Simeon's systems never were stream-lined and updated in the way that would actually have suited such an efficient and hard-headed man.

The room was dominated by a partners' desk, with an arch in the middle for two pairs of knees, and drawers running down on either side. This desk brought out Simeon's inclination to behave like a Victorian papa. When Hester's school report arrived he made her sit opposite him and held her gaze as he slowly read it aloud. Only when he had finished was she allowed to comment. It was somewhat farcical, as her reports contained little criticism, but the exercise had what she supposed was the desired effect in fostering a sense of awe. And her father's voice had a way of tarnishing even the most glowing words of praise. Now, on this June afternoon when Hester and her mother had united to change the nature of this room for ever, to dispel the awe and gloom and free the place up to become whatever the new owners wished it to become, the vast tooled-leather surface of the desk was clear except for a vase of flowers. They startled Hester, she had never seen flowers in the study before. These were the darkest of dark red roses, the ones that climbed up the side of the house that was faced with pale grey stone. They had always reminded Hester of the beginning of the story of Snow White, when the mother pricks her finger and a drop of dark blood wells up and falls on to the snow on the window ledge. Those roses were like beads of blood unfurling. Verity had arranged them in a granite-coloured vase; she had mixed them with euphorbias of a stinging acid green. Blood and poison. Hester couldn't take her eyes off them.

Another difference was that the chairs had been removed. The high, ladderback chair that had always stood on Simeon's side of the desk, and the smaller, uncomfortable, cushionless one that faced it. Hester's report-reading chair. Both had gone. It meant that mother and daughter would not sit facing each other across that desk. There was to be no echo of the way things had been done in Simeon's time. It began to dawn on Hester that her mother was organizing things her way.

'Well,' said Hester, 'where do we start?' She looked round the room. All was orderly, contained, but each box and drawer concealed, she knew, a skein of complexity. She looked at the unreadable books, the dictionaries, the legal tomes. All the books one might enjoy picking up were elsewhere in the house. The books in her father's study brooded on the shelves like punishments. 'What about the books?' Hester asked.

'Oh, don't worry about those. I rang the second-hand shop in Westbeech and they're sending a man round. They're going to deal with them all. I'll tell him we don't want to keep any, shall I?'

Hester nodded. 'And the files?'

'Yes, the files,' said her mother. 'But let's start with the desk. I think that's where the most important things will be. Shall we take a drawer each, Hester? We could pull them right out.'

They did so. In the absence of chairs they knelt on the carpet. The first drawer Hester took was full of unused stationery, some of it printed with the address in the days before people used post codes much. It was excellent quality, thick and creamy. 'You'll want to keep this,' she said.

'I don't think I will. I won't be here much longer, and the new people won't want it. They'll be the curly cursive type.'

Hester looked at the handsome Roman font with an uncharacteristic tinge of regret. 'So, we'll throw it away?'

'I think so. If it wasn't printed I'd give it to the surgery for the children to draw on, but . . .'

The thought of keeping scribbling paper for unborn grandchildren must have flitted like a summer shadow through both their minds. Hester piled the sheets of paper together and slid them into a black bin bag.

'The envelopes too?'

'Let them all go.'

It was the same with the next drawer, which held glue, Sellotape, ring reinforcements, Tipp-Ex, pencils and those mysterious tags where two tiny metal bars are held together by a piece of green string, which every desk owner buys but few find a use for. Verity wanted none of it. 'I can't pack all this stuff up and take it with me,' she said. 'I'll start afresh.' Her attitude surprised Hester. It was the one Hester would have taken herself, but Verity had spent her life scraping bacon fat on to crusts to give to birds and reheeling shoes fit only for the dustbin. As Hester embarked on her third drawer she stole a look at her mother. Verity was flicking through a folder of ten-year-old bank statements, but there seemed to be a taut excitement about the set of her shoulders, a faint bloom of colour on her cheeks, that Hester couldn't interpret.

The third drawer Hester chose was the middle one, the one that would have covered her father's lap. The contents were neatly arranged. They seemed to be mainly bundles of school reports, secured by thick rubber bands. Hester was warmed, for a moment, by the thought of her father taking so much care over her, saving and ordering her reports as if the opinions of a harassed needlework mistress in the mid 1970s should have a lasting impact on posterity. She wanted to reread them, but at leisure. 'I'll keep these,' she said, 'if you don't want them, Mum.'

'Which ones?' asked Verity, sharply. She craned her neck to look at the school crest. 'Oh, The Turrets. Oh, yes, darling, of course those should be kept. By one or the other of us. What about the others?'

Hester picked up another bundle. These folders were not the same as those used by The Turrets; they were a little larger, a little more sumptuous. There was the usual crest and motto stamped on the front, but these were the proud, assertive emblems of a famous public school for boys, a boarding school in the West Country, very different from the faintly apologetic Turrets. Hester read the name, mystified. 'Sebastian Oakes? Who on earth is Sebastian Oakes?'

Her mother said nothing.

'It must be some long-lost cousin of Dad's. But why have we –?'

'Look underneath,' said Verity.

Hester pulled out a large brown envelope, with nothing written on it. The flap was sealed.

'Open it.'

She had never heard her mother's voice resonate like that. She opened the envelope. She didn't know what she expected – some particularly horrible pornography, or evidence of a crime – but it felt as if the envelope was something dangerous to touch. She drew out photographs. A sheath of photographs of boys' football and cricket teams. She rejected those in favour of a clutch of smaller pictures. A toddler in dungarees, dark ringlets, gender not obvious. A little boy in a soldier's uniform as if on his way to a fancy-dress party, saluting the camera, his cheeks puffed out, bursting with self-importance. A baby in its mother's arms, the mother unfamiliar to Hester. She turned that one over. On the back it said, 'Sebastian. Six months old.' She didn't know the handwriting.

She laid them on the desk and turned to her mother. 'I don't know who these people are.'

'Can't you guess?' Verity's voice was a stretched wire. Her face was almost unrecognizable; there was an intensity about it that was almost a glare. Hester looked away.

'What am I supposed to –?'

'Look again.'

She obeyed. That in itself was alien. All her life, if she had followed her mother's instructions it had only been because she happened to concur with them. This time, she felt compelled to obey.

She looked at the baby. Sebastian, aged six months. It was in colour – her own baby pictures were black and white. Whoever this child was, he was of a younger generation. He wore a light blue knitted jacket, he had a bald head and a gummy grin. He looked much like any other baby, to her inexpert eye. His mother – or rather, the woman who was holding him – was dark and, from the little that could be seen, slim and lithe. Her large eyes were heavily made up, her thick hair fell to her shoulders from a middle parting. Her mouth was full, her lower lip especially prominent, like a shelf. She wore what used to be called a 'skinny-rib' jumper, cream-coloured, with a polo neck. Hester couldn't see, but she would have expected her waist to be girdled by a chain belt. She looked uneasy, and attractive. Hester didn't like her.

'And the next,' said Verity, her breathing audible. Hester turned to the toddler in the denim dungarees.

'Is this the same child?'

'They're all the same child.'

The toddler's ringlets looked silky and unusually dark. His face was charming, elfin; big eyes and a pointed nose and chin. He bore no resemblance that Hester could see to his plump six-month-old self. He wasn't looking at the camera, but was focusing intently on the cart he was pushing along a garden path, the kind of cart that holds coloured bricks. She turned the picture over. There was no name on this one, just a pencilled date: 13/6/72.

She looked at the team photographs. The names of the boys were printed underneath. 'S. Oakes' featured in all of them, but he was never the captain, never the huge furrow-browed boy in the middle cradling the ball or the bat. S. Oakes was usually standing in the top left-hand corner, arms folded, dark hair, still curly, half obscuring his eyes. In his sporting mode he didn't interest her terribly, but in among these pictures was one that looked as if it was taken at a school play. There were only three performers on the stage, and it was easy to identify S. Oakes. The stage was heaped with rubble, broken bricks, old bicycles. S. Oakes wore torn jeans and some kind of patchwork waistcoat; beneath it, his lean young torso was bare. He looked about sixteen, fully grown but not filled out. His hair had been greased back from his face for the part, and despite the almost clownish stage make-up she could see the mixture of strength and delicacy in his features. In contrast, the other actors looked lumpen and immobile. Whoever he was, S. Oakes had presence.

'What's this?' she said to her mother, trying to detach herself from a suspicion that was swelling inside her. 'It looks like Samuel Beckett or something.'

'Turn it over,' her mother said.

She did so, and the suspicion peaked and burst and washed through her in a hot wave. 'To Dad,' she read, not aloud. 'Thanks for coming. Hope you enjoyed the show.' She dropped the photograph. 'No!' she said, under her breath. 'This can't be –'

94

'Yes,' said her mother. 'He's your brother, Hester.'

'Dad –?'

'Yes. Your father's other family. I'll leave you. You've got a lot of catching up to do.' And she slipped out of the room.

Why did I do it that way? Verity wondered, sloshing cutlery in warm water for a final rinse it absolutely didn't need. It was cruel, and she was not a cruel person, but she didn't regret it. Or perhaps she did have a cruel streak – perhaps everybody did, it was just that some got more opportunity to demonstrate it than others. Certainly, forty and more years of living with Simeon had driven all sorts of feelings and impulses into underground tunnels, where they lurked, unseen, but they didn't go away. Something rose up in her when Hester was looking at the photographs, something pure and hard and vengeful. It felt like a vision, an angel made of fire and air.

She dried the cutlery and put it away, and began peeling vegetables for supper, far earlier than she needed to. Here I am, she thought, I'm in the kitchen scraping carrots, and Hester's in the study letting Sebastian into her life. Already she could feel the pressure lifting. For thirty years that boy had lived inside her, not growing, not threatening to escape, but taking up too much space. There was a medical condition – she couldn't possibly remember the name of it – where the doctors remove what looks like a cyst, and find it's a ball of flesh and bone and hair, fat and teeth and even fingernails, all the ingredients for a twin that somehow never got made. Well, Sebastian had been like that inside her, only not like flesh and bone. A ball of emotions, ugly and tender and harsh and sweet. Feelings that were hers and yet not hers, feelings to which she had no right but from which she couldn't escape. And now, it felt as if there might be movement. Would she miss that ball once it had rolled away?

She'd never met Sebastian. She didn't know anything about him now, where he lived, what he was doing. For all she knew, Simeon might have some grandchildren by now. She chose not to think about that. There was no mention of him in Simeon's will; that had surprised her, but she was also relieved. That would not have been a good way for Hester to find out. Simeon must have made that decision when Paulina married, must have decided that the stepfather could provide. Verity knew she'd married in 1978. She used to listen to telephone calls, sometimes, and read letters. Not often, but she needed to know, in spite of the pain. Knowledge was power, and power was something of which she'd never had her fair share.

She'd never met Sebastian, but she had seen him, once. It was Paulina she'd wanted to see. This was during the period when she came closest to leaving Simeon. Hester was about thirteen; she needed less and less of her mother's attention. Simeon was at the height of his career. He'd just been made a judge, and he hardly ever seemed to be at home. There were endless important dinners to keep him in London overnight. Sometimes that would have been true, but other times he was with *her*, of course. Verity was used to that; over the years it had settled into a pattern of twice a week, mutely acknowledged by both of them, never discussed. Verity had been amused to notice that after the birth of Sebastian – which Simeon hadn't told her about, she found out for herself – he spent more time at home. She even wondered whether the baby would ring Paulina's death knell. But no, once Sebastian was beyond the newborn stage things picked up again between them. Presumably she found a nanny, and got her figure back.

So when Simeon became one of the great and the good,

and found himself much in demand, there didn't seem to be any question that Verity would ever accompany him to any of these grand functions. On one level, she wouldn't have wanted to. She'd always been daunted by dressing up, and she'd never enjoyed exposing Simeon's irritation with her to the eyes of the world. Oh, no, she would tell any friend who asked, let Simeon deal with all those Londony things. Just leave me alone with my house and garden, she would have said. But that was only true on one level. One idea began to hollow out the core of her mind – that he was taking Paulina with him to every big occasion, that she was being presented as the real partner for him in his grandeur. The thought came to possess her. It was jealousy, she supposed, and she'd always told herself that she didn't suffer from jealousy, not truly. Simeon did, he was always jealous of her, even when he didn't really want her. She knew he was jealous of Paulina, and as for Hester – she didn't like thinking about it. But Verity always maintained that she didn't properly know what jealousy was. She saw it as weakness. She was very insistent on this. In her own mind, that is. She didn't share such thoughts with anybody.

If Simeon was presenting Paulina to the world as his wife in all but name, then, Verity reasoned, it would be time to leave him. She had always thought this. Once the colour and the taste of another woman started seeping through the fabric of their shared life, then Verity would have to fight, or lose herself altogether. She didn't want Simeon to go. She didn't want anyone but him. The only other men she wanted were fantasies, clusters of characteristics of the type one might find in a lonely-hearts column – gentle man, caring, seeks soul mate, loves animals and flowers. Such men, she decided, did not exist, or not for her.

She had to know. She had to go and look. If I could just

see her, just watch her, Verity thought, I would know what to do. From her occasional forays into Simeon's desk and briefcase she knew what Paulina looked like, and where she lived – a flat in Notting Hill. She didn't know how she spent her days, didn't even know whether or not she had a job, but that didn't much matter. Verity was patient, she could wait, and besides, with so young a child it was unlikely that Paulina would be very late back.

It was May; the evenings were long. Verity chose a day when Simeon had told her where he was going – to a banquet in the Guildhall, in honour of the Attorney-General, or some such person. She would watch to see if he called for Paulina. She arranged for her mother to meet Hester from the station and provide her with supper and company. She considered taking the car, but rejected that plan. If Simeon did turn up he would recognize the car, and if she had to park some way off to avoid him then she might as well be on foot.

It was hard to know how to conceal herself. Paulina, as far as she knew, had never seen her, but Simeon kept photographs of her and of Hester in his wallet, and if Paulina was any kind of approximation of a normal woman she would have pored over those. Then, of course, if Simeon turned up, as she almost wished he would . . .

She went to some lengths over her disguise. She found a summer mac at a jumble sale, light enough to wear even on a warm evening. It was a dreary garment, dirty olive in colour, and not at all the sort of thing she would usually wear. She bought a plain brown headscarf from Marks & Spencer, and resolved to exchange it after its outing for something prettier; it went against the grain simply to throw it away. She bought some cheap sunglasses from a market stall. They would look eccentric, but they would be an effective disguise; Simeon wouldn't associate her with sunglasses because she hardly ever wore them, disliking the way they changed the colour of everything. Footwear was a problem. Most men would not be able to identify every pair of their wife's shoes, but Simeon was very observant about some things, and clothes was one of them. She thought about tennis shoes, which would be quiet and comfortable, but decided they would make her look just too dotty. She had a pair of low-heeled navy court shoes, the sort of thing absolutely anybody might have; she settled for those.

She took no bag. She wanted to be as unencumbered as possible. She stowed money and keys in the mac's capacious pockets, and took only the newspaper to read on the train. She held it in front of her face, but didn't take much in.

It was only a couple of years since she'd stopped living in London, but already she felt like a stranger. She arrived at Charing Cross mid afternoon, and dithered about how to reach Notting Hill. The Underground, once so familiar, now made her nervous. A taxi was an unwarrantable expense, and besides, it would be too obvious, drawing up in a quiet street in the middle of the afternoon. The rattle of a taxi makes people look out of their windows. That was not what she wanted.

She could get a bus – a Number 11 – to Victoria, then change to a 52. Or she could get an 88 all the way, via Oxford Street. Couldn't she? She found she was no longer certain. She liked London buses, liked the confidence of knowing them properly, liked the way people swung on and off at traffic lights, but she no longer had that confidence. She thought, I'll walk.

It was a beautiful afternoon, a Friday; one of those late-spring days when the only thing that spoils one's consciousness of how marvellous London is looking is the thought that the country will be looking even better. She walked through the parks, where the horse chestnuts shook out their crumpled ball gowns and the weeping willows draped their veils over the young couples entwined at their roots. She didn't linger to look. She wasn't yet forty, but she felt sure that no one would ever take her in their arms quite like that again, and time had proved her right.

She walked quickly and steadily, and became far too hot. She took off the mac and walked on with its awkward bulk bundled over her arm. Her shoes rubbed, but there was nothing she could do about that — she was hardly the type to go barefoot. She began to regret the enterprise; she was sweaty and uncomfortable, at odds with the rustling, murmuring Maytime world.

She made it, at last. She stopped in Notting Hill Gate and bought some sticking plasters, went into a café for a cold drink and, in the cramped lavatory, peeled off her tights and stuck the plasters over the incipient blisters on the backs of her heels. Putting the tights back on was not pleasant, nor was checking her appearance in the mirror above the basin. She had made up her face, as she automatically did when she went to town. The heat and exercise had caused her foundation to rearrange itself in orange grooves. She did what she could to repair the damage, and sallied forth again, mac, scarf and dark glasses in place, annoyed that she had allowed herself to arrive in a state that would put her at a disadvantage, even though her intention was that Paulina would not see her. The walk had taken a long time; it was nearly five o'clock by the time she reached 84B Allington Grove. She had meant to allow herself a lot more viewing time than that.

Allington Grove was wide and long and elegantly curved. Behind the terraced houses were enormous communal gardens. They couldn't be seen from the road, but Verity knew they were there because she'd had friends who'd lived there in her Chelsea days. Like Verity and Simeon, they'd moved to the country, so there was no danger of bumping into them. They hadn't been very great friends, but she felt a little nostalgic ache for them now. Roger and Penelope Pritchard. He was a stockbroker. Verity remembered sitting in the communal garden with Penelope on just such a day as this, pink cherry blossom overhead, their babies kicking on rugs, she and Penelope picking laburnum pods out of the grass in case they made their way into the babies' mouths. Laburnum and pink cherry blossom were the hallmark of Notting Hill and it was obligatory to admire them, but Verity remembered despising those bunchy pompoms, like tutus for sugar mice, and privately pining for the fragility of the wild white cherry with its fluttering insect-wing petals. On this particular afternoon the trees were past their peak but still triumphant, and there had still been a breath of lilac in the air. Verity remembered how, in Chelsea, she used to push Hester in her pram through the summer dusk and pick at random roses that had spilled over front-garden fences. She did this when it was too dark to see what colours the roses were. She laid them over Hester's pram blanket, and when they got home, in the light, their colours flowed into life. She could never have told Simeon that she did this. He would have thought it eccentric, and pointless. 'I can buy you roses,' he'd have said, in that voice of his with its growly catch. 'We can afford all the roses you want.' Did he bring Paulina flowers? More, or less often, since this baby son was born?

She positioned herself opposite Number 84B. There was a low front-garden wall and she sat on that, feeling conspicuous. She wished she had brought something to do. Anyone observing her could reach only one conclusion – that she was watching a house. Possibly she looked as if she'd lost her keys and was waiting for someone, but if she hung on for as long as she intended, that would seem like a strange decision.

But she didn't have to wait long. It was only about ten minutes before a young woman with a pushchair came round the corner. Verity knew at once that it was her. What struck her immediately was that she and Paulina had nothing in common. Sometimes she looked at the mothers of young children and felt a kinship, a sense of shared experience, but under no circumstances could she have had any fellow feeling for Paulina.

She was small – shorter than Verity by half a head, but plumper, or rather, curvier. Her thick, dark hair swung to the nape of her neck, and was pushed back from her face by a broad band. She wore a close-fitting dress the colour of egg yolk. It had no sleeves; her shoulders were round and smooth, like fruit. Even Verity felt an urge to touch them. Her legs were bare, too, and the dress was short. They were not long legs, but they were so very – shaped. Everything about her formed a shape, firm and yet pliant, as if she would at once yield and rise to a touch. Compared to Paulina, Verity was flat and lean, disjointed, poorly assembled, pale.

Verity felt herself shrinking within her waterproof carapace, drawing in her wound like a prodded sea creature. But she went on looking. The child was asleep in his pushchair. Sebastian. He had on a stripy T-shirt and not much else. His knees, like his mother's, were round and smooth, his long hair fell in soft curls round his tilted head, and Verity had to admit that he was very beautiful. No look of Simeon was immediately apparent, but then he was very young, and on the other side of the road, and asleep.

Paulina hesitated at her front gate, as if deciding whether

to lift the child out and risk waking him, or whether to lug him in the pushchair down the steep stone steps to her basement flat. Simeon's basement flat, presumably. Verity was pretty sure he'd paid for it. Paulina stooped to lift the whole thing, and suddenly she was at a disadvantage. She would have to bend, she would have to struggle, she would have to grunt. Verity made no conscious decision, but she found herself across the road in a second. 'Excuse me,' she heard herself saying, 'can I help with that?'

Paulina looked up. Her eyes were as dark as could be, and the lashes were extraordinary, an upwards lick of black paint. She revealed, then concealed, her surprise in the space of a blink. 'Thank you very much,' she said, in a deep voice that held just the trace of a lisp. 'If you wouldn't mind taking this bit here – can you manage?'

They grunted down the steps together, which even at this time of year were dank and treacherous with lichen. 'I remember what it's like,' said Verity. 'You don't want to wake them.'

'He's only just fallen asleep. We've been to the park.' Paulina pulled her keys out of the bag that was slung across the handlebars. At any moment, the flat would swallow them up and Verity would never see them again. She didn't want that.

'Could I possibly have a drink of water?' she asked. 'If you wouldn't mind bringing it out here . . .'

Paulina sized her up – an odd woman, she seemed to conclude, but harmless. 'No, no, come in,' she offered. Now she had revealed herself as a risk-taker, and Verity rose to her challenge.

'That's very kind,' she said. 'I'm visiting a friend, and I'm rather early.' She followed Paulina and the pushchair into the flat.

There was one big room, a combined kitchen and living room. Despite being a basement it was not gloomy. The late-afternoon sun sent shafts of light into the far end where there was a corduroy-covered sofa strewn with toys. The furniture looked new, but not expensive. The colours were clean and light – blond wood, clear glass. A white vase crammed with red and purple tulips stood out of toddler reach on the construction which Verity believed would be called the 'breakfast bar'. The tulips were new; stiff, and waxy. Verity touched one with a fingertip. 'What beautiful tulips.'

Paulina looked appreciative. 'They're from Sebastian's father. He's very good about flowers.' She handed Verity a glass of water, then glanced at the still-sleeping child, and moved to open a food cupboard. 'I'd better get something ready for when he wakes. He'll be starving.' She paused, considering the situation. 'And I was going to make myself some coffee. Would you like some? I'm afraid I don't drink tea.' She reached for a packet. Verity recognized Simeon's favourite brand.

'Coffee would be lovely, thank you.'

'Won't you take off your coat? It's such a warm day.'

'Oh, no. Thank you. I've just had an operation.' If the non sequitur puzzled Paulina she didn't show it. Verity tapped her dark glasses in what was intended to be an explanatory manner. 'Could I use your bathroom, do you think?'

'Of course.' Paulina pointed it out. Verity could see a bedroom, temptingly, beyond, but the kitchen door was left open so she didn't dare peep. The bathroom was luxurious, more so than the rest of the flat. Two long shelves were stocked with more jars of expensive creams than Verity had possessed in her entire life. A bottle of Oil of Ulay and a hank of cotton wool – that was her beauty routine.

She eased open a cupboard, trying to make no sound. Some packets of the Pill – so how had Sebastian happened? Tweezers, razors, hair-removing cream. Ha! That had never been a problem of hers. Smiling at this small triumph, she spotted a pair of Simeon's cuff-links. They were gold, set with a tiny diamond. His best cuff-links. Verity had assumed he bought them himself, but perhaps Paulina had given them to him. How? Saved up her child benefit? It struck Verity that she knew virtually nothing about her rival. She might have money of her own. She didn't look rich, but not poor either, and too proud, surely, to depend utterly on a married man. A man who was going to stay married, she decided as she pocketed the cuff-links.

The coffee was ready when she returned. She drank it quickly. Simeon might turn up at any moment. 'This is most kind,' she said, 'but am I holding you up? You're going out tonight, I expect?'

Paulina was sipping black coffee and smoking. 'No, I'm not. I don't get out much. Babysitting's a problem.'

'Oh,' said Verity. 'His father –?'

'Doesn't live here. No, we don't see so much of him.'

'It sounds like a very modern arrangement.'

She shrugged her beautiful shoulders – a most un-English shrug. 'Or else the oldest story in the world,' she said, and Verity realized in a flash that Paulina was in love with Simeon, and that she was lonely. She rose to go, before she could begin to feel sorry for her. As she scraped her chair on the tiled floor Sebastian's eyes flew open, and she caught, for an instant, his father's hard and furious stare.

'Now we're for it!' Paulina started to laugh, and swooped to unbuckle her child. 'He'll scream for twenty minutes, I promise you.' She held him to her, laughing into his hair.

'He's beautiful,' said Verity, as it were in return for the cuff-links. She twittered her way out of the flat in a flurry of thanks.

The weather had changed in the short time she'd been indoors. Thick soft clouds had blown up, and fat raindrops thudded through the sighing trees. She limped as far as Westbourne Grove and then hailed a taxi. She had seen what she wanted to see. She would never need to set eyes on Paulina or Sebastian again. But she was unsettled, knowing for certain now that there was a woman in the world who loved Simeon better than she did, not because she hadn't intended to love him, but because she wasn't particularly good at love. She'd kept him, simply because she'd got there first. He was with her on the last day of his life. If he'd been with Paulina, she wouldn't have been on the lavatory when he died.

She waited a couple of weeks until she knew he'd have missed them, then she put the cuff-links in a bowl on Simeon's dressing table, a bowl that tended to hold foreign coins and stray buttons. She listened to him dressing that morning, and heard his shout of surprise. 'Everything all right?' she called.

'These cuff-links! I thought I'd lost them.'

'Which ones?'

'With the little diamonds. I haven't seen them for weeks. I thought I'd left them at the club.'

'Those? They've been lying about for ages. Oh, Simeon, you are getting absent-minded.'

Oddly, perhaps, it was Sebastian who stayed with her after that encounter. Sebastian, who had slept almost throughout, who had granted her only the merest glimpse of himself in that moment when he opened his fathomless eyes – he was the one who lodged inside her, and grew. Paulina didn't grow, didn't change. She remained constant, an opponent but no longer an enemy. Every now and then, as little as once a year, Verity would check up on her by riffling through Simeon's things, and she usually found a few clues to satisfy her; a letter, a photograph, the receipt for an expensive dinner. All the usual things. There was a hotel in Venice, once, mid-week; three days. She barely begrudged it. All those years as Simeon's satellite and no real holiday. Verity wondered how she sorted out the babysitting. She thought it unlikely that Sebastian went too.

So she followed the story of their affair from a distance, rather like watching a soap opera intermittently, and when it came to an end she rather missed it. She didn't find out exactly what happened, but she gathered that Paulina met someone else who was prepared to marry her and take on Sebastian. Simeon, she believed, severed all direct contact with her, though there must have been some continuation of his relationship with Sebastian, because the school reports kept coming. Presumably Simeon paid the school fees. That wasn't the sort of thing Verity minded about. She read all the reports, as carefully as if they were Hester's. And Simeon thought he'd hidden them so well!

And that was it, really. Or rather, that had been it until now. Now she was letting go, and Hester was taking it on. And she would have to take it on, wouldn't she? Even cool, compartmentalized Hester wouldn't be able to brush this aside. A brother – and she never thought she'd have one. She had some sort of adventure ahead of her. Verity envied her. Almost.

Hester was hardly aware that her mother had left the study. She looked at the piles of stuff in front of her and just thought, there's a lot to get through. She had to get on top of this bewildering information, subdue it, thrash it into shape. She read the school reports, not every single one. She established a system, reading one for each year of her new brother's school career. Behind the bundle from the grand boarding school were some from his earlier years, bearing the name of what Hester took to have been a West London prep school. It took her about an hour to boil Sebastian's scholastic career down to its bare essentials.

Her brother, she learned, was an attention-seeker. He was imaginative, but his spelling was atrocious. For a couple of years he was considered to be mildly dyslexic, but that seemed to fade away – the public school would have no truck with such a notion. Maths was an area of weakness, though he coped with science. When he was thirteen, his scientific career was enlivened by 'dangerous behaviour' in the chemistry lab. He was good at sport, though not a natural team player. He excelled at art. He needed to take Scripture more seriously. He shifted from being 'too easily led' to being 'a born leader who must take responsibility for the power he exerts over others'. He was untidy, disorganized, charming; he tried hard with his music (electric guitar). He was not allowed to give up Latin. His performance as Perdita in *The Winter's Tale* (age: 12) was 'remarkable'. He represented the school in a debating competition. Singing lessons were quickly abandoned.

His mock O-level grades were 'uneven', his A-level choices 'appropriate'. He had 'flair' for English, 'enthusiasm' for Russian; History was an also-ran. He spent too much time on his art. And then he disappeared. There was no report for what should have been his final term, his A-level term. His housemaster commented the previous Christmas that he hoped Sebastian would come to appreciate the importance of a solid academic degree. Hester could only guess that Sebastian had not.

She searched the drawer again, looking for clues. There were a few letters, all addressed to her father at his club, in large and loopy black writing. It was obvious who they were from. Hester tried to read them, but her eyes swam, not with tears, but with the kind of phobic reaction some people get when they catch sight of a snake or a spider. It was as if her body was ordering her to look away. There was one in the pile in a different hand. She opened that one. 'Dear Dad,' it said, 'Mum has told me to write to you, so I am. I'm all right, don't worry about me. Mum and Ralph don't want me at home so I'm going to doss with some mates. I just couldn't go through with all that A-level shite. It'll save you a lot of money, anyway. Seb.'

Hester wanted to know more. The note had a Captain Oatesy flavour that made her worry for her unknown brother. She went through the contents of the drawer again, but to no avail. The story seemed to end there, at least as far as that drawer went. But what else lay hidden in this room, in this house which had suddenly turned into a box of surprises?

She stood up, stiff from kneeling, hardly aware of the length of time she'd spent in that position. A petal from one of the black-red roses dislodged itself and fell to the desk, the sound almost as loud as the beat of a clock in that motionless room. Her mother had not opened the window, despite the heat of the day. It occurred to Hester that she never remembered the study windows being open, not ever. She crossed the room to investigate. They were jammed shut, with fingers of ivy reaching over them from the surrounding wall.

She remembered that there was a world outside that

room, that sequestered space which housed the story of the life that paralleled and undermined her own. Beyond, there was her mother, waiting in the kitchen. Her whole being would be quivering in anticipation of Hester's reaction. It dawned on Hester, slowly, that this information could not have been new to her. These neat bundles of reports and photographs – her father would not have left them that way. Verity had arranged the discoveries of the afternoon, as carefully as she arranged her flowers. What kind of reaction should Hester choose to present her with? It was up to her to fulfil or to disappoint.

She put everything back in the desk drawer and closed it. There was plenty more to sort through – files and folders and quantities of boxes – but she'd had enough for one day. And besides, she was beginning to suspect that her mother had been considerably more focused and efficient in her sorting-out than she had assumed. Briefly, the weight of her father's long betrayal oppressed her as it must have daily oppressed her mother. But thinking about the pair of them, always so ill-assorted, how could one have imagined anything other than a faithless marriage? She was astonished to find she had never truly considered the matter.

She shuddered with one of those strange, not unpleasant spasms which Grandma Evelyn used to say was a goose walking over your grave. Why a goose? She'd never asked. It was gone six o'clock and she had knelt too long in that sunless room. She went upstairs to fetch a jacket. She could hear her mother moving about in the kitchen; then, when she heard Hester's footfall on the stairs, she stopped. Hester could feel her listening. She spent a few minutes in her bedroom, smoothing her hair, checking her voicemail for messages. Then she went down to join her mother in the kitchen. She had chosen her approach.

'Drink, darling?' asked Verity solicitously, as if Hester were an invalid.

'That would be nice. I brought some wine with me. I'll open a bottle of that.' In Simeon's absence, bringing one's own wine was a wise precaution. Her mother tended to have a bottle 'on the go', which meant the cork would have been drawn at least a week before. Her white was invariably an acid Muscadet, her red a dullish Côtes du Rhône. Forty and more years with her epicurean husband had taught her remarkably little in such respects. Hester took her time over drawing the cork, selecting glasses. She wasn't going to be the one to broach the important subject.

At last her mother could bear it no longer. 'Well?'

Hester couldn't say 'Well what?' as she would have done at fourteen. She said, 'Have you always known?'

Verity nodded. Her feelings were choking her. That felt ugly to Hester.

'Is there anybody else who knows?'

Verity got her voice under control. 'I don't think so. I've never told anyone and I wouldn't have thought your father –'

'No, I wouldn't have thought so either. But the – the – whatshername –'

'Her name is Paulina. Yes, of course, I'm sure that her family, or friends . . . but they are not people we know.'

'Is she –?'

'I don't know what happened to her. She might be dead.'

'That's not likely. She can't be very old.'

'Early fifties, I suppose. She was quite young when – well, she could be dead. She smoked.'

Hester suppressed a smile at this semi sequitur. 'You knew her, then?'

'No, no. Certainly not. But I know she smoked.'

Hester pictured her mother sniffing at her father's clothes, analysing her smoke, her scent, her sweat. She remembered her father's hair as it used to be, thick lion's hair. The smoke from her cigarettes would have woven its way through his hair, and then he would have laid his head down on the pillow next to her mother's. She thought of Guy, and the time when she found a streak of somebody else's foundation across the front of his jacket. The time she unwound a long, golden hair from one of his buttons. Had her father been careless, like Guy? She could imagine that he was.

'So you never met her?' she asked.

Two chicken portions lay side by side on a sheet of foil, each bearing a spike of rosemary like an emblem. Her mother tucked them into their silver bed as she replied, 'I didn't see the point of meeting her.'

'And –' Hester had avoided Sebastian so far, because he was already precious to her, and she needed time alone with the idea of him. 'And the boy?' she asked, carelessly. 'Did you ever –?'

'I've never spoken to him. I don't know where he is now.'

Hester braced herself. 'We need to find out.'

'Do we?'

'Does he know that Dad's died?'

'Possibly not. He wasn't mentioned in the will. Though he might have seen it in the papers.'

Hester had, naturally, read the will. It was very straightforward. Everything was to go to her mother, and to herself should her mother have predeceased her father. There had been no special requests, nothing except a letter of wishes mainly concerned with funeral arrangements. The omission of Sebastian seemed extraordinary. 'He should have been mentioned,' said Hester.

'Darling, why?'

'Because he was my father's child.' She was conscious of raising her voice. 'Just as much as I was.'

'No, Hester. Not just as much.'

'Of course he was. It wasn't his fault. He didn't ask to be born.'

'Hester, you're getting hysterical. Your father hardly knew this boy. He had no contact with him after he left school. You were his child, you were the one he –'

Don't say 'loved', Hester thought. Just don't say it.

'– brought up. The boy was an accident. It's completely different.'

Her nonchalance had evaporated. 'Yes,' she said, 'I was the one he brought up, and, for all his faults, he did bring me up to be fair. He was a judge, remember. And the will is unfair, and it's even more unfair that he – this boy – hasn't been contacted about his father's death. His own father!'

Her mother pressed her lips together and said nothing at all.

'If it was me,' Hester went on, 'if I had Dad's money, I'd transfer half of it to him.'

'*Half* of it?'

'Yes, half of it. But I don't. So I can't.'

Her mother resumed her silence. Hester was unnerved. Since the dawn of her conscious mind it had been her mother who had been coaxing responses. Over the last forty years she had, she thought, perfected the art of inscrutability. Now, for the first time, her mother held interesting information, lots of it, and she craved a glimpse. Verity must know far more about this shadow family than she had yet admitted. She must have some idea about Sebastian's fate, or whereabouts. Verity was passive, but still she was a human being.

Verity spoke, suddenly. 'Have you finished with those reports and things, Hester? Because if you have, I think we might as well throw them away. I can't see any point in keeping them. Can you?' There was a challenge in her voice.

Hester very, very much did not want them thrown away. In the short hours she had known she had a brother her desire to hang on to them had increased to the point where it seemed as if she must have been quite empty before, if this new feeling could find so much space in which to grow. 'I'll deal with it,' she said, not sure that her mother was convinced by the insouciance of her tone. 'I'll clear it all up. There's no reason why you should have to.'

'Oh, I don't mind,' said Verity. 'It's all dead to me now. Just a pile of dead leaves, really. But – just as you like.'

'I'll do it now. Before supper,' Hester said.

The chicken portions still waited in their chilly silver bed. 'Oh goodness, I forgot these,' said Verity as she took the roasting tin and slid it into the oven. 'They'll take half an hour.'

'Fine,' Hester said, 'I'll get rid of that stuff, and then I've a couple of calls to make. All right?'

'Of course, dear – absolutely fine.'

7

It was difficult for Hester to stay at Knighton after the discovery of Sebastian. She'd arranged several days off work in anticipation of a spell of humdrum activity, emptying wardrobes and cupboards and helping Verity to focus on what she really wanted or needed to keep. She was going to direct the sort-out; she was to have been in charge.

Then Sebastian moved into her life, and everything changed. Had something been given to her, or had something been taken away? Had she been cheated of her uniqueness, the special aura of the only child? Was there less of a family for her now than ever, now that she knew so much of her father's emotional life had been lived elsewhere? And her mother – no longer a soft, pale backdrop for Hester's clear-cut assertive actions, but a controller, a planner, and a keeper of secrets. To have the strength to hold on to secrets – that was not unpowerful. Did that make her more or less of a mother to Hester?

She went to bed early that Saturday night, but she didn't sleep for ages. She kept trying to do emotional calculations in her head, but the sums couldn't come out right because she didn't know whether she was adding or subtracting. And the next morning she couldn't look at Verity. She couldn't bear the excited twitching. After lunch, though, during which Hester was as uncommunicative as a teenager, it was Verity who suggested an early return to London. 'You've a lot to think about,' she said in a confidently maternal tone that was new to both of them. 'I can manage things on my own. Don't worry about me.'

Hester was grateful. 'I'll come back soon,' she said. 'I'll leave my things here.' That seemed to suit them both. To pack up all the clothes and shoes that she'd thought out so carefully, arranged so neatly – that would have felt like a failure of some kind. So she left those things to wait for her, but all the Sebastian stuff, the letters and reports and photographs, she took with her. She hadn't finished with Sebastian yet.

The London she returned to was sticky, dull. The glorious late-June heat had congealed; the sky was a glutinous grey. Entering her flat was as unpleasant as opening a bag of chips in a crowded tube carriage. She opened all the windows to let the staleness out. A few drops of fat thunderous rain smashed on the balcony, like the beginning of the Egyptian plague of frogs. The red eye of the answerphone was winking at her as if to say, you know, you're never alone.

She tipped a bottle of mineral water to her mouth as she pressed the button for the message. The voice she heard made her splutter. Lines of water ran under her collar and down her neck. 'Hettie, it's Guy. I'm coming to see you. I'll be there at seven. Check out the date.' Guy. Her ex-husband, still assuming that she was at his disposal. 'Check out the date.' Ah! Their anniversary. Or would have been. Thirteen years.

'I'll be there at seven.' It was ten to now. She had abso-lutely no time to escape. She ran into the bedroom, changed her wet shirt, shoved the briefcase with all the Sebastian things in it into the wardrobe – Guy was hardly likely to look inside, but her instinct told her to keep Sebastian properly concealed from everyone – and then the bell rang.

'All right,' she said into the intercom, 'come in.' She tried to sound as if this was a considered choice. In came Guy, holding a ridiculously large bunch of not very special flowers. Too many carnations and bits of stiff green stuff, like plastic fans. Guy had never been very good with flowers. She thanked him without warmth and laid them to one side.

Guy's lanky public-school-boy shape seemed to loom disproportionately tall in the flat. She'd often thought of the high-up flat as like a nest; now it seemed as if an alien bird had landed, absurdly large, and caused the treetop to rock. He looked round, scanning book titles, running a fingertip along her immaculately ordered compact discs. 'All very nice,' he said. 'And tidy. As usual. Nothing changes.'

Actually, she thought, quite a lot does, but she didn't say it. She stood with her arms folded and demanded, 'What's all this about? I've only just got in.'

If Guy noticed the chilliness of her tone he chose to ignore it. 'I've come to take you out,' he said, 'because you deserve it, after what you've been through. Even strong women need pampering sometimes. Go and get changed. I've booked a table for eight o'clock.'

When Guy wanted something from her he always used the well-worn phrases of soap-opera sympathy. Hester quickly weighed up the pros and cons of accepting his invitation. Caution urged her to turf him out, but curiosity and a sudden distaste for her unpeopled flat pulled her the other way.

'Where have you booked?' she asked. The kind of restaurant he had chosen would tell her something about the extent of his designs on her.

'Don't make me tell you. I want it to be a surprise.'

'How do I know what to wear?' To her dismay, the conversation already seemed to be bordering on the flirtatious.

'That's easy. The best.'

She laughed, she hoped a little derisively, and went to

change. She didn't offer him a drink, or even ask him to sit down. She didn't put on 'the best', but chose a well-cut dress made of thick oyster-grey silk, high-necked, a perfect fit but rather prim. She didn't bother with proper make-up, just pale pink lipstick and the merest touch of mascara – enough to show she was an adult, no more. She wore her very beautiful Emma Hope grey suede shoes with diamanté buckles, which she loved as though they were a pair of greyhounds, but which she knew were not the sort of shoes that Guy appreciated. His imagination never got further than black and spiky. When she came out of the bedroom he said, 'Very nice,' but she could tell that what he really wanted to say was 'Very Julie Andrews.'

At twenty to eight the doorbell rang. He'd ordered a taxi. He'd thought of everything. He wanted something from her, something quite big. She was intrigued; she resolved not to drink too much. When she came back into the living room he was still standing and she wished she'd told him to sit – hearing him pacing the flat had made her agitated. She was glad when they were out through the door and into the taxi. Guy ushered her with a gentlemanly hand cupping her elbow, but she sat on the edge of the seat, as far away from him as possible. She was determined not to fall back into the old habit of physical familiarity. A series of images of the pair of them in different forms of transport flashed through her mind; their bikes, nose to tail as they cycled out of Cambridge towards Grantchester, Guy in front, turning his head to shout encouragement to her. The top deck of a London bus, the back seat, in the days when people still smoked on buses; both of them wanting to pay the other's fare, Guy taking his cigarette out of his mouth to kiss her. Their first car, a third-hand Mini Metro, mustard-coloured, the gear stick ragged from the teeth of the previous owner's

dog. They'd paid £150 for that car. The flight to their
Caribbean honeymoon, the baby on the seat in front setting
up a wailing at take-off that would last the whole journey,
or that was how it felt. 'Jesus,' Guy had said, too loudly.
'Let's not ever let ourselves in for one of those,' and she
hadn't allowed herself to acknowledge the little chill his
words gave her. On the motorway, in his company BMW,
on the way to visit his mother in Shropshire, him laughing
and spitting nicotine gum out of the window, her nagging
him to slow down. The pair of them bickering after a dinner
party about whose turn it was to drive home, their voices
quiet but corrosive; some wilful harming instinct that prevented them from ordering a taxi and cutting down the
argument at root. And now another version of them, in this
taxi, not touching, but not so the driver would notice. What
would he see if he cared to look? A handsome couple off to
dinner together, just beginning to taste freedom again after
the childbearing years? Guy was in good shape. He'd kept
his luxuriant curly hair; there was silver in the brown, but
not much. His eyes slanted sideways and down, sleepy lazy
eyes, like a sloth's. The folds round them were becoming
more pronounced, but that didn't make a man less attractive.
A well-matched couple, that's what the taxi driver would
see. He wouldn't see what Hester saw, the day she came
home early from a week away and found him in their bed
with a Spanish waitress from their local tapas bar. He
wouldn't see the spare bedroom in their little Clapham
house, the room the estate agents described as 'the nursery',
which Guy had almost aggressively filled with computer
equipment – boys' toys. He wouldn't see Hester going
through pockets, analysing the telephone bill, gathering
evidence. No one else had seen any of that.

The restaurant he'd chosen was, as he'd intended, a

surprise. Hester had heard of it, but she wouldn't have expected Guy to know of it. Usually, his touch was not as sure as he liked to think. But this place was the business. It was tucked away somewhere in Mayfair, it was called Saison, and from the outside it was so discreet as to be virtually invisible. There was a small sign over the door made of claret-coloured wood, on which was painted in cursive pewter lettering the single word 'Saison'. There was nothing so vulgar as a menu in the window. You have to be special to find us, the restaurant murmured. Hester was surprised there wasn't a password to get in. She was even more surprised that Guy had been sufficiently organized to book a table.

Even though it was Sunday evening the dining room was full, and Hester counted five celebrities without even trying. She was herself a minor celebrity, almost a household name, at least in households of a certain type, and it occurred to her that Guy would have used her name to secure a table. But she was not recognized, because she had very little to do with television and nothing at all with *Hello!* magazine. One diner did catch her eye. She had interviewed him once – someone high up in the world of opera, something to do with Glyndebourne. His name escaped her. He nodded and smiled. She was beginning to regret the modesty of her attire. Guy stole glances at her to see whether she was impressed. She kept her eyes averted.

The menu was in French, handwritten, too grand for English translations or even for prices. The wine list was small, thick and leatherbound, like an old-fashioned diary, and Guy peered into it with as much circumspection as if it were indeed a private document. He muttered something to the waiter, without consulting her. She guessed, correctly, that champagne was on its way. She thought of their early days, of the curry houses of Cambridge, of the greasy plastic tablecloths of the Trattoria Roma near Stockwell tube, of chicken Kiev and side salad with a wet egg sliced into it, of dusty grissini and a litre carafe of house red.

They talked, without apparent direction. She deflected inquiries about the aftermath of her father's death. She couldn't bear the puckering of the eyebrows Guy used to denote intense concern, so she brought the conversation round to her job, and to news of old acquaintances; babies, divorces, promotions. When they'd parted they'd tried to make sure their friends didn't have to take sides, and the result was that a number of them seemed to have fallen down the gap in the middle. Hester didn't find she minded very much. She'd kept ringing some of them just long enough to ascertain that they didn't think much of Selina, the woman he'd left her for, but once this palled she'd given up on all but her most intimate friends. Guy hadn't done any better, but between them they managed to rake up enough tepid gossip to last them through their hors d'oeuvres – Hester's was a particularly delicate pike soufflé. She already knew that Guy and Selina had parted company. She now learned that his most recent romance had also foundered, and that he was bored of the business he ran, which was an upmarket mail-order accessories company. Cuff-links and jokey socks for him, earrings and faux-Prada bags for her. In Hester's experience of Guy, which was still probably more extensive than that of anyone else apart from his mother, announcing he was bored of something meant that it was not going as well as he had hoped. She thought she detected the reason for the star treatment she was getting this evening. Her father's will. Guy would have been thinking about that from the minute he'd heard of his death. How could she have been so slow?

He declared that he was thinking of putting his Earls

Court flat on the market, perhaps in favour of an East End loft conversion. She said, 'Aren't you a bit old for one of those?' He ignored this mild jibe, and said he might not bother to sell the flat but just let it out instead. 'I'm getting itchy feet,' he said. 'Because I've hit forty, I suppose. It seems to happen to everyone, in some shape or form. I want to take a few months off to travel, see all those places we missed out on first time round. That's my number-one plan at the moment –' he swallowed the last forkful of his steak tartare – he always was a show-off when it came to food. 'Unless . . .'

There was a meaningful pause. Hester obliged. 'Unless what?'

'Unless you'll have me back.' He looked her straight in the eye, in the king-cobra way he had tried to use so often with her in the past, with diminishing success. 'I want you, Hester.'

This she had not expected. She'd been sure a request for a loan was coming, or at least an introduction to one of the influential people she met through work who might be useful to him in some way. She said, 'Guy, what are you talking about?' and that was the first time she'd used his name that evening.

'Hester,' he said, with more seriousness than he was wont to muster, 'I'm talking about us. It was such a disaster that we ever split up. Do you remember what Paul said in his best-man speech? That we were made for each other?'

'Well, he would say that, wouldn't he? To coin a phrase.'

'But the way he said it. After all the jokes. Don't you remember, he had everyone wetting themselves with all those stories, and then quietly, right at the end, he said that bit about us being made for each other, and everyone knew he was right.'

She couldn't deny that she was impressed, even touched, that Guy had retained such a vivid impression of the speech, which in her memory lingered with only the most muffled of echoes. Guy must have seen some softening in her face, for he renewed his entreaties.

'He was right, Hettie. Paul was right, the bastard. It was my fault we split up, and I've regretted it ever since. I was just so immature. I'd lost sight of what a special person you are, and I'm really, really sorry.'

Hester had never before heard Guy apologize for anything in the entire time she'd known him. She watched him, narrowly. If he'd reached out to take her hand at that point he'd have lost her, but he didn't. He just sat there with his hands in his lap, like a child accepting punishment.

'I wish we'd had a baby,' he said. 'You know, we still could.'

'But, Guy, you always said –'

'I know. I know what I said. I was wrong.'

She thought of that little room that should have been a nursery. Her throat felt tight. She thought of the things she'd found in that room: unpaid bills, cocaine, pictures of splay-legged girls. And, once, a pair of black knickers, rolled up, not hers. She pushed back her plate. That was about twenty pounds' worth of truffle shavings she was leaving. 'I don't want any pudding,' she said, 'or coffee. Could you get a taxi? No, make that two taxis. Don't contact me again, Guy. I'll ring you. I need quite a lot of time to think.'

Back at the flat she paced. She made coffee, because she didn't want to sleep. She stood on the balcony and felt the rain; she let the drops burrow through her demure grey silk. She felt her skin crawl and tighten as it cooled.

She went back into her bedroom, drew out the photograph

of Sebastian in his play, touched the bare young midriff, and said, aloud, 'My brother.' Then she hid it again, even though she was alone. She picked up the telephone.

'Solly?' she said. 'It's me. I'm back.'

8

Sunday lunch at the Wilkinsons' was always a good idea. Rosie and Robin understood what family life can and should be, and they put what they knew into practice. Though Hester had never truly had such a life, she recognized it, and enjoyed it – in small doses. Half past twelve until tea time, about once a month, was just perfect.

Rosie was short, not fat, but fatter than she had been when Hester first knew her, and fatter than she would have wanted to be. Not that she was going to do much about it. There was a little grey in her bouncy dark hair, but Hester didn't think she was going to do anything about that, either. She was very good at making pastry, very bad at putting on make-up. She looked charming in floaty frocks, dumpy in trousers. Her garden was a beautiful mess, her kitchen a messy mess. She and Robin met in their first year at Cambridge. Robin was six foot four, bearded and smiley. He had once resembled a beanpole, but these days he had a soft fold above his belt that Rosie liked to poke a finger into, like dough. He worked in advertising, producing promotional videos, though you wouldn't guess that from looking at him. He loved making things, like tree houses and hat racks. He and Guy only ever pretended to get on.

Rosie and Robin had four children, and there was always the threat of a fifth. At their wedding they had had a tidal wave of tiny bridesmaids and pageboys, and Hester remembered how Rosie couldn't stop beaming at them. She liked children of all ages, but she liked newborn babies best. She couldn't get enough of wrinkled downy heads and small bendy limbs. Whenever Rosie got near a newborn, she would snuff at it like an animal. Hester suspected that Robin would willingly forgo a fifth, but that he would go along with whatever Rosie decided. Their adoration was mutual.

The four they had already started with Becky, Hester's twelve-year-old goddaughter. Becky had fine dark hair and eyes that were violet triangles like Vivien Leigh's, but her bumpy nose and her brace kept her from realizing how beautiful she was, which Hester thought was probably a good thing. Next was Angus, who was ten, and Paddy, seven – both sturdy, freckled, smiley like their father. They had broad hands and feet and they were always fixing something. Paddy's front teeth were missing; Angus's gap had been filled by great slabs of tooth that seemed to have been stuck in at random. Angus and Paddy were very similar, apart from a few inches in height. Then there was Bud, nearly five, who still had the flaxen hair and rounded tummy of infancy. Bud's real name was Benjamin, but when he was born he was thought to resemble a bud, and he was rarely called anything else. All three boys were thoroughgoing Wilkinsons, cheery and loose-limbed, practical and energetic. Becky was different, rather tall and dreamy, given to writing poetry, shy with strangers. When she was six or seven she made a notice that said HEAR IT IS PRIVAT and stuck it on her bedroom door. Rosie might have liked to have a girl who more closely resembled herself, thought Hester – that was what she was hoping for, when Baby Number 5 came along. Not that she didn't value Becky for what she was.

The Wilkinsons lived in a big house in Wandsworth. The children could scramble over the fence at the bottom of their garden and make their way to the common without crossing a main road. Rosie never worried about their being on the common as long as they were all together. They'd lived in the same house since Angus was born, and they knew all their neighbours. Paddy said that if his parents ever tried to move he would lie down in the road in front of the removal van.

Hester went to lunch at Anderson Road a week after her evening with Guy. She'd tried not to think about Guy's proposal in the intervening time, because she wanted her subconscious to do the work for her. But now she went to Wandsworth with the specific intention of sounding Rosie out.

The weather was glorious, the garden spilling over with roses, and lunch had gone Middle Eastern. There were two cold chickens, burnished with saffron, a mountain of rice studded with pistachios and sour cherries, a salad of broad beans, each slipped out of its khaki skin, lying in a dressing of lemon and dill with the dull gleam of sea-rubbed glass. There was a passion-fruit sorbet, home-made, and little almondy biscuits shaped like crescent moons. 'I don't know how she does it' was what people often said about Rosie when they looked at the variously insistent demands of the house, the garden, the four children, the husband, the cats, the guinea pigs and the immense number of societies and committees she belonged to, but Hester did know how she did it. She did it because she loved it. On this particular Sunday Hester was the only guest, but Rosie made the same effort for her as she would have done for anybody else, and she would know it would be appreciated.

So there they sat under the sunshades on the decking – Rosie and Robin were naturals for decking – sipping the thick black coffee that Robin had brought for them, still picking in a desultory manner at the debris of the meal. That was something Hester particularly liked about being at

Rosie's. There were always leftovers, and you could go on picking. A cold roast potato, a sliver of garlicky lamb, a strip of pie crust. One never had proper leftovers when one lived alone.

Becky lay in the hammock some way off reading *What Katy Did*, which Hester had given her. Becky was a satisfactory goddaughter because she would read absolutely anything. Paddy and Bud were pushing tractors in the sandpit reasonably amicably, and Angus was in the kitchen with his father, washing up. The Wilkinsons had a rota – one child and one adult to wash up, and that included Bud, who had to be stood on a stool to reach. Rosie ought to write a book on How To Do It, Hester thought.

That left the two women, languid in the heat. The plumbago shuffled in the lightest of breezes and dropped its blue shooting stars on the table. Hester picked one out of her coffee. That kind of warm repletion always made Rosie want to talk about babies, and for once Hester wanted to talk about them too.

'You know, we're really seriously thinking about having another one,' said Rosie, refilling their cups.

'No!' Hester exclaimed, spreading her hands in mock astonishment.

'But we are. In fact, we're more than thinking about it. It would be great to have another girl, you know, just to round things off, so I keep taking my temperature and counting, and then when the moment's right I have to ring Robin and summon him home from work.'

'I didn't realize it was such an exact science.'

'Well, it isn't, really, but Robin loves being summoned. And now that Bud's at school all day . . . there's nothing better than going to bed in the middle of the afternoon, don't you think? It just always feels so right.'

Hester was impressed. She didn't imagine that many women would feel that way about their husbands after – what was it? – twenty years. She was shot through with a sudden pang of loss for everything she might have had – if circumstances had been different, or if she had been a different person? She said, 'Rosie, guess who took me out to dinner last night?'

'A lovely, lovely man, I hope.'

'Not exactly. It was Guy. He took me to Saison.'

'Good grief! He must be in the money. Whatever brought this on?'

Hester's mouth felt twitchy, but whether with embarrassment or with a quiet kind of triumph she wasn't sure. 'He wants us back together again.'

'Guy said that?' Rosie's amazement would have been unflattering, if she hadn't known the protagonists so well. 'He wants something. It must be money.'

'What he says he wants is children. Me, and children, in that order.' Hester smiled at her astonished face. 'That's what he says.'

It was easy to read the struggle that was going on in Rosie's generous soul. It truly pained her that Hester, her greatest friend, had no children. She would have loved Hester to match her, baby for baby. She often spoke with politely feigned envy of the benefits of having freedom and a career, but Hester knew that she wouldn't have exchanged places even for one day. So Guy's offer to impregnate Hester felt almost like an offer made to her. But she knew Guy, almost as well as anyone did, and when the marriage ended she'd said, 'Put it behind you, Hester. Guy was a mistake.'

Now she asked, hopefully, 'Do you think he's really changed?'

'Do people?'

'Surely they do. You have to give them a chance. Otherwise, what's the point of –'

'Should I give Guy a chance?'

'Oh, God. I don't think I can answer that question.'

They fell silent. All round them, the South London Sunday hummed. Hester shifted her chair and let the sun stream down on her upturned face. Rosie bit her nails, as she always did when she was thinking.

'How much do you want children, Hester?'

Hester considered Bud and Paddy's red-faced exertions in the sandpit and thought, not so very much. Then she looked at Becky's thin brown leg dangling out of the hammock, and at her narrow foot and fragile coltish ankle, and thought, yes, I want them a lot. Becky, wading uncertainly through the shallows of late childhood out into the roaring ocean of the adult world, was fascinating to her. Becky would take things forward. Her childless life seemed static, dry. She said, 'I do want them. But I can manage without.'

'I've never understood why you haven't met anyone else. I'd have thought you'd have been besieged.'

Rosie didn't know about Solly. No one did. That was the whole point of him. 'There just aren't many single men around,' she replied, in the breezy manner she'd taken with so many other questioners. 'And the ones there are – well, it's usually easy to see why they're single.'

'What happened with that photographer Judy set you up with? He was quite nice.'

'Oh, him. Absolutely nothing. He took my number, but he didn't call.'

'They're scared of you, Hester. They must be. Perhaps you have to make the first move.'

'Frankly, if they're going to be scared of me, then I don't think I want to know.'

'You're too fussy. Nobody's perfect.'

'So I should have Guy back, then?'

Rosie chuckled. 'They don't have to be *that* unperfect.'

'Well,' Hester said, 'in the five years since Guy and I split up, I haven't met anyone who really grabbed my attention. What's the tally? Let's see – Hugo, that poncy art dealer with the pink cords. Jean-Marc, who couldn't cope with having his hair ruffled because he always had to look immaculate. And whatshisname – that estate agent who looked like a farmer – oh, you know, you met him.'

'Sandy?'

'Yes, Sandy. What a dreadful name for a man. No wonder I've forgotten it. Three short-lived affairs, though "affair" is too grand a word for them. The thought of all of them makes me cringe. I'm forty, and I've got to be realistic.'

'It sounds as if you've already made up your mind to have him back.'

'No, not at all. But it's either that or no children. That's what I've got to be realistic about.'

Rosie's expression had become dreamy. 'Say I get pregnant in the next two months, I'll have finished being sick by Christmas. Then it'll be born next spring. That's the nicest time to have a baby, because you just loll around feeding it all summer. Then if you and Guy get a move on, you could have one not long after me. You'll only be forty-one. That's nothing these days. There's a child in Paddy's class whose mother was forty-five, and it was her first. When it goes to university you'll still be in your fifties.'

'Late fifties. And I'll be stuck with Guy for the rest of my life.'

'Well, yes, there is that.'

Robin emerged, screwing up his eyes after the darkness of the house. He'd brought out a slopping mug of tea for himself and a jug of iced water for the women. He was wearing baggy khaki shorts; there was a pimple on his thigh. He flumped down between them, and Hester noticed what a lot of space he took up, and how warm and moist that space felt, like mulch. She shifted a little, drew her knees up.

'How's your mother, Hester?' Robin asked. They'd avoided the subject of her parents during lunch because Bud had got to the stage where he was worried about death.

'She's fine, thanks. Coping really well.'

'Is the house and everything sorted out now?'

'More or less. This banker couple have put in an offer, and she's starting to pack things up. I think she's almost enjoying it. She's throwing away much more than I thought she would – I'm quite impressed.'

Hester knew that this was the closest she would come to telling Robin and Rosie about the revelations of her father's desk. They were her dearest friends, but Hester kept her friends for a variety of functions. Feeling affection for someone put her under no obligation to tell all.

'It's so sad about the house,' said Robin, who loved houses.

'Oh, is it?' chipped in Rosie, whose instinct was to iron out sadness of any kind. 'I think it's rather good. I'm very impressed that Verity's making a new start. I think she'll love being in a smaller place.'

Hester was struck by Rosie's choice of words. Hester never talked about her mother in terms of loving anything. She never considered her in the context of love.

'But what about you, Hets?' urged Robin. 'That house! I mean, all that family history. Won't it be a wrench? God, I'd buy it myself if I had the money.'

Just like that, Hester could see light bulbs winking on over both their heads as if they were characters in the *Beano*.

They did have the money. Robin saying they didn't was just a reflex. They could buy it. They could sell Anderson Road, and Robin could commute, or do something altogether different, as he'd often claimed he wanted to do. And the garden would be brilliant for the children, and the state schools would be usable, and Rosie would redecorate everything with a new baby perched on her hip . . . Hester felt a great lurch in her heart, and she wanted them all to be there, infusing Knighton with the sense of family that it had always deserved. But something else warned her to cut them off. It wouldn't do to have anyone too close on her heels.

'Why didn't we think of it before?' said Rosie, enraptured. 'It's so obvious.'

'Is it too late?' asked Robin. 'Has your mother –?'

She could have told them that the sale was all but complete, that it was a great pity but their plan was too late. One pinch, and she could nip it in the bud. But though she was good at keeping things to herself, direct lies didn't come naturally to her, especially not where Rosie and Robin were concerned. She said, with some hesitation, 'Well, I don't think anything's been signed. I'm not sure. You could ask.'

'You don't sound very enthusiastic, Hets.'

'Give me time,' she said. 'It's a new idea.' She rose, and brushed invisible crumbs from her clothes. 'I'd better go. I'm taking root here.'

'Hey, it's only half past three. Stay for a cup of tea.'

'No, really. I've got a mountain of things to do. I'm still writing letters to people about Father.'

'Poor old you,' said Rosie. 'It must be tough, being the only child. If you had a sibling you could spread the load. I don't know what I'd do without Millie and Soph.'

'Oh, it's not so bad,' said Hester aloud. 'Just time-consuming.' But in her head she said, ah, but I do have a sibling. Somewhere in the world, there's a brother waiting for me. All I have to do is find him. If that's what I want, of course.

Rosie made the telephone call that evening. For Verity, it was as welcome as it was unexpected. She'd always liked the Wilkinsons, who reminded her of the illustrations in the Ladybird books of Hester's childhood – an apple-cheeked family at play in a garden where the grass is slick like fresh paint and the hollyhocks and lupins rise tall and bright, miraculously free from slugs. Not that there was anything too perfect or goody-goody about the Wilkinsons, as there was about the Ladybird family. They were not bland people, in Verity's opinion. It was more that they gave one a sense of knowing where they stood in the order of things. And they all thoroughly enjoyed being alive.

They had often stayed at Knighton for weekends, more often when Hester and Guy were still married. Hester seemed to like to have other people about when she brought Guy home, to provide some kind of padding, because Guy and Simeon never really hit it off. It was hard to imagine any escort of Hester's who would have met with Simeon's approval, but it certainly wasn't Guy Harrison. Simeon called him a hollow man, though not to his face. There was rarely any open quarrel between them. After the separation, Simeon said something to Verity in private implying that Guy was the sort of person who could have followed the Nazis. He expressed it obliquely, but it was of course his strongest condemnation. And though Verity told him not to be so silly, she did know what he meant. Guy would talk himself out of any position of principle. He always followed his own best interests.

So friends were quite often produced to make conversations more general. Verity was glad; it was company for her, and a relief from the heaviness of life with Simeon. Of all the friends, the Wilkinsons were the most frequent visitors. She put Hester and Guy in Hester's old bedroom, Robin and Rosie in the best spare room, the one that had been her mother's private sitting room, and all the children were crammed into the narrow attic – they liked the sloping ceilings and the fact that there was an antiquated fire escape that one was supposed to throw out of the window in an emergency, not that any of them could have reached the window. There was an old cot up there, though the littlest one usually ended up between Rosie and Robin in the big bed. The little girl, Becky, loved Hester's old doll's house. Verity was sure she played with it far more than Hester ever did. And for the boys she filled a couple of boxes with toys, little things she found at jumble sales or what have you, because though she'd kept most of Hester's old toys there'd never been cars or trains or things like that.

Summer evenings were lovely times. Robin and Guy would walk down to the village pub – they were hardly soul mates, but they could bear to share a pint – and Hester would make supper while Verity gave Rosie a hand with bathtime. The children loved the deep old-fashioned bath with legs shaped like curved dolphins. Verity had a photograph Rosie had sent her of Becky and Angus sitting in the bath holding Paddy when he was very new – you could still see the dark clot of umbilicus. They looked as if they were playing pass the parcel with him. Rosie was a cheerful mother, singing and laughing and telling them stories, absolutely non-stop. Verity would have liked to have been that kind of mother, but never quite was. Her instincts were there, she felt, but something got in the way of them . . . Where would Simeon have been during these sessions? In the parlour with the newspaper, Verity supposed. But when the children were in bed and the adults took their drinks out to the terrace to catch the last of the sun, he was always bonhomous, and the Wilkinsons seemed to regard him as a charming host. Verity hoped so. Or rather, she thought she hoped so.

And now, what did she truly feel about this plan of theirs? It was obvious what she would be expected to think. How wonderful that Hester's friends want to buy it; Verity puts on a brave face but it would have broken her heart to lose it altogether ... she could hear the Beryl Barbers of this world humming over their morning coffee. So lovely that it'll be a family home again, so marvellous to know they won't do anything awful to it; how could anyone disagree? But privately, part of Verity felt it to be less the perfect solution, more a fencing-in. Perhaps life was just a country park, she thought. When you think you've got to the wild bit, when you think you've broken free, then there's a fence with a notice on it reminding you most politely that you are, after all, expected to remain within the parameters of the park. Trespassers will be prosecuted. And the park is very pleasant, not dull at all, pretty, even beautiful in places. But just stay inside. Don't even think about escape.

9

Verity had been Simeon's secretary. That was how they'd met. Or rather, she was a secretary at his chambers, dogs-bodying for all the barristers; she wasn't especially assigned to him. It was the first job she took after completing her Pitman's secretarial course, and that training, which she undertook at the urging of her friend Stella, was the last of the various courses she had fiddled about with. Clever, forceful, feminist Evelyn had assumed her daughter would go to university, but Verity didn't want to. She didn't feel clever, just intelligent enough to know what cleverness was, and to know that she didn't possess it. Her mother, who made all sorts of assumptions, was taken aback to find that the school's opinion of Verity coincided with Verity's opinion of herself. She never excelled at school. She hadn't struggled, either; she'd just done what was expected. She did best at those tasks that required neatness and patience. She liked biology, because she enjoyed copying the diagrams out of the textbooks and labelling them with little ruled arrows; geography, when she filled maps in with pale shaded colours; and needlework – her blanket stitch was singled out for praise. She was good at tasks that had clear boundaries, and she was meticulous about finishing things. She had wondered whether these traits were inherited from her father – her mother could hardly have been more different – but he had died when she was eight, and she had never felt she knew him well, but she didn't have the impression that he was particularly neat or patient, either. Perhaps she was what they called a throwback.

She didn't know why her mother had chosen this particular boarding school, which struck Verity in retrospect as a singularly dull one. Only a handful of girls went on to university, and she could see from early on that she would not be among them. The university girls fell into two groups. There were those who wore their uniform untidily, took a perverse pride in getting a conduct mark, read huge Russian novels and affected to be moved to tears by them, asked the mistresses questions they couldn't answer, and dominated the dining hall with their bold, loud laughs. Then there were those who never spoke a word, whose eyes swivelled sideways as they scuttled along the corridor walls. This type kept their hair short, and greasy; any escaping strands were brought into line by Kirby grips. These girls tended to be keen churchgoers who didn't seem to notice what they ate. It was easy to overlook their existence until the form orders were posted on the noticeboard, and then there were their names, always at the top, in the science subjects at any rate.

Verity fell into neither group; and she had no illusions about her status. Her life at The Pines was tolerably pleasant. She had some placid, good-hearted friends. She still wrote to two of them, visited them occasionally, and felt a calm affection for them that never needed to be probed. When she moved to the new cottage she planned to have them to stay. They would talk about gardening, and books they had enjoyed, and they would both tactfully try to avoid the subject of their grandchildren. She would look forward to their arrival and their departure in almost equal measure. Erica Dawes and Gillian Braithwaite. Her mother could never remember their names.

Erica, Gillian, Verity and a few others walked to church

in a group, won prizes for keeping their dormitories tidy, grumbled about prep but completed it on time, and were sometimes selected to play for the second teams. Erica was mildly musical, Gillian was horse-mad. Together they trundled through the long, eventless boarding-school years attracting little attention. Verity had wondered whether the headmistress was disappointed in her – how could the product of such comparatively exotic parents have turned out so dull? Or perhaps she was relieved. Certainly, Verity was relieved once she felt sure that her camouflage was sufficient to protect her from the glare of her mother's talent and halfway fame. But somehow, Evelyn herself took a long time to notice that her daughter had inherited none of her flair or her father's adventurousness. Perhaps she thought it was latent, lying dormant, and if so, she could have been right. Now, in her sixties, Verity felt the stirrings of something unfamiliar. If it emerged, would she recognize it for what it was?

Evelyn must have assumed that any child of hers would shine, and when it was time for Verity to leave school with only modest grades for Higher Certificate and the dimmest of ambitions, she was quite alarmed. She spent the rest of that summer trying to galvanize Verity, who found herself receiving more of her mother's attention than she had in her life before, which was not an unmixed blessing. Evelyn marched her off to art galleries and theatres, got her intellectual friends to engage her in conversation – a thankless task, reflected Verity, which must have stretched their bonds of loyalty to the limit – and even took her to Florence for two weeks that September. She seemed to be making up in those few months for years of – would 'neglect' be too strong a word?

Verity enjoyed Florence, though she quailed before the

rich friends in whose villa they stayed – a pair of hard-edged American writers, chain-smokers, who drank Martinis for what she would have called elevenses. She liked the piazzas, the fountains, the ice creams which were so unlike anything in her war-disrupted gastronomic experience. She liked the shoes and handbags in the shop windows, the precision of their silhouettes, their muted shine. She liked the grieving faces of Giotto's monks, the building-block simplicity of the Pazzi Chapel. Best of all, she liked the monastery of San Marco, where Fra Angelico had given each cool narrow cell a painted extension into another world. She liked it enough to venture that she would be willing to take a course in the history of art. So back in England that was arranged. She was to live at home, at Knighton, and travel by train to London for her studies, at the end of which she would be taken on in some lowly capacity by one of the great auction houses, from which position, her mother said, she could 'work her way up'.

Because of course it never entered Evelyn's head that her daughter would not have a career. Evelyn Albery, novelist, poet, journalist, and the youngest suffragette to chain herself to the railings outside Number 10 Downing Street, had earned her own living until her lateish marriage. She had famously broken into the masculine world of the radical political journal the *Eye* by signing her copy using only her initials so that the editor, the vastly respected Leslie Stonestreet – later to become her friend, mentor and (it now occurred to Verity) perhaps her lover – believed her to be a man. How could such a woman produce a daughter who had no more ambition than a hedgehog? Verity had come across a postcard not long ago, inside a book she obviously hadn't opened since the early 1950s, a novel by Lettice Cooper. The postcard was a snapshot of the relationship between mother and daughter at that time. 'Did you send your bread-and-butter letter to the Finkelsteins?' demanded Evelyn's thick-nibbed fountain pen. 'If not <u>do</u> <u>so</u> <u>at</u> <u>once</u>! Just going to dine with Lady H. at her club. Awful bore as have cold and throat coming. Have bantams hatched yet? All love, M.' The postcard, inexplicably, was a black-and-white – or rather, grey-and-yellow – photograph of the Fruit Department of the Army & Navy Stores.

In the fullness of time the history of art course was completed, and an interview at an auction house was arranged. This would have been about a year after Verity left school. Her mother took her shopping for something suitable to wear. They came home with a stiff smart suit, sea-green; Evelyn said the colour enhanced Verity's eyes, but Verity thought it made her look ill. She was thin and flat-chested; the deep darts in the jacket were like arrows pointing to where her breasts should have been. She loathed the suit, but she put it on, and the uncomfortable shoes that went with it, and set off for the interview. It was a hot day. She took a bus from Charing Cross. Someone had dropped chocolate on the seat, and she sat on it. She twisted the skirt round, and tried to scrape off the chocolate with the edge of her return railway ticket. It left a pale stripe. She got off the bus and dashed into a department store, where she found the Ladies and rubbed at the stain with damp paper towels. Tiny white paper worms rubbed off the towels and clung to her skirt. The chocolate remained. She took off the skirt, stood there in her slip and stockings, and held the dirty patch under the tap. She squeezed and squeezed, but when she put the skirt back on it just looked as if she'd wet herself. She tried wearing it back to front, but the fastening looked most peculiar. She was already five minutes late for the interview and some distance from the auction house.

She let it go. She crouched in the lavatory for another half-hour, hoping her blood heat would dry the wet patch, but it didn't. Then she crept out, and somehow made her way to the park, where she sat on a bench with her skirt on the wrong way round and let it dry in the sun.

She told her mother that she'd failed the interview, and, in case Evelyn made further investigations, declared she'd lost interest in it. She wanted to do something else. And what might that be, inquired Evelyn. Verity thought of needle-work at school, calm and snug, and said she wanted to learn dressmaking. Evelyn wasn't impressed, but seemed to think it better than nothing. The patch on the skirt dried to a different colour. Verity bundled the suit to the back of the wardrobe and never wore it again.

So dressmaking followed history of art. Less interesting, but more soothing, and possibly more useful, as she retained the habit of making some of her own clothes, though Simeon would have argued contemptuously against the use-fulness of that. She enjoyed making clothes for the child Hester. They used to plan them together, sorting through the packets of paper patterns, McCall's and Butterick. When they'd made their decision they'd go on an expedition to the haberdashery department of Peter Jones or Derry & Toms to choose buttons and braid. Verity liked haberdashers, the tininess of everything, the doll's-house neatness of rolled ribbons, thimbles, skeins of embroidery silk. All those reels of coloured cotton – golden cinnamon, pale salmon, pea-cock, eau-de-nil, tangerine. Hester, too, would pore over those names, enchanted by their precise poetry. It was all so carefully considered. The exact shade one would want for some particular button holes; perfection for one tiny moment. There was a nevermoreish quality about a leftover cotton reel that was really quite melancholy.

Verity used to mend clothes as well as make them. Like many war children, she enjoyed 'making do'. It drove Simeon wild. 'Buy a new one, forgodsake! We're not paupers!' He had a way of saying 'forgodsake', all in one word, as if he didn't understand what it meant, and this made him sound like a foreigner, which of course he was. He never liked the clothes she made, either; he used to tweak at them and tell her to open an account at Harrods. And he was right. Money was not a problem, not even right at the beginning. Verity never needed to make or mend a thing. So, no, her dress-making apprenticeship was never truly useful. She had a mental image, one she held on to for years, of herself sitting in her armchair, darning or hemming, bent over her work like Vermeer's lace-maker, and of her husband gazing at her as if he found the sight reassuring, graceful, even moving. But Simeon was no such husband.

She lived at home for several months, and then her mother found her a flat in London. It would never have occurred to Verity to do so. She didn't actively want to live with her mother, but to move out would cost money, and she wasn't earning any. She was unobtrusive at home, and it did not cross her mind that she might be cramping her mother's style. Nothing much did cross her mind in those days. She floated along in a little dream of nothingness. Then one day Evelyn made the announcement, without preamble. Verity was to share a flat in South Kensington with another girl. The rent was to be paid out of her allowance, which was the interest from a lump sum her father had left her. The amount had increased now she was eighteen, though she would not have full access to it until she was twenty-one. 'I suppose Father thought you might go wild,' said Evelyn with a sarcastic smile. Verity hadn't known about this money. Naturally she knew she had an allowance, but she had never inquired into its origins. When she looked back on her youthful self, it seemed to her that she had absolutely no gumption.

Her flatmate was the daughter of a friend of a friend. Her name was Stella Penn, she was a year older than Verity, and she was reading law at London University. The flat belonged to her parents. The two girls got on well. Stella was tough and intelligent – not intellectual, but competent and ambitious. A supremely sensible person. She didn't look down on Verity, but accepted her completely for what she was. It could be, thought Verity, that she was the only person in my life who has done that. Her boarding-school friends, the Gillians and the Ericas – yes, their acceptance was and remained unquestioning, but she held back from them – and still did – so their sense of what she was or what she had become was necessarily partial. But under Stella's benign authority, she blossomed. Stella knew how to lay down rules for everything – she didn't understand any other way of operating – but her rules were flexible, and fair.

The flat had one large bedroom, which they shared, and a living room with what was known as a 'kitchenette' in one corner. There was no muddle, no confusion about their belongings. They had two drawers each in the chest of drawers, and half the hanging space in the wardrobe. Stella used shoe trees and knew how to fold her jerseys properly. She arranged her books in alphabetical order, by author, and recorded every halfpenny she spent – postage stamps 6d, bus fare 3d, athlete's foot powder 1/4d. She wasn't mean, just orderly. And she could be teased about it. Once, when they invited a couple of young men to supper, Stella wrote down everything they spent on the evening, right down to 'approx. ½oz Coleman's Mustard'. Verity used this as an affectionate jibe for years.

They shared a social life, and this was perfectly satisfactory. Stella made friends with other students and Verity gathered a few people along the way, on her various courses. There were very few girls reading law, so Stella made friends with men. Unlike most girls, she was good at establishing friendships with no romantic undertones, but there were a couple of boyfriends, too. There was Tony, who reverted to Anthony and became a highly successful QC, and Alan, who looked as if he might become, as Stella put it, 'Mr Stella Penn', but he didn't. He did offer, and Stella agonized. 'I don't think I *can*.' Verity could still hear her voice. 'He's too dull, and he's only going to get duller.' Stella never did marry. She died in her late twenties of Hodgkin's disease. She was Hester's godmother.

Verity had a few followers of her own, but no one very serious. It took some effort, now, to remember their names, let alone their faces. They were escorts, really; they took her to the cinema, or sometimes to dances. The fact that Stella and Verity shared a bedroom wasn't a problem at all. It was all very chaste. Hands were held, kisses were sought, but not much more. Verity never even considered herself to be in love, until she met Simeon, and then – well, that was love of a kind.

It was because of Stella that Verity met Simeon. Not through her, but because of her, so it wasn't her fault. Verity had continued to shilly-shally, as her mother would have put it. She finished the dressmaking course and was taken on as an assistant by a firm of couturiers, but she quailed at the sight of all those polished nails and silken shins, and lost heart. She signed on with a temping agency, but as she had no office skills the jobs that came her way consisted of little more than making the coffee and watering the plants, with wages to match. She wondered about becoming a librarian, but did nothing about it. Then one day Stella said, 'This is silly. Learn to type, and then work your way up. If you can type, the world's your oyster.'

'Work my way up what?'

'What about the law? You don't need a degree to get a perfectly decent job. Legal secretaries earn good money, and respect, too.'

Verity's imagination didn't catch fire, but Stella organized her, and she had no better suggestion. Evelyn saw secretarial work as servile, so it was under the shadow of her disapproval that Verity learned her skills and specialized in legal shorthand. Her first job application was successful, so she started work in Simeon's chambers. She was there for a few weeks, not particularly noticing him – she was more interested in another young barrister, actually, a thin, dark, poetic-looking type, though she was careful to give no sign that she harboured tender thoughts. But then one day Simeon slapped a pile of papers down on her desk, and she saw his hands, his big, curved hands, and they reminded her of the paws on the lions in Trafalgar Square. She noticed the golden hair curling from underneath his cuffs, and, quite suddenly, she saw those two big hands covering her naked breasts. She was not aware of having had such a thought before, about anyone. It would have been more like her to look down, but for once she looked up, and caught his eye.

It was early spring when they began what for want of any better word could be called their courtship – February, actually, but spring comes earlier to London. He took her out to lunch that day, the day she noticed his hands. He insisted on wine. When she walked back to the flat that evening she noticed clumps of snowdrops in the front garden, spiky and brave, and crocuses sending out soft purple flares in the damp dusk. The next day was 14 February, St Valentine's

146

Day. The doorbell rang before she was even dressed. There were no entryphones to the flats in those days; the front door was left unlocked, and callers just came up in the lift. She answered the doorbell in her dressing gown. It was twelve red roses, and this was before he'd even kissed her. Stella put down her slice of toast, and stared. 'Good grief!' she said. 'I didn't know Philip had it in him.' Philip, the last of Verity's chaste escorts, had always been shadowy. Now he was dissolving like a sandcastle broken down by the tide.

'He hasn't,' said Verity. 'Got it in him, I mean. It's – someone new. You don't know him.' Stella looked a little hurt. 'I don't know him either,' she blathered. 'Not really. This is – well . . .'

'Lucky old you. I shouldn't think Alan will even notice the date.' She cleared her breakfast things, punctual as always. 'Lucky old him, too, of course. Tell me about him tonight.' She winked, but a little veil was drawn between them, and because Simeon didn't go away, that veil was never completely lifted.

That evening he did kiss her, and the evening after that and the one after that. For a long time she felt as if it were a case of mistaken identity, as if when he was embracing her he might suddenly look over her shoulder and let go of her and say, 'Ah – here she is. So sorry, my mistake.' He was older than her, already successful, handsome, appallingly clever. He met his friends in fashionable bars where they made witty comments about difficult films. In the company of his friends she spoke very little, but that seemed to be how Simeon wanted it. In time, she introduced him to the friends she shared with Stella, but they didn't register with him. He just couldn't take them in.

Simeon had a flat of his own, within walking distance of his – their – chambers, therefore on the opposite side of town from South Ken. For quite a while she made excuses not to go there. She was frightened of being alone with him. They were never truly alone anywhere else – one isn't, in London, not in any park or restaurant or cinema, and in her flat there was always either the presence of Stella or the possibility of her imminent return. On the somewhat unyielding wooden-armed sofa Verity would let his big lion hands make their way under most of her clothing, and she listened to his protestations of love and his talk of the shape their lives would take – he talked of marriage and children very early on – but still when he asked her to come 'home' with him she made excuses. It wasn't just the sex. She was nervous about that, but only in what she still regarded as a perfectly normal, virginal way. It was Simeon himself she was afraid of. When she was a child she had peeped into a book her mother had of the works of William Blake. She saw the image of a man, full face, straight on. He was coming out of the page at her. His eyes were huge and terrible, and there were flames, or the suggestion of flames. She slammed the book shut, thrust it away from her, and never looked at it again, but she knew that face was still coming towards her. The face was Simeon's. On her own territory, or in a shared, public space, she could avoid looking at him straight, but in his own flat there would be no escape from revelation.

With Simeon, he was all there was, and that made it all the more intense. Verity's other admirers had had doting mothers and quarrelsome sisters and pipe-smoking grand-fathers who made faintly suggestive remarks about her role in their grandson's life. She had been taken home for Sunday lunches, even once shared a week's boating holiday on the Norfolk Broads. No family had quite clasped her to its bosom, but she had received the impression that she was generally acceptable. The sons of these families in no way deviated from the template laid out before her. One could see so clearly the pattern of life, the kind of future on offer. Even Verity, who did not regard herself as either clever or perceptive, could see precisely the section of the pattern waiting to be filled by her, or her like. And there was nothing wrong with this kind of life, its security, its predictable pleasures. Nothing wrong, but not quite enough right, either.

Simeon was not part of a pattern. The structure in which he had once belonged had collapsed in dust and rubble, and nothing was left, not even a little pile of bones. Simeon was a Jew, the only survivor, as far as he knew, of a once-prosperous Viennese banking family. His parents, complacent, padded by their wealth against the slashing persecutions of the 1930s, failed to take action. Verity never talked to Simeon much about them, but she did once ask, naively, why they couldn't see it coming. 'They weren't intellectuals,' Simeon said. 'They were capitalists. Every-where they looked, they saw only mirrors.' A family friend, a gentile, talked Simeon's mother into parting with her only son. He was tall, fair-haired and blue-eyed; false papers were found for him, and he left Vienna. His friends took him as far as Amsterdam, then he crossed the sea to England on his own. He had never seen the sea before, and he found the crossing the most alarming thing. He was fourteen – too young, perhaps, to comprehend the scale of the greater threat. This was in 1938. By then, most of the family's fortunes had been stripped from them; his father, deeply shaken, died of a heart attack in the spring, a few months before Simeon's departure. Simeon left behind his mother and Elisabeta, his younger sister. His rescuer persuaded him that the best thing he could do would be to study in London so that one day he could make a home for them there, but within months of his arrival in Muswell Hill, where he lodged with another family contact, their letters stopped coming. He did not find out that they died in Ravensbrück until he was a man.

Verity's other suitors, the Philips and the Davids, the Andrews and the Jeremys, had framed family photographs, aunts who sent them postal orders, savings accounts opened for them at birth. They borrowed their fathers' dinner jackets, dined at clubs with their bachelor godfathers, mourned the demise of their family dogs. They had in-jokes and obligations and memories of camping holidays. Simeon had none of this. He had nothing, not even one photograph. The food, the customs, the language of his childhood – none of it remained. Even his name – 'Eichenbaum' – had become English 'Oakes'. 'Simeon' was all that was left. He'd considered 'Simon', but held back. With 'Simeon' he could just about scrape through.

Simeon was defined by loss. He spoke about it rarely, but the scorching pain of loss had left him somehow purified. He believed himself to be absolutely strong, and if energy is strength, then he was. It was loss that drove him to Verity. She might well have asked 'Why me?' but in truth she knew why. She was safe, predictable. She had little discernible personality. She was, at least in the early days, under his control. She wasn't going to disappear. And time proved him right. It was Verity who was with him when he died. Under the same roof, at any rate.

The day of course came when she did go back to his flat. She found it hard to think about this – hard in the way that looking at a naked light is hard. Because she knew that it would have to happen, she did a little tentative research into contraception, via a friend of Stella's who had married young, and she learned that to be fitted with a Dutch cap she would need to present herself to the doctor as a married woman, or at least a fiancée. She knew of bold spirits who provided themselves with cheap rings from Woolworth's and blagged their way through, but she was not a blagger. And she knew the doctor would examine her and find her virgo intacta, so a ring would be unconvincing. No, she decided, she would go ahead and take the risk. If she became pregnant, Simeon would marry her. She didn't know if she wanted him to. She almost hoped she would become pregnant, because that would make up her mind for her.

So, she was more calculating than Simeon knew. In later years he would often boast to friends that he had swept her off her feet, but no one and nothing had ever done that. She chose the day, she chose the time. It was a hot evening in early summer. 6 June. A private anniversary of hers, though not one she was inclined to celebrate. After work they had walked through the City, still dusty with the rebuilding work of the post-war decade. They neared St Paul's. Verity said, 'Do you know, I've never been inside?' and Simeon said, 'Neither have I. Let's go.' That vast barn full of stored space and time was cool after the sticky city air. 'It's astonishing they never hit this,' said Simeon. They stood hand in hand under the great dome and stared, up and up, until she felt as if her soul had left her body and was spiralling up into the roof. She leaned against Simeon and said, 'I think I'm going to faint.'

He scooped her up and carried her out, her legs draped over the crook of his arm, and they crossed the threshold as brides are supposed to be carried over the threshold of their new homes. Except they were doing it in reverse. Everything looked green and silver, but she saw the staring faces of onlookers as if they were photographic negatives, and she was aware that people moved back to let them pass. He set her down on the steps outside and she lolled against his shoulder. He said, 'A taxi? Back to your flat?' and she said, 'How far are we from yours?'

They walked there, his arms so firmly supporting her that she felt as if she was swimming. He carried her again, up the shared staircase – an old wooden one, like in a university college. His living room was also his bedroom – she took that in at a glance. He set her down on the armchair, not the bed, and inquired tenderly whether she needed a doctor. She asked for water. He went to fetch it from the kitchen across the landing, and she looked about her.

There was little that she could not have predicted; nothing to catch her off her guard. His books were neatly divided into two cases; legal tomes and other works of reference in one, the other for general reading. Novels, some plays, a little – a very little – poetry. No history. Thomas Mann in German – that rattled her, rather. The bed, neatly made, was covered with a kind of fitted counterpane so that it could double up as a sofa. There was dust, but no mess. Nothing had been left on the floor. The wardrobe doors were properly shut.

Beyond the uncurtained window the sky pulsed with the heavy uncertain white of urban summer heat. It had to rain. She longed for it to rain.

He came back in with two glasses, one of water, one of brandy. She stood up, quite steady now, and took both. With the back of his forefinger he stroked her arm, bare below the short cuffed sleeve of her summer frock.

'You're shivering,' he said.

She swallowed the water, handed back the glass. 'Not with cold,' she said. Then she raised the brandy to her lips and let it all run down her throat.

*

Afterwards, it did rain. They lay on the bed, with nothing on at all, and no cover over them. His leg kept hers pinned down; her cheek was pressed against the dense springy hair that covered his chest. Below the rumble of the traffic thunder growled and, war children that they were, they both tensed. Then the rain began, and there was nothing else; just their skin and breathing and the high window full of rain.

10

8th May 1980

My diary-keeping resolution has not grown stronger with age. Few things do, except querulousness and regret. I'd meant to work at this steadily, even daily, until I'd told all there was to tell. But several weeks have passed since my birthday outing to Sissinghurst, and I haven't lifted a pen. At my age, one might imagine that the rumble of time's wingéd chariot would spur one into action, but, on the contrary, I seem to pass my days in a kind of waking dream.

The war in Europe ended thirty-five years ago today. Three young men from the village had been prisoners of war, two of them brothers, one a nephew of Mrs Apps. They'd come home within the last week or so, all thin, one limping, all three grinning all over their faces. We had a special service at evensong time on the 8th. I took Verity. The three young men were there, the church was packed, and everyone was bursting with pride and excitement. I was, too – I squeezed Verity's hand very hard, and she returned my squeeze, which wasn't the sort of behaviour we usually went in for. But it wasn't my war. I felt myself to be only on the fringes of the jubilations. That brought home to me, I think, that when Jack died a shutter rolled down between me and a large part of shared emotional life.

Just look at the day! Isn't May marvellous? Bluebells, red campion, cow parsley, crab apple blossom, everything frothing and foaming up out of the earth, every stalk swollen with juice, every leaf uncrumpling like the fist of a newborn baby. The beauty is almost too much to bear. I remember that feeling, thirty-five years ago, and looking at my daughter, and thinking, I hope that all this juice and all this joy means what it ought to mean for her, because it's rather too late for me.

When I was writing – properly writing – I always had an upsurge of creative energy in spring. I love that Herbert poem: – 'I once more smell the dew and rain/And relish versing.' He was talking about spiritual renewal, but my response to the seasons is the closest I can get to spiritual. I always found the first two months the hardest part of the year to write in. I would have a little burst just after Christmas, an upsurge of some puritanical work ethic, but once that had died back it was like plodding through mud. It ought to have been easy – socially the quietest time, and with little to do in the garden, what is there to prevent one from sitting and writing by the fire? But for me, there has always been a block. The world slows down, like the pulse of a hibernating animal. Thoughts seem muffled, buried like a squirrel's hoard in places you can't quite find again. At Knighton, during the early years of my marriage to Lionel, I would stare out of the window and see no colour, no light, no promise of anything at all. The unwaving trees were the same grey-brown as the empty fields. The sky was that thick and toneless grey that seems to suck the life out of everything. In spring and summer, birdsong seemed to crowd against the house; in January it was replaced by a woolly silence. Mrs Apps threw out leftovers for the birds, but the magpies seized the lot. I watched the magpies from my bedroom window. The showiness of their black and white, that metallic slash of blue, was like a mockery. They would laugh, and bounce away with the crusts in their beaks. No other bird had a chance.

Every season has its compensations, but, city child that I was, I needed more than snowdrops and catkins and the embers of the occasional sunset. I was off to London whenever I could manage it. Lionel rarely accompanied me. He huddled in his north-facing study, wrapped in a shawl the colour and texture of which were nearly indistinguishable from his beard. He looked as reproachful as an injured owl, though he tried not to mind my going. Any guilt I felt at leaving him quickly converted to irritation. I left the house in a bad temper, issuing a stream of instructions over my shoulder to poor Mrs Apps. Once I was on my own, on the train, my mood changed entirely. Out came my book or my writing pad, and ideas crowded to the front of my mind or the tip of my pen. It was something to do with the rhythm of the train, the smoke shadows floating over the frostbound fields, or the scatter of human activity across the unrolling landscape – a rider, children running, a man with a gun. I've always thrived on change, visual, geographical – every kind. Verity is unlike me in that respect, as in so many others.

At Knighton, the story of my life was for so much of the time held in suspension; on those train journeys it could continue to unfold. This was the story of my other life, you understand; not my married-to-Lionel-country life. Not my literary-friends-in-London life, either. No, I mean the story of the life I might have led, had circumstances been different. I realize that in my earlier paragraph I wrote 'during the early years of my marriage to Lionel'. 'To Lionel' ought to have been superfluous, for I was never married to anyone else. But in my other life, I was married to Jack.

One of the purposes of this diary is to write about Jack, which is something I've never done. Here am I, an old woman, writing in 1980 when we've a woman Prime Minister and no Empire and my only grandchild is fully grown, and

I've never had the courage to write about Jack, who died in 1918. Sixty-two years ago. Have I thought about him every day for sixty-two years? It's quite possible. I forbade myself to speak of him, but I put no constraint on my thoughts. And it's more than likely that in my mind I have turned him into something he never was. I worry about this. I have very little of him. Half a dozen letters, that's all, and the brown petals of a dog rose he picked in Flanders and folded in his last letter to me, because, as he said, he had nothing else to send. I don't even have a photograph. Because, you see, Jack Addington was never mine to keep. He was engaged to somebody else, and, in wartime, breaking engagements to sweet and faithful English girls was not a thing one did.

Jack's fiancée's name was Dora Smithson, and she lived in a village in Kent. Her father was the local solicitor; her parents and Jack's were firm friends. She was his childhood sweetheart, and she became more than that, because his parents both died, one of tuberculosis and the other of influenza, before he was out of his teens. So the Smithsons became his substitute family. When war broke out there was no reason for him not to propose, so he slipped his mother's engagement ring on her finger and off he went to the Front, and she rewarded him with letters and tobacco and bits of knitting. He showed me a photograph she'd sent him, with her hair gathered in a soft bun and her sweet round face held wistfully to one side. He showed me this the first time I met him, which was on a train. 'She's a good person,' he said. And then he took my hand.

I saw Dora, once. It was about five years after Jack's death. I remembered everything Jack had told me about her, so it wasn't hard to track her down, because he'd told me plenty. He was always trying to talk himself out of love for me and back into the bond of faith that we both knew she deserved. I decided to go and see her because five years of not talking was stretching me thin and brittle, and I thought, if I can't set eyes on someone else who knew him I will snap. Because if you can't mourn someone properly it's as if they never existed, and I had to continue Jack's existence for me, otherwise nothing made any sense.

I thought about writing to her first, but then I didn't, because that would give her a chance to run away. I didn't think she was the running-away kind, but I couldn't take the chance. Besides, I had only the memory of an address I'd seen on the top of her letters to Jack. He'd shown me some of her letters, I suppose to impress on me – and on himself – the reality of their engagement. It hurt me, but it was a wound I wanted to bear. With Jack, I had to see what was happening with clear eyes. I needed to know how wrong it was, and how right. So I looked at the photograph, and read the letters, and when Jack talked about her I never stopped my ears. The address I'd seen was only 'The Gables', and then the name of the village. It didn't seem quite enough. So one warm day in July I took a train, and asked directions from the station porter.

The village was larger than I had expected. There was a row of small shops, two public houses, and a duck pond on the green. The walk from the station was at least three quarters of a mile, and the heat was considerable. The porter had told me to turn right by one of the pubs, but whether it was the Coach and Horses or the Green Man I was no longer sure. I bought a bag of currant buns at the baker's shop, and asked the woman who took my sixpence whether I would be likely to find Miss Dora Smithson at The Gables. 'Miss Dora? She's Mrs Hardwick now, madam. Oh, no, you won't find her at The Gables on a Tuesday, that's Mrs

Smithson's day for Maidstone. You'll most likely find Miss Dora – Mrs Hardwick, I should say – at home on a Tuesday, at Keeper's Cottage, up the hill, past the church, just not quite opposite the rectory. There's a green-painted gate, and a sign on it that Mr Hardwick had made. Keeper's Cottage. You can't miss it.' She paused. Her forearms had the waxy colour and the bumpy texture of suet pudding; she rested on them, on the counter. I could see she was longing to ask me my business, but couldn't quite justify the inquiry. I traded a small opening for her information, which was all I was prepared to offer. 'Mrs Hardwick,' I said. 'Thank you for telling me. I'm glad to hear she's married.'

'She's luckier than some. Mr Jack was a sad loss. Still, he wasn't the only one. I thank my lucky stars I only had daughters. The Sprays at Jacob's Farm lost their four lads, all within a month, and Mrs Duffin at the Mill House lost three. She's only got the cripple left. Oh, well, you've a fine day for your visit, madam. You'll find Mrs Hardwick at home, I'm sure.'

I thanked her, and set off with my bag of buns and a thumping heart. The road past the church was little more than a track. A crest of grass sprouted down the middle; sprays of butterflies rose as I brushed against the flowery grasses of the verge. Jack's absence was oppressive in this place where he must have walked so many times, but never with me, never with me. By the lychgate the horse chestnuts spread their flat green hands above my head as if to ease my burden. I turned and entered the church. The heavy door fell shut behind me, its own momentum overruling my guiding hand. The wooden latch clunked in that solemn way that tells you how much you are alone.

It didn't take me long to find the brass plaque. 'Sacred to the Memory of Second Lieutenant John Addington, Killed in Action June 1918. He Who Would Valour See/Let Him Come Hither.' I had come hither, but was it fair or right that I should add other, more complicated, emotions to poor Dora's estimation of Jack's valour?

I left the church. I retain no memory of its interior, except for that plaque, but I have the clearest possible picture of the flagstones of the path, the splats of lichen like tiny broken eggs, a red soldier beetle braving the open space between the shelter of one hillock of moss and the next. That moment has become for me the epitome of all summer stillness, all time gone. I continued up the lane to Keeper's Cottage. There was the green gate, quite freshly painted. There was a wrought-iron sign with the black letters curling round the silhouette of a man with a dog and a gun. The front garden was long and narrow. The path to the cottage door was a series of shallow stone steps set into the grass. Above my head, above the gate, was an arch of honeysuckle, booming with bees. There was nobody in the garden, but two striped deckchairs were waiting, with a plaid rug on the grass between. On the rug was a coloured rubber ball, and a stuffed toy dog, an Airedale, mounted on wheels, with a handle. The dog lay on its side. The door of the cottage opened. I stepped back into the shadows. A family of three came out. Dora, soft and bosomy, her white frock sprigged with pink flowers; Mr Hardwick (I presumed), a stocky, broad-faced young man with high colour and sandy hair and – yes – one empty sleeve tucked into his shirt front. And the third, the plump owner of the ball and the dog, a curly-headed cherub of indeterminate gender with a clean smock and its mother's round face, waddled its way to the rug, lurching like a sailor, its mother's forefinger sucked into one small doughy fist. Its father righted the dog with his good arm, and before he lowered himself into his deckchair he kissed the top of his wife's head, and she smiled up at him – she was very short. Her light brown hair was still coiled in the same loose bun I remembered from the photographs, and her cotton frock reached nearly to her ankles. My hand strayed to my own shingled bob. The first time – which turned out to be the only time – Jack saw my new hair, he had been dismayed. I pushed that memory away. I felt empty of every feeling save gladness that, for Dora, all was well. I made to move away, but something rustled, and her husband saw me. He rose. 'Can I help?' he called, and his voice was agreeable.

'Could you tell me the way to the station?' It was the only thing I could think of.

He looked a little surprised, but he told me, with laborious repetitions and many gestures of his one hand. I thanked him and moved off, slowly, realizing that my only regret was that I had not heard Dora's voice. But then she called, 'It's quite a walk. Can I fetch you a glass of water? It's such a hot day.' Her voice was gentle, rather girlish, with the hint of a lisp. She bent over the child, saying, 'Johnnie, stay here with Dada, while I fetch the lady a drink,' and I was moved because she had passed Jack's name on to her first-born; I was moved almost to tears. I took the water and my throat received it gratefully, but I declined her offer to come inside. I now knew that she was kind, and loving, and that she had been very sad when Jack died, but that she was happy now, and there was nothing complicated in her life at all. And I knew that to intrude on that contentment for the sake of some emotional assuagement of my own would be a dreadful thing to do. So I went on my way. I regretted my conversation in the baker's shop, because next time Dora went in to buy her bread, or a gingerbread man for Johnnie, the mysterious visitor would be mentioned, and the wondering would wriggle in her mind and cause her some unease. But I could think of no way to undo that small harm.

I made my way back to London in a trance. When I reached my flat in Golden Square I found it airless and full of grit. I was still clutching the bag of buns and the top of the bag was damp and softened from my hot hand. I put it down on the kitchen table and Peggy, puzzled, said, 'Are we expecting anybody?' and I said, 'No. Nobody. We're not expecting anybody at all.'

I set out to write about Jack, and I haven't. I've written about Dora instead. But that's as it should be, because the subject of Dora can be dealt with in one sitting, and I'm not so sure that Jack can ever be dealt with. And it seems I may not be ready to try.

I never saw Dora again. When I moved to Knighton, seven years later, I realized that our two villages were separated by a distance of no more than twenty-five miles. But I never sought her out, and the glimpse I'd had of her left me with the impression that she would not wander very far from home. On the rare occasions I attended farmers' markets or Christmas bazaars in the small towns that lay between us, I would find myself looking hard at any small, round-cheeked woman with fair-headed children, but none of them was ever Dora.

Before I embarked on Jack, from which embarkation I am now temporarily in retreat, I was describing my little winter escapes from Lionel and from Knighton. The sad truth is that though Lionel was a good man, even a man with a touch of greatness about him, I never chose to spend time with him, and rarely sought his company for comfort or for pleasure. Over this I feel guilt; it was a cheerless life for him, despite my acting. Even at the time, I felt ashamed that I needed to escape, since he put so little pressure on me. I always had my separate bedroom, right from the start, though I was expected to accept his nocturnal visits. These were not frequent, but neither were they regular, and when I heard his footfall in the corridor it was like an ambush. So in time I rearranged things, I can't remember on what pretext, and I would go to him in his cold hard bed.

Other pressures were no greater than those which came of sharing a life with any other human being. Companionship was part of our deal, and I gave Lionel an approximation of that, and he gave some back to me, to the best of his ability, though companionship is not something I've ever needed much of. And then there was the housekeeping, which was more than adequately managed by Mrs Apps. The pressure there came from my sense that Mrs Apps only consulted me at all because her sense of hierarchy obliged her to do so. But perhaps the strongest pressure came from the feeling that, though I came to love Knighton, I didn't truly *live* there. It wasn't until Lionel's death that I managed to rid myself of this feeling. After that, the place became my own.

I didn't have an especially strong sense that I belonged anywhere else. London was my playground, London filled me with energy and made me laugh. But once I'd left it I never yearned to live there again, despite my need to get on that train and put Knighton behind me and guzzle down great gulps of sooty London air. No, it wasn't that there was any other place where I felt I was truly living, unless it was in my head, in my other life, on the train.

When I reached London, what then? Well, that varied. Sometimes I did respectable lady-up-from-the-country things, like visiting exhibitions at the Royal Academy and lightly lunching with a female friend. Sometimes I had a professional pretext for the journey, such as a meeting with an editor. I gave up journalism when I married Lionel, but in the course of the 1930s I published three novels, two volumes of short stories, and a slender collection of poems entitled *The Shadow on the Lawn*; the poems I think are best forgotten. From time to time there'd be a literary party, to which Lionel would also be invited, but he abhorred that kind of thing so I had no qualms about leaving him behind. These parties took place in the early evening, and afterwards I would go on with friends to the cinema, or out to dine, or even to a jazz club. I was no longer very young but I still liked late nights and going back in a group to somebody's flat and drinking black coffee and whisky into the early hours.

It was on one of these evenings that I met Giles Delaney. The day had been a particularly chaotic one, but pleasantly so. I'd arranged to meet my old friend and fellow author Leonie Vickers for lunch at her club, and I'd waited there for a while, wondering whether I'd got the day wrong, when the waitress approached with a message. Leonie had twisted her ankle and couldn't move, but she hated the thought of my wasted lunch so she was sending her friend Nora Hazell instead. She was sure we'd get on. And just as I finished reading the message, Nora Hazell turned up, and I was rather intrigued because she was the faintly notorious owner of a left-wing bookshop; she had, it was rumoured, Sapphic leanings. I had somehow never managed to meet her and was pleased to be given the chance to do so. Nora was tall and angular, with grey flannel trousers, a cigarette holder and an Eton crop. We got on rather well, though there was no hint of Sapphism in her dealings with me. She delivered fierce wisecracks through drifts of cigarette smoke, ate almost nothing, and ordered a Brandy Alexander, which Leonie's muted gentlewoman's club was unable to provide. She'd read everything I'd written, which cannot fail to gratify. At last she looked down her long, almost translucent nose at the sad remains of my rissoles and said, 'Have you finished with that? Because if you have, come back to the shop with me. There are a couple of people I'd like you to meet.'

We walked to her shop, Nora Hazell Books, which was in Soho. It was hard to imagine that it made anything other than a considerable loss. The small windows were almost wholly obscured by posters advertising meetings of various socialist leagues; most were out of date. There were portraits of Lenin and Trotsky, beetlebrowed against blood-red backgrounds. More books were displayed – if 'displayed' is the word – in piles than on shelves, and several of the piles were crowned with ashtrays or coffee cups. Nora Hazell led me to the back room where through the smoke and dust I made out three young men with knitted ties and floppy fringes, and a couple of women who were slightly less eye-catching versions of Nora. I was introduced. Only one of the young men rose to greet me. 'This is Giles Delaney,' said Nora, 'who is going to run for parliament next time round. He'll probably stand for Bermondsey, if we can get him selected.'

'How do you do?' I said, and I held out my hand. For the first time, I understood what people meant when they said 'My heart missed a beat.' Giles Delaney looked startlingly similar to Jack.

I'd come in upon a meeting; they were putting together some pamphlet or other. I suppose Nora hoped I'd join in the discussion, but it didn't work that way. We were soon drinking tea and planning how we would spend the evening. We started in a bar in Greek Street, where we were joined by some acquaintances. Somebody said they were hungry, so we all went to Bertorelli's and ate veal escalopes. Some-body else said they knew of a party, so off we went, and as we left the restaurant I slipped my hand under Giles's elbow. He looked startled – I was a married woman, fifteen years his senior – but he quickly changed his expression of surprise into a welcoming smile. He was a very polite young man.

The party was lots of smoke and noise and people shout-ing at each other in corridors. I hollered into Giles's ear, 'I'm too old for this' – I thought I might as well touch on the subject of the age gap – and he nodded and smiled, and steered me out into the foggy street. 'I know a club –' he said, and I said, 'Do you want to bother with a club?' and he chuckled in a way I particularly liked and said, 'Whatever you say, Lady Conway.' So I hailed a taxi and took him back to the pied-à-terre in Kensington that Lionel had kept on largely to spare me the indignities of the last train home.

It took me by surprise that I became pregnant straight away. There, I've said it now. Verity, you'll read this one day. Lionel Conway is not your father. Ought I to apologize?

11

The Wilkinsons had colonized Knighton less than two months after Hester's Sunday-lunch discussion with Rosie and Robin. They sorted everything out with amazing speed, or with speed which would amaze somebody who didn't know them well. But, as Hester knew, they were really very focused. The clutter with which they surrounded themselves was misleading. The secret was that they did everything together. No time was wasted on disagreements, or squabbles over territory. Rosie would say, 'Robs, we're going to have to put in a shower. I just can't bear not having one,' and Robin would say, 'Great, we'll do that on Saturday.' Then off they would go together to decide where they should put it. Rosie would make the telephone calls, Robin would set aside time for the DIY, and by Saturday evening they'd be showering in it together, giggling, with an open bottle of wine and a couple of glasses balanced on the edge of the bath. So it wasn't surprising to Hester that by the end of the summer they'd packed all their things, their pine chests of drawers, their kelims, their skateboards and tents and well-used Le Creusets, into a couple of removal vans, or that Rosie was busy sewing name tapes on to a whole set of new school uniforms: Ewes Green Primary for the boys, The Turrets – Hester's alma mater – for Becky.

They'd all wept as they drove out of Wandsworth, as Rosie later described to Hester, but by the time they'd lost – and recaptured – one of the hamsters in a Little Chef where they'd stopped en route, spirits were restored, and by the time they reached Knighton they were all raring to embark on the next step of the Famous Five adventure that was Wilkinson family life. The children raced round the garden like greyhounds before setting up stepladders in the orchard and picking pounds and pounds of the most delicious wasp-cracked greengages. Listening to Rosie's account, Hester almost wished she had been there.

There was lots of furniture left over after Verity had taken everything she needed. Her new cottage had narrow doorways and low ceilings, so she didn't even consider the big glass-fronted bookcases, the oak refectory table in the dining room, the grandfather clock, or Lionel Conway's display cases filled with fossils and blown birds' eggs, all labelled in his cramped and fine-nibbed hand. The Wilkinsons liked all of it, with an enthusiastic absence of discrimination, and offered to buy everything in a single swoop, which Hester didn't really think they could afford. But her mother refused any money. 'Keep it,' she said. 'Look after everything, in case Hester ever wants it, though I don't suppose she will. You'll be doing me a favour. Truly.' So the furniture remained, even some of the pictures and curtains. And Paddy and Angus pored over the fossils, and Bud rammed his tricycle into the grandfather clock, and the kitchen dresser was refurbished with the bright chunky crockery that had been so familiar to Hester at Anderson Road, and it seemed to her that, after all, her past was still with her, and she wasn't sure whether she liked that or not.

She had been a little surprised that her mother had not chosen to move to the cottage in the village where Grandma Evelyn had lived for the last ten years of her life. It had never been sold, only let. Simeon had explained the tenancy agreement to Hester at one time and, being a lawyer, he had been careful to ensure that no one tenant could stay there for too long. It was currently let to a childless couple who worked in London all week and used it as a weekend bolt-hole. Verity would not have felt unduly conscience-stricken about giving them notice to quit. When Verity first mentioned selling Knighton, Hester had made the assumption that this was what she had in mind, but she'd said something like, 'Oh, I don't think so, dear. I always found it a little poky.' A lot of people would not want to move into a house strongly associated with their own mother's old age and death, but Hester had never had Verity down as the fresh-start type. Hester minded, just a bit, though of course she didn't say so. Visiting Grandma Evelyn there had been an important part of one stage of her life. She'd have liked the chance to be inside that cottage again.

The night before they left Anderson Road, Robin and Rosie managed to fit in a house-cooling party as a farewell to their London friends. Hester arrived early, to help them set it up, but there wasn't a lot to do. All the furniture had gone. There was nothing left in the house except the mattresses they were going to sleep on that night, which were to be dumped in the skip the following morning, and a kind of shanty-town of hamster and guinea-pig cages huddled in the front hall ready for exit. Emptied of its furnishing, the house felt vast, like an empty barn. The living-room walls, terracotta-coloured, looked like Rothkos, patched as they were with fuzzy faded places where book-shelves had stood and pictures had hung. Hester and Rosie stuck candles into bottles, spiked the garden with barbecue flares, laid out cheese and bread and paper plates on the kitchen work surfaces. 'It's like that ghost house,' said Rosie, running a loving finger over the speckled pocks in the door of the airing cupboard, where she'd allowed the boys to hang their dartboard. 'You know, Hester, that house in Bow or somewhere that got filled up with concrete by that artist woman with frizzy hair. And you could see where the wall sockets had been, and everything. I took Becky to see it, she loved it. She scrambled all over it.'

The evening was warm. People brought bottles to the party, and children and dogs, and quiches and pavlovas that they'd made themselves. They drank out of plastic cups and broke off chunks of cheese with their fingers. Their cigarettes hissed out their last gasps in empty beer cans. It was quite unlike the twelve-different-canapés-and-champagne parties to which Hester had allowed herself to become accustomed. It could have been an undergraduate party, except for the tide of children that surged in from the garden and out again. In the middle of the floor in what had been the playroom, a couple of forty-somethings, investment bankers by day, sat cross-legged on the floor, rolling joints. Hester wasn't sure whether the sight inspired her with scorn or affectionate nostalgia. I'll see who's in the garden, she thought, and turned to go, and there was Guy.

'Jesus!' she said, wrong-footed. 'You made me jump.'

'Didn't Rosie tell you she'd asked me?'

It was obvious that she hadn't, so Hester didn't pretend. Her disadvantage angered her. She said nothing. Guy touched her elbow, and then withdrew his hand. 'You were making for the garden,' he said. 'You always run away at the first whiff of dope.' His smile was fond.

Hester gestured at the cross-legged bankers. One was running his tongue along the side of the trembling, bulbous, inexpert joint. She thought about that City tongue, furred with years of claret and stilton and cigars. 'It's a little grotesque,' she said, 'but if you want to join them, don't let me get in the way.'

Guy's blue linen shirt intensified the colour of his eyes.

Hester noted the fact with annoyance. Despite everything, Guy somehow managed to pull it off. 'I'd much rather come with you,' he said.

She shrugged, and edged her way out into the garden. Guy followed. She felt the palm of his hand on the small of her back. They stood on the terrace, under the canopy of jasmine and plumbago. The scent of the jasmine was an intrusive cliché. From the bottom of the garden, where the laurels were thick, children's voices rose and fell. The borders attracted her, with their sombre late-summer tangles of asters and rudbeckias and montbretia, but she stayed put. To wander further from the house would imply a romantic intention. Here on the terrace there were plenty of other adults, braying and squealing. Some of them knew her and Guy. She could feel their wondering glances between her shoulder blades, like pressure points. She sipped her wine, and said, 'How did Rosie get hold of you?'

'Oh, easily. Through Steve and Rach. I still see a fair amount of them, you know.' He stood closer, so that his upper arm pressed against hers, just as close as if they were swaying together on a crowded tube. He said, 'Hester, I had to see you. I can't get you out of my mind.'

She could have moved away, but she didn't. She looked at the August moon, swelling over the rooftops, the colour of apricots, its soft rim frayed like felt. She could feel the tension flicking in the body of this tall man next to her. She could feel his physical strength. For years now she'd stood at parties without anyone by her side.

Inside the house, people were dancing. Hester found that dancing at parties felt awkward these days, a forced good humour like competing in a charity game where you might have to get covered in shaving foam or fall into a tub of water. She usually avoided it. The music was some kind of

171

Greatest Hits compilation. She could feel a twitch in Guy in response to the same insistent two-tone beat that had animated their Cambridge days. 'Mirror in the Bathroom'. She'd always associated that song with him. 'Guy,' she said, 'I'm not going to dance with you.'

He kissed her on the mouth.

The kiss was extraordinary. He hadn't kissed her like that for more than five years. It was like the first time and all the other times – at once wholly familiar and utterly unknown, like the kind of dream where you open a door in your own house and find yourself nowhere that you recognize. The flick of his tongue was like the picking of a lock. She pulled away. 'Upstairs,' she said. 'You first. The au pair's room. At the top.'

Guy went. Hester moved through the dark garden, crumbled a head of lavender and sniffed her fingers, paused to chat to a gaggle of acquaintances who she would be unlikely to see again now the Wilkinsons were leaving London. She made her way to the kitchen, bestowed pecks on the cheeks of two departing couples, took a plastic cup, half filled it with vodka, swallowed it neat. Then she went to the foot of the stairs. Guy would be up there, in that converted loft designed as a private space for the au pair who never quite materialized. The room would be empty, just the bare floorboards and the uncurtained skylight framing the night. And Guy, waiting. He was three flights up, but she could almost hear the tick of his heart. Desire surged through her in a blood-thickening rush. She laid her hand on the banisters, then turned and left the house. She left him there. Let him wait. She walked home, all the way.

*

It all happened so quickly, thought Verity. Rosie Wilkinson rang her in late June, bubbling with plans for taking over at Knighton, the meniscus of her eagerness only just held in check by her wholly genuine desire to take Verity's feelings into account. And Verity, not famed for decisiveness, had agreed with what must have seemed like surprising speed. Indeed, she reflected, I'm not famed for anything. I'm rather unfamed for things. But, yes, she said, yes, and the lawyers whirred into action, and by mid August it was all sorted out, and the great cheerful Wilkinson caravan had rolled up.

The Wilkinsons reminded Verity of those big Victorian families who every so often would pack themselves up into a large coach and trundle off round the Continent. Wandsworth to Ewes Green was hardly a continent, but there was something splendid about the way they travelled, with animals in boxes and children hanging out of the window and lots of stuff strapped to the roof. They arrived at teatime, and Verity made a big tea, because children like that were always hungry. She didn't know what modern children ate, so it was rather a village-hall sort of tea – bridge rolls and wafer biscuits and things – but they gobbled it up. Paddy said, 'I felt sick in the car and then I was starving and now I feel brilliant,' so that was nice. The very first thing they did when they arrived was make sure their animals were looked after – several hamsters and guinea pigs, and two cats who they barricaded into one of the bedrooms so they wouldn't streak out into the garden and vanish. The children had been promised a dog, too, once the move was completed – a dog from a rescue home. Verity did wonder if it would be a case of out of the frying pan into the fire for that dog, going to live with all those bouncy children, but she liked the idea of a dog at Knighton. She still resented Simeon for not letting Hester have more pets when she was a child.

After tea they all ran about the garden. The weather was glorious. There was something static about August, in Verity's opinion – she preferred months with more movement to them – but this was the right kind of immobility, that syrup-coloured light that turns the afternoon into the best kind of childhood experience, like a Polaroid of memory. In the orchard, the greengages were dropping off the trees like blobs of jam. The children filled box after box, and Verity said, 'They won't keep,' so little Bud said, with five-year-old solemnity, 'That means we'll have to eat them all tonight! There's at least a thousand each.' 'Will they freeze?' asked practical Rosie, and Verity said she thought they would if they were stewed first, but privately she thought that she wouldn't want to do that. Part of the glory of greengages was that they only belonged to late summer. Some years they didn't come at all. It depended on the weather at blossom time. They needed to grow near some other fruit tree, a plum or a damson, to make them bear. They didn't do well on their own. When Verity bit into the flesh, like soft sweet bronze, she thought of her mother, because they had been her favourite fruit.

Verity's cottage wasn't quite ready. It was called Wisteria Cottage, which was an irritating whimsy as there was no wisteria in sight, but it would have to stay. She didn't feel up to changing the name of a house. She'd been emphatic enough over the last few months; now she felt the need to retreat to her shadowy self. The cottage was an unassuming, two-bedroomed, early Victorian brick-and-tile affair, with enough garden but not too much. There was a little greenhouse, which she was pleased about, and she was considering putting in a pond. The best tree in the garden was a fine old walnut. In high summer the almost bluish sheen of walnut leaves was the kind of colour you could get lost in. What was that lovely poem? 'Annihilating all that's made/To a green thought in a green shade.' That made perfect sense to Verity.

Yes, she was looking forward to the cottage. She would enjoy setting out her bits and pieces. She had left an awful lot behind, just as her mother had left it behind for her. Only Rosie, of course, was not her daughter. Sometimes she was almost on the point of forgetting that. Rosie and Robin seemed genuinely happy to take it on – great big bookcases and chests of drawers, and that refectory table she never really liked because they never seemed to have enough people for it. It was probably all quite valuable. The Wilkinsons had offered to buy everything, but there was no need. Verity had all the money she could ever want; she was quite happy for Rosie and Robin to act as guardians. It was Conway stuff, most of it. Verity found she didn't feel much connection with it. The things she'd take to Wisteria Cottage were mostly the furnishings of the mews house she and Simeon had had in Chelsea. The scale was about right, and on the whole the associations were pleasant. Then there were a few of her mother's 1930s pieces – classic Heal's. Not very cottagey, but elegant and well made.

It was all sitting there in the cottage, waiting for her, but it would have to wait for a couple of weeks longer because the drains needed renovation and she didn't fancy subsisting on a single cold tap. So she'd taken herself off. Dear Rosie had urged her to stay on at Knighton for as long as she needed to, but she'd declined. She knew they wouldn't really want her there. The children wouldn't mind. They seemed to regard her as benevolent, certainly unthreatening. But Robin and Rosie needed to be left alone to line their new nest in the way that most suited them. It felt good to Verity to have a child population in the house. The echo in the walled garden had been silent for too long. Now the children's voices were filling the air like dust motes dancing in sunlight. And before too long there would be another little voice to join them. Rosie had that dreamy look; she was sure to want another baby. If so, it would be the first baby at Knighton since Verity's own arrival, nearly sixty-four years ago. Verity would be glad. A house needs a baby, every now and then.

So, no, she didn't want to hover around while all that colonizing was going on. Any one of her old friends would have taken her in, she had only to ask, not to mention Beryl Barber or at least a dozen like-minded neighbours. But none of them appealed. She was a woman of means. She had been for years, though she'd never behaved like one. And since Simeon's death she was accountable to no one for the money she spent. So she had booked into a London hotel. Very central, in Pimlico. Comfortable, but not flashy. Used mainly, she would imagine, by adulterous MPs. Here she would stay until Wisteria Cottage was ready, and here she would watch.

She had no inkling as to what Hester had done with the information she had put into her hands. She had thought she would not care. She had thought that telling Hester would ease her own burden, that thoughts of Paulina and Sebastian and all that consciousness of Simeon's double life – which, she now recognized, had had the effect of halving her own life, of halving *her* – would curl themselves up tidily and roll away, and that she would be allowed to retire from having feelings at all. But she found this was not the case. She was restless. She wanted to know what Hester would do. It seemed that she had something invested in Hester, and she needed to follow it through. Of course it was possible that Hester would do nothing, but Verity didn't think so. And so Verity had taken herself to London, where she was very near Hester, and here she would wait, and watch. Would one call it spying, or merely finding out?

I 2

27th May 1980

Since I finished the last entry in this book I've been pondering on the implications of letting Verity know that the man she called Father was no relation of hers. Of course I haven't told her, and I won't. I've taken the coward's way. I've written it down, and that means that chance still plays a part. This house might burn down, with me and the diary in it. It could be destroyed in a flood – not likely, I grant you, since nothing approaching a flood has afflicted Ewes Green within my memory, but anything's possible. I could leave the bath running all night – as I become deafer and more forgetful that becomes increasingly likely – and the water could pour through the ceiling and obliterate every word I've written. If that were the case I certainly shouldn't write it all again. I could lose my wits – no sign of that so far, but perhaps I would be the last to notice – and shove the diary into the Rayburn, or tear it up and use it as lavatory paper, or thrust it into the hands of the next Jehovah's Witness who rings the doorbell. What I intend to do is to leave it in an obvious place, with a note addressed to Verity and Hester, calling their attention to it. That way, whichever of them finds it will not be able to make the decision of whether to burn it or throw it away, because it will not be their exclusive property. They could. Either of them could just dispose of it and say not a word to the other, but I don't think that will happen. Both of them have too much probity for that.

I don't have to leave it to chance, either. The information is still within my power, though only just. At my age, one's grip is weak. If I have regrets about this revelation, if the disclosure of it was really more for my immediate benefit than for any sense of obligation to tell the truth, then my only safety is to destroy the diary at once, while my hands still have the strength to rip or tear or strike a match, and my mind still has the power to tell my hands what they should be doing. But it seems that this is not what I want to do.

And so it must follow that I want to pass the truth on to my daughter. In which case I owe it to her to give as full a picture as I can of the man whose blood flows in her veins. Lionel may not have been demonstrative towards her, but he was solid, real; if I rob her of Lionel, and replace him with a couple of paragraphs about Giles Delaney from which the only information she can glean is that he was younger than me, that he was involved in radical politics, that he was socially adroit – though that is perhaps more a value judgement than a fact – and that any scruples he had about adultery were easily waived, this would be less than fair. Oh, and the other piece of information I've given her is that her father looked like someone called Jack Addington, of whom no photograph survives. Poor Verity. She needs more.

It feels like a chore, though, to set down much more about Giles Delaney. Giles didn't truly interest me very much. I took him because at that moment when he rose to his feet at the back of Nora Hazell's shop, I saw Jack again, rising to greet me through the fug of a little restaurant in the Strand where we used to meet when he'd come back from seeing Dora in Kent. Like all those coincidental physical resemblances, it melted away once the details were examined. Jack's nose had a bump in it, Giles's was straight. Jack's eyes were sometimes green, sometimes grey, and they moved a great deal, and when they moved they glittered, which gave the impression that emotion was never far beneath the surface. Giles's eyes were close to blue, and he had a level gaze. Verity, it may interest you to know that Hester has Giles's eyes, except that his conveyed primarily kindness and candour. He lacked his unknown grand-daughter's cool intelligence. But the colour and the shape are the same.

Giles was fairer than Jack. They both had fine, straight hair, of the kind that is plentiful in youth, but in either case I doubt it would have lasted long. Both already had little inlets at the temples, like bays, that I used to trace with my fingertips. Giles was the taller, Jack more thickset. So, no, they didn't look so very much alike. Why should they? They were nothing to do with each other. But there was just that moment when Giles stood up, and there was something about the line of the jaw and the set of the shoulders, and he held out his hand, and I thought Jack, Jack, you've come back to me. So that's how it happened. And Giles was nice; he was young and appreciative and there was no harm in him. He was interested in all the right things, and he tried to give me what I wanted, even though he wasn't quite sure what that was, and he didn't expect too much in return. But somehow he was less than the sum of his parts. I am sorry for this, Verity. I've taken away the father you thought you had, and I'm not managing to fill the gap with anything very satisfactory.

You'll need more than this. Material facts will be of more use to you than a limp account of my emotional responses to the man who was your father. I'll set down all I can remember. His name was Giles Erskine Delaney. I remember his middle name because it was rather unusual. I remember discussing the whole business of middle names with him, how parents slip in little horrors as booby traps for their children in later life. Not that 'Erskine' is so very dreadful. It was the name of one of his uncles, who was killed at Ypres. There you are, Verity, that's a nugget of information that could send you scurrying through the ant-hill of genealogy, if you felt so inclined. Though I'm afraid I don't know whether this uncle was on his father's or his mother's side. I never met any of Giles's family. Ours was not that kind of affair. The Delaneys were army people, from Somerset, I think. I know Giles had terrible arguments with his father. He was the only son. There were two sisters, both younger. He was fond of them. Yes, Verity, it's perfectly possible that you have two living aunts, not to mention cousins. I've cudgelled my brains to retrieve the names of the sisters, but they simply won't come.

Giles was a public-school boy – Sherborne, was it? I'm pretty sure it was Sherborne. He didn't go to university. His father wanted to put him through Sandhurst, but he rebelled and went off to New York and worked there for a year or two, which I must say was rather enterprising. He worked in bars and hotels. Giles was never afraid to get his hands dirty. It was in New York that he first became involved in radical politics. He had a natural sympathy for the common man, and a clear, almost naive, belief in the evils of capitalism. He was such a straightforward person. I'm afraid that's why I found him dull. Oh dear, Verity, it'll be of no help to you to learn that I found your father dull.

What else can I tell you about Giles? He was a popular young man; not a leader, but people always liked him. He came to Knighton several times, always in a group. During the spring and summer it was usual for me to entertain house parties at Knighton. Lionel took little part, but he looked on indulgently. He saw no difference in my treatment of Giles to that of any of the other guests – or if he did detect a difference he gave me no sign. I put Giles in the attic bedroom, so that I could slip in to join him in the middle of the night with little chance of being overheard by Lionel. Verity, I'm not proud of this.

The only reason I have for doubting the completeness of my pretence is that Lionel was a little distant with you. I don't know whether you felt this, or minded if you did. Perhaps not; children have no means of comparison. But one might have expected a man who had lived through a long, unhappy, childless first marriage, and who in old age was presented with a baby daughter – one might have expected such a man to . . . well, to dote. And Lionel didn't dote on you, poor Verity. He was fond of you, and concerned for your welfare; do you remember how anxious he was, that time you had scarlet fever? He made you that little story book about his Polar voyages, with those rather good drawings of icebergs and walruses, a different episode for each day of your convalescence. He did treat you like a daughter, in a detached sort of way. But he didn't live and breathe you, the way some fathers do. It could be that he was simply too old, too tired. Whatever the reason, I think you had a lucky escape. Lionel's passions could be burdensome.

To the world at large, you were Lionel's child. Indeed, I did my best to ensure that you might really be his. After that first night with Giles I went straight home, and for the next few weeks I surprised Lionel with my unprecedented ardour. This was in January; it was hard work, I can tell you.

There was no central heating at Knighton in those days. I didn't really believe in the efficacy or even in the existence of Lionel's sperm, but I had to give them every chance.

I had an easy pregnancy. I knew I was pregnant very early on, because everything tasted different and I felt – not ill, but just changed all over. No one would ever have put me in what people would now call the earth-mother category, but I enjoyed my pregnant body. I drifted about the garden all through that summer in a sort of sailor top and a vast blue skirt, cutting flowers and helping Mrs Apps pick fruit. Mrs Apps found my condition embarrassing. She had got all that sort of thing over with in her early twenties. Mrs Apps was not much older than me, but she had reached a sort of timelessness that had nothing to do with youth, but could not fairly be described as middle age. She could hardly bring herself to mention the subject of you before your birth, though she was devoted to you from the minute you arrived. And she knitted for you, great lumpy matinée jackets; your tiny fingers caught in the stitches. Poor Mrs Apps, she must have been horrified when she found she had to deliver you. But she rose to the occasion with great dignity.

Giles knew about the pregnancy from early on. I told him that it could have been Lionel's, but I don't think he believed that for one minute. How could a handsome man of twenty-five look at a rival like Lionel and seriously consider that he'd been pipped in the potency stakes? Giles was enthusiastic about the idea of fatherhood. I told him that I took full responsibility, that I expected nothing from him, that I had no intention of leaving my marriage, and he accepted all of this, but he had the idealism of youth, and he imagined that somehow he could be a loving father to you without anybody else knowing anything about it. He was such an affectionate boy. He adored me when I was pregnant. I remember how his tongue would follow the veins on my breasts, like blue rivers. Oh, you don't want to hear about that.

What on earth did I imagine was going to happen? Was I so arrogant, or so deluded, that I thought I could manage all this, the deceived husband, the eager young lover who was not going to write himself out of the script? Did it not occur to me that a triangular parenting structure is not one that any species, including the human, has ever favoured? I can't answer, because I can't remember. I think I drifted along with a sense that everything would work itself out. I didn't panic. It's difficult to panic when you're pregnant. I have only a limited experience of the condition, but it does lull you, doesn't it? It's as if the mother is held in a sac of fluid, just like the baby. One attaches importance to nothing, and to everything. I thought it was a lovely time.

Your birth was a lovely time, too. You came early, on the most perfect September morning. I was in the orchard . . . but you've heard all about that. You were small, because you were early, but you were neat and perfect. Five pounds. A good round sum. You had no problems with sucking or breathing, you were quiet and sleepy, and I often had to wake you up to feed you. You hardly ever cried, just gave a little mew. I didn't pick you up in between times. You slept in your white wicker cradle for hours and hours, barely visible under the muslin drapes. There seemed to be no need to take you out of it, except to feed and change you. Perhaps I was wrong about that.

I knew straight away that you were Giles's baby. In novels it's usually the eyes that betray the paternity, or sometimes a convenient 'shock of red hair', but with you it was your toes, or more specifically your little toes. You know how your little toes are doubled over, curled into balls so you can hardly see the nail? Well, Giles's were like that. His little toes were as round as marbles. Lionel never remarked on your toes. He was rather in awe of your physical details. I put you into his arms, as one is meant to, but he always looked as nervous as if he'd been handed an osprey's egg, though he did like to feel your little digits hooking round his thick forefinger. I tried to keep your feet hidden in knitted bootees, but there was no need. After all, how could Lionel know what Giles's toes looked like?

Giles never saw you. He went off to Spain at the end of the summer to fight in the Civil War. He was killed almost straight away, about a month after your birth. I don't even know whether the news of your arrival reached him. I wrote to him, but I had no way of finding out whether he received the letter. He was killed when the building in which he was taking shelter was bombed. It was somewhere south of Madrid, somewhere beginning with M. I could find it on a map. I will – I'll find it, and write it down. People like to know where and when things happen. The date was 4th October 1936. I hope this is of some help to you.

He did leave you one thing, Verity, apart from his little toes. He left you your name. The last time I saw him, which was in late July, we talked about names. We met in London; we walked in St James's Park and sat down by the water. We ate sandwiches and threw our crusts to the pelicans. We drank beer out of brown bottles. We both liked doing things like that. Giles said, 'If it's a girl, I want to call her Verity. Because truth is important, even though we're not behaving as if it is.' So you have the name he chose, Verity, and Amelia, your middle name, belonged to Lionel's mother. Which is irrelevant to you, and therefore, not truthful. And I think it's interesting that your married surname, Oakes, was changed from the German. It was Eichenbaum, wasn't it? And Oakes sounds so stable, so English, so enduring. Your names – all of them – express considerable ambivalence. I'm sorry about that, my dear.

What does come through, though, is that your father was a good man. Good, and brave. I didn't love him so very much, and though I wept when I heard of his death my sorrow didn't stop me from thinking, well, that simplifies things. But he was sincere when he chose your name, and, had he lived, he would have had no difficulty in loving you. I hope this gives you comfort.

13

The affair across the road looked as though it was coming to an end. He'd decided to go back to his wife, or else the girl had delivered an ultimatum about having a baby. She was about twenty-nine, he was in his fifties. She was pretty; when she walked, her yellow hair swung about her shoulders and her haunches shifted in rhythm beneath her short leather skirt. Physically, he hadn't much to offer. An inch or two shorter than her, paunchy, balding. The usual story. His face looked familiar; he might be a TV anchorman (wasn't that what they called them?) or an MP. Or perhaps it was just the generic face of the middle-aged man surprised at his own success; defensive, as if he didn't quite believe in it; greedy, which is why he wanted the girl. When he was a schoolboy, he wanted his neighbour's portion of treacle pudding; his own was never enough. Unpopular at school, a slow starter in the race for girlfriends, but with some sort of doggedness that had taken him nearly to the top of his profession, from which lofty eminence he had looked down on his own history and rearranged it.

Oh, I'm rabbiting, thought Verity. That was an odd word for chat; rabbits are the most silent of creatures, but she supposed it referred to running pointlessly in all directions. And the silence of rabbits was appropriate to her, because here she was chatting in silence – she had no companions here at this small hotel in Pimlico. She'd been in London nearly a fortnight, and she'd not spoken to a soul except for pleases and thank yous and excuse mes. To a 'soul' – why did she use that word? People used it in that context, didn't they, when they were alone. 'I haven't seen a soul all day', 'There wasn't a soul in sight.' One never said, 'I invited four souls to dinner last weekend,' or 'The bus was packed with souls.' Did being alone make one consider the essential in people, did it strip away the peripheral, the mundane, leaving only the eternal part? Or did solitude force one into habits of self-contemplation, so that, with only one's own soul for company, one came to regard others, too, as wraith-like beings, wandering over the world? Here, in this quiet hotel, she'd had plenty of opportunity to inspect her own soul, and what she had seen was not edifying – a withered, twisted little thing, a frayed and dusty shadow. Goodness, Verity admonished herself, how I do go on! If I were to write a diary, what tiresome reading it would make!

Beauty and the Beast – who'd been given ample chance to turn into a prince, but who had failed to do so – lived opposite the hotel, in the top half of a white-stucco-fronted house. When Verity sat at her window, which she often did, she could see straight into their living room. They had a balcony, and she didn't; she had watched them leaning on the iron balustrade, looking out, holding drinks. She had seen him slip a hand under Beauty's skirt; she had seen Beauty remove that hand, politely but firmly. She imagined it was his flat, for weekday use. His wife, she supposed, lived in the country and minded her own business; there would be oldish children at boarding school or beyond. But now, as Verity surmised from a tearful late-evening exit (Beauty's), it was over, and he would be obliged to make other arrangements. It wouldn't be long, if he was the creature of habit she took him for. Did Simeon replace Paulina? Yes, undoubtedly he followed her up, though Verity didn't think there was ever such a quasi-domestic set-up again. Simeon needed female admiration the way people need oxygen, and his marriage alone would have left him gasping for breath.

For the first few days of her London vigil Verity had had an uneventful time of it, regarding Hester. She had developed a routine. She had always been a great one for routine, which had infuriated Simeon. She rose early, used the dismal little tray of hotel equipment to make herself a cup of tea. Kettle, teabags, instant coffee, UHT milk, sugar or some sort of substitute in a pink sachet, all set out like medical paraphernalia, like the things nurses bring to one's bedside when they want to take blood or suchlike. She sipped her tea as she sat in the armchair by the window. She tucked up the net curtain to give herself a clear view of the street. Not much happened before eight in the morning. A few men in suits escorted their briefcases out of their flats, as if they were walking the dog. The Beast left early, once or twice, and Beauty would wave to him from the balcony, clutching her lilac silk robe across her chest. That was the nicest thing Verity saw them do. Next door to their flat there was a nurses' hostel; she watched the girls leave in pairs, giggling companionably in their capes despite the earliness of the hour. Twice a week the barrow boys set out their wares – fruit, fish, flowers, and a rail or two of bright synthetic clothing. She had heard other guests complain about the scraping, the bangs and the shouts, but that kind of noise suited Verity.

She sat and watched, and drank tea – no radio, no newspaper, nothing. Unbidden, a strange kind of drama unfolded, interposing itself between the scene in the street and her mind's eye. The drama was a procession of scenes of Simeon's life with Paulina, a series of tableaux, almost. A handful of photographs, letters, a few telephone conversations overheard, and of course that single occasion when she had made her way into their flat; that's all she had to go on, but it seemed her imagination was more fertile than she had supposed. She tried to manipulate the action to her own satisfaction, but scenes of passion, scenes of tenderness between her husband and his other wife – such scenes would spring up, however hard she tried to scorch them with rows, slash them with difficulties, poison them with humiliations. It was as if Simeon was director of operations, even now.

But Verity did have some control over him, too, because she could do what she had always done, which was to shut him out. She could sit in the armchair for as long as she chose to be possessed by the life they stole from her, and then when she'd had enough she could switch them off. She would stand up, wash, dress, fold her nightie and hang up her dressing gown. She wore the clothes she had bought in preparation for this vigil; anonymous clothes, not so radically different from what she would usually wear, but unfamiliar to Hester. The most extraordinary thing was the wig. She considered a hat, but hats are eye-catching, and as the weather was still warm a hat might seem particularly eccentric. Even a straw hat was not usual in London in late summer. So she bought herself a wig, by mail order – there were advertisements for the most peculiar things in the back pages of the Sunday papers. It was an expensive one, made of real hair. Dark brown, quite springy – for the first time, she saw a resemblance between herself and her mother. The elegant Evelyn Conway of her earliest memories, that is – the suffragette-turned-literary lady with her neat belted waist and her head cocked to one side, not the uncompromising, rheumy-eyed, grey-headed Grandma Evelyn of later years. Verity was rather pleased with her wig. It made her look ten years younger, she thought. She'd even attracted glances from a couple of the male guests at the hotel. She assumed they were glances of admiration, rather than alarm.

She breakfasted in her wig – indeed, nobody at the hotel had seen her without it. She took breakfast in the dining room – the butter, the marmalade, everything imprisoned in those awful fiddly capsules, so one could never have the amount one wanted, one was obliged to take too much or too little. She was usually the first to arrive in the dining room, and she ate quickly, because she needed to take up her position in time to watch Hester leave her flat. There was a Peabody Trust estate near Hester's flat – rather an interesting design, built between the wars, at a guess, or possibly even earlier – and this provided her with walls and corners where she could stand and watch. She didn't have long to wait. Hester's habits, like her own, were regular. She hardly knew why she bothered to watch in the morning. It was not spectacular. Hester left for work, looking well groomed and preoccupied, and that was it. Verity had not seen anyone leave with her. So far the only variation had been at the weekend. On Saturday she appeared an hour later than usual, in what Verity thought were called workout clothes. She bought a newspaper and some milk from the corner shop and then returned to her flat. On Sunday she didn't emerge at all. It was a fine morning and Verity didn't mind waiting. But she felt foolish when, after an hour and a half, she looked up and saw Hester reclining on her balcony, her long legs extended to the sun.

Hester took the bus to work. Verity took the next bus, and then followed. She didn't know why she did this, either, since on all but one occasion, when the buses were nose to tail, she arrived too late to see Hester enter the building. She pottered about in shops and public gardens, and there was a library near by, which was useful. At half past twelve she positioned herself so that she could watch the doorway of Broadcasting House. Three times she'd seen Hester leave in the company of a man, but from the way she conducted herself it seemed most likely that they were all people she would need to talk to over lunch, for her programme. None of them looked remotely like a lead to Sebastian.

The afternoons hung heavy. A morning of pottering was quite enough. Once Hester was back from lunch, she didn't re-emerge until early evening – at least, that was Verity's assumption. She'd only kept her vigil for one entire after-noon, on the first day. Then she decided that, of all times, a weekday afternoon was the least likely to provide any brother-tracking activity. So she would go to a gallery or a museum, though she found it hard to concentrate. She would sit on one of the big seats in the middle and watch the people, and if any dark-haired, actorish young man appeared she would think, could that be Sebastian? Which was rather nonsensical, because it was Hester who should be having such thoughts, not her. Since that long-ago May afternoon in Notting Hill she'd taken no steps in his direc-tion, and yet now, if Hester was to do nothing, the frustration would quite possibly be too much to bear. What would Verity do if she met him? Should she, as Hester suggested, hand over half of Simeon's estate? That would be a grand gesture, one that would be thrilling to make. Excitement was something that seemed to matter to Verity now. Strange, when she'd done without it for so many years.

She'd seen several likely young men in the galleries – she'd had to remind herself not to bother with the very young ones, since Sebastian would by now be thirty. But she still kept latching on to the studenty types, which suggested, perhaps, that she was more interested in fantasy than in reality. When she'd settled on one she would follow him round the gallery, at a discreet distance at first, then moving in swiftly to ask her question. She'd made it her rule to ask each man one question, but only one. Could you tell me the time? Do you know where they keep the Leonardo cartoon these days? I wonder whether you could possibly let me have two 5ops for a pound? They all looked surprised; one of them said, 'I don't work here, you know,' and another turned out to be deeply foreign, and spread his hands in a clownish gesture of incomprehension. And of course, none of them was Sebastian, and it would have been extremely surprising if they had been. They were just bit players in her funny little game. One thing Verity felt sure of; if she did meet Sebastian, she would know.

She didn't always go to a gallery. One afternoon she went to a cinema. She hadn't seen a film in years; she didn't even bother to watch them on television except, very occasionally, an Ealing comedy or something black and white from Hollywood. Something like *High Noon* – that was her idea of a good film. Whatever it was she sat through in Leicester Square did emphatically not come into that category. She selected it at random; she might as well have wandered into a cinema in Shanghai for all she understood of it. The action – there was a lot of action – moved between an American city, possibly Chicago, and somewhere in the East – Vietnam, perhaps? And lots of it happened on aeroplanes, whatever 'it' was. Of course she didn't understand a word they said – she never did understand the way Americans talked. But what surprised her, even alarmed her, was that she understood so little of the emotional drama, either. There was a man and a girl, as always, and they went to bed, though they took quite a long time to get round to it, and it seemed that one was hoodwinking the other, but which way round it was, or where the audience's sympathies were supposed to lie, was beyond Verity. She sat there in her wig all that sultry afternoon waiting for the moment when it would all fall into place, but it never did.

She was back outside Broadcasting House in time to see Hester leave. This was never before six, sometimes nearer seven. Twice, she had gone straight from work to meet friends, to a bar down the road, the sort of smart urban establishment where one can order cappuccino or vodka or a fancy sandwich with equal ease at any time of day or night. Such places hadn't existed in Verity's London days. She had glanced through the window to see who Hester was meeting. She hadn't dared go in. Wig or no wig, at close quarters a girl would recognize her mother. There's the way one holds oneself, the shape one makes in space. It takes a skilful actor to disguise that. Verity would recognize her own mother if she came back from the dead. So she just hovered out-side the bar and cast a few glances. She identified a Cambridge friend of Hester's, Katie Pickles. She particularly remembered her because of her pleasing surname. She became a solicitor, something like that. This was on the Friday night; there was quite a gang of them, but Katie was the only one she knew. There was much laughter, and several bottles of wine on the table. They weren't going anywhere in a hurry. Verity took herself off to a vegetarian café round the corner where she did battle with a wholemeal pizza with an impossibly high crust. When she'd finished she came back and they were all still there, talking loudly, the men blowing smoke in each other's faces, as if they were all still young.

On one occasion, Hester gave her the slip. She had a taxi waiting for her, and she was off. Verity looked for another taxi – she liked the idea of telling the driver to 'follow that cab' – but in vain. So she went back to the hotel and watched television, and tried not to torment herself with the thought of what she might be missing.

There were logistical problems in the life of a stalker, for a stalker, she had to admit, was what she had become. It was a natural career progression, really, for a person who gave up any semblance of useful employment more than forty years ago, and who had spent most of her time hovering on the margins of other people's lives. One difficulty stalkers had, Verity found, was how to move quickly enough to keep the quarry in sight. The stalker waited in a particular spot, and then the stalked was off, they didn't wait. When Hester went straight home from work, Verity was never in time to watch her arrive, the first few evenings, because she'd hop on the next bus, which was pointless. Then, after the evening Hester went off somewhere and Verity missed her altogether, she changed her strategy. She sat in a taxi, meter running, from six o'clock. Once she was sure Hester was on the bus, they'd be away, and Verity could be in position opposite the flats with ten minutes to spare. It cost a great deal, but that didn't matter. Verity enjoyed spending Simeon's money to obtain the rather dilute satisfaction of seeing their daughter enter the block of flats blameless and alone.

The first high point of Verity's stalking career had come two evenings ago; she was back ahead of Hester, standing in a shadowy doorway opposite, when she saw another taxi pull up in front of the flats. The door slammed, the taxi rumbled off, and there was Guy. Her former son-in-law, the man she had assumed would father those grandchildren of hers, who had never been born. At the sight of him a shiver of surprise ran through her, as it does when you see a dead animal lying in your path and for a moment it feels as if your eyes are turning round in your head. Guy; tall and rumpledly handsome, or handsomely rumpled, and not a bit changed. Except that, as often with men of boyish appearance, the onset of middle age made him look something of a sham. It was the merest touch of disappointment, like catching sight of an interesting painting that turns out to be a reproduction. He was still a handsome man, but the passage of time was giving him the air of a has-been. A has-been who never was.

Guy stood there whistling and looking about him, and several times he ran his fingers through his hair – still plenty of it, Verity noticed. Then he stepped to one side of the main entrance, so that when Hester approached she wouldn't see him at once. He didn't have long to wait. Unknowingly she strode towards him, her hair bright in the slanting sunshine, as neat and fresh in her pale grey suit as when she had left that morning. Guy stepped forward. Hester started visibly. Verity could hear their voices, but the murmur of traffic made it impossible to distinguish what they were saying. He laid a hand on her arm. She shook it off. His stance, his tone, which had seemed angry, changed, and became – as far as she could tell – pleading. Hester hesitated; she had her keys in her hand. She made for the door; he moved in front of her. Spread his hands. She shifted her body – it wasn't exactly a shrug, but it implied acceptance – and they entered the building together.

Verity was footsore and hungry, but it was impossible for her to desert her post. She had no idea that Hester was still in touch with Guy. Any tentative inquiries she'd made about him since their divorce had been brushed aside with 'I've no idea,' or some other adult equivalent of the pouting child's 'I don't care.' And now the sight of him made Verity feel almost panicky. Trust Guy to turn up and ruin things! For Verity was convinced that he would find out about

Sebastian, interfere with whatever plans Hester had made, make an issue of it for his own amusement – or benefit. If Guy scented money, he'd be on the trail. Of course he would get back in touch with Hester after her father's death. He'd be in a fever to know about the will.

He was there for an hour. Verity waited. She didn't know whether it was low blood sugar, or the cooling evening – the weather had stayed fine, but the merest touch of autumn had fingered its way in – but she felt a rage banking up inside her, a rage aimed as much at Hester as at Guy. What was she doing, allowing him to get in the way? The search for Sebastian was the path of the future; Guy was history. She thought of the wolf and the three little pigs. Hester had believed herself impregnable to his huffing and puffing, but now it seemed as if her brick house was after all no more than straw.

What could he be doing in there? Need one ask – how could it be anything else? They could hardly have much to talk about, those two. She remembered Simeon, and how, over and over again, in spite of everything, he broke her down. She denied him a second child. She denied him comfort, tenderness, affection – or rather, she offered him only the palest reproduction of those things. She staked out her own territory, fooled herself that she could keep him out of it. But always, always, if he wanted it enough, she'd find him grunting away on top of her, and her soul, her self, whatever one wanted to call it, coiled up small as a tape-measure, tucked in a corner of her head where the messy process couldn't touch it. Even up to the end, she let this happen – the last time, not a week before he died. Oh Hester, she thought, oh, my daughter, save yourself. Don't give in.

She was on the brink of ringing the bell. She could pull

off her wig, shove it in her bag. 'Hello, darling, it's only me. Gillian and I thought we'd have a day in town. Guy, what an unexpected treat! How *are* you?' Several times she took a step forward. Her voice on the intercom would certainly put a dampener on things. But she held herself back. Her quest, for whatever it was, was not yet over. She did not know quite what she was looking for, but she knew she would recognize it when she found it.

It was almost dark; her ankles were swollen and her shoulders ached with waiting. Then there he was, in an instant; Guy on the pavement. A victorious Guy? By no means, though not defeated either. He was whistling; that loud, toneless whistle of his which, when Hester had first known him, Verity had taken to denote good cheer. Over time she had come to realize that it meant no such thing. The whistle was a warning, an unconscious warning; Guy Harrison was not entirely pleased with life, but Guy Harrison would keep battering away until he got what he wanted. Off he strode, up the street, looking for a taxi, most probably, his hands in his pockets, still whistling. He didn't glance up at the balcony; nor did Hester appear.

Back at the hotel, Verity snipped open one of the sachets of bubble bath and squeezed it under the hot tap. She ran the bath as hot as she could take it, lowered herself in, and closed her eyes. The hotel did not serve dinner. She didn't want to go out again, so she tried to persuade herself that she wasn't hungry, that she could nibble on the little biscuit that came with the coffee tray, the flat dark thing that looks like something one might have found aboard a sailing ship. But her body was unconvinced, and as her stomach heaved and gurgled under the foam she realized that she would not manage the night without food.

She dressed again; wearily. She pulled on the wig. It was

now pitch dark. She put on a light coat. Once out of the hotel she found her feet heading her back in the direction of Hester's flat. Oh, come on, she said to herself with irritation, you're like a teenage girl who keeps checking to see whether the postman's been, even though you know he won't come, not now. One part of her brain told her feet that she was looking for a cheap, anonymous restaurant, while another part chimed in that there were plenty of those much nearer the hotel. And her feet kept going while this dull little argument droned on. Then there she was, back in front of the flats – no need to lurk at a distance now, she was under cover of darkness – and, good heavens! What a day! There was a man, not Guy, ringing Hester's bell. The girl kept them stacked like aeroplanes. Verity moved close, so that she could be sure which bell he was ringing. She looked at him hard, almost spoke to him – she even opened her mouth to do so, and then moved away. He must think me odd, she thought. He was a rough-looking character, not tall, thickset, even running a little to fat, Hester's age or a shade younger. His dark hair was longer than it should have been, his profile blunt, his face unshaven. He wore oily jeans and a battered leather jacket. His expression was open – he didn't make Verity nervous – but his general appearance was hard to connect with Hester and her world.

'Hi, doll,' he said into the intercom. 'It's me.' She heard Hester reply, 'Sol. Come on up.' Doll? A man smelling of engine oil and cigarettes was calling her 'doll' at ten o'clock at night? Verity was astonished, but she didn't feel like waiting this time. She took her astonishment off to a little Turkish café that must have once been a Swiss restaurant – a shadowy Heidi could still be seen on the red plastic menu cover; she'd had a belly dancer superimposed on her. Here, most uncharacteristically, Verity ordered a beer, and sank her teeth into a sprawling kebab – she didn't even pull out the raw onion. She exulted. For surely this lank-haired Sol, whoever and whatever he might be, would keep Guy Harrison at bay. Whatever was going on was bringing her no nearer to Sebastian, but she could only hope, and assume, that it was bringing her nearer to Hester.

14

Hester hadn't begun to look for Sebastian before he was found. It was Guy who found him; her ex-husband found the brother that he never knew – never would know – she had. It was one of those astonishing coincidences, Hester thought, that make you think perhaps coincidences aren't, after all, so very astonishing; that what people called coincidences were really only a question of noticing. You often see, on your travels through London, say, a man with a badly burned face, and you think how surprising it is that you see him so often, but then it dawns on you that you must often see the same people in the street, time and time again, but it's only the burned face that you remember. So the freakishness of Guy finding Sebastian wasn't so very freakish after all. And he couldn't truly be said to have found him, because he didn't know he was lost.

When Hester walked away from Guy that hot valedictory evening, when she left him stewing in the attic room in Rosie's emptied house, she knew she hadn't seen the last of him. Guy wouldn't admit defeat so easily. She knew she'd nettled him, but she also knew that Guy rather liked to be nettled. He enjoyed a game, an intrigue; anything was better than boredom. So when Hester reached her flat one dusty evening about ten days after the party and Guy sprang out at her from the shadows the shock was only momentary. And her instinctive and genuine irritation was shot through with a certain pleasure; pleasure of the kind she used to feel when Guy was her tall and handsome boyfriend and she used to see him waiting at their agreed rendezvous and feel quite wobbly with pride.

He started off with a show of anger – what the hell did she think she was doing, messing him around like that? Didn't she understand that he had feelings? He was laying himself on the line and she was treating him like a piece of shit. Hester kept her voice level. She said, 'Have you just come here to shout at me?'

Guy laid his hand on her arm and said, 'No, Hets, I'm here because I want you. You've got to believe me.'

She shook off his hand. 'Guy, I've heard it all before.' She moved away from him, told him to leave her alone, but they both knew that the lines they were speaking belonged to a radio play, and they also both knew that she was going to let him in. So when he stepped in front of her, to bar her way, she put up only a token protest.

She offered him a drink. He refused, which put her out; the gritty end-of-August city air made a glass of white wine particularly appealing. But she couldn't drink if he wasn't going to. She couldn't afford to have a muzzier head than his. She poured fizzy water into two tall tumblers, added ice cubes and slices of lemon. She wanted to remind him that she did things properly. Though the flat was stuffy, she didn't open the doors on to the balcony. She wanted to avoid any possible romantic implications. Nor did she kick off her shoes, which was what she usually did the moment she was home. Instead she perched on the edge of an armchair, sipping water, as if she was preparing for an interview. Guy sat on the sofa, silent, in an I've-a-right-to-an-explanation mode. And then Hester thought, yes, that's what I'll do. I'll interview him. She interviewed people all the time for work, and she was always in control.

She began. 'Guy, at what point did you decide that you'd

like to patch things up with me? Was it before or after my father's death?'

Guy was taken aback; she could see that he understood exactly what she meant. There was no innocence in Guy. He summoned up a touch of righteous indignation. 'Your father's death doesn't have a lot to do with it. Except that hearing about it made me think about you. Made me think about you even more than usual.'

'You didn't come to the funeral.'

'You wouldn't have wanted me there.'

'But you didn't write or ring. You didn't write to me or to my mother. A letter – now, surely, that's normal, if you're thinking about somebody in their hour of need?'

Guy smiled uneasily. 'I never know what's normal or what's not when it comes to writing those kinds of letters. You always took care of that sort of thing – lots of other things as well. You spoiled me.' She wasn't sure whether he meant this as a compliment or a reproach. With Guy, the two were often confused.

'But I could hardly be expected to write my own letter of condolence, Guy.'

'Oh, God. You're right. Of course I should have written. But I thought you might have wanted me to leave you alone.'

'You didn't think anything of the sort' – still her tone was level, pleasant. 'You didn't give it any thought at all. You registered that Papa had died, and then later – quite a few weeks later – you scented some advantage to yourself and –'

'Hester, that's outrageous! You ought to know me better than that.'

'Oh, I do know you, Guy. Quite well enough.' She left a silence for him to fill. He obliged.

'If you're implying that I am in any way interested in your father's money –'

'I'd have thought there was only one way of being interested in another person's money.'

'Well, perhaps I wouldn't know, because I'm not.'

She smoothed her skirt, then looked him in the eye. 'So it would make no difference to you to learn that Papa left the bulk of his money to an American institute for Holocaust research.'

The lie direct. How rarely one has a chance to use it, thought Hester; how delicious it tastes when that chance comes one's way! Guy flinched, almost imperceptibly. The speed of his recovery was impressive. He cleared his throat.

'It wouldn't make any difference to me whatsoever.'

Hester ended the interview, and rewarded him with a smile. 'Now, how about that drink?'

He followed her into the kitchen, but he didn't attempt to touch her, nor did he aggravate her by taking the corkscrew out of her hands. They drank their Pinot Grigio in the kitchen, standing up. Guy said, not entirely with conviction, 'Well, I hope that's cleared the air?' and Hester said, 'Absolutely. What are you doing on Saturday night?'

She remembered that she liked making him smile. He said, 'Taking you out, I hope. Wherever you want to go.'

'How about the theatre? I haven't been for ages.'

'Good idea. What would you like to see?'

'Oh, anything, as long as it's not Lloyd Webber. Or too fringey. Not that there's much danger of that with you.'

He left, soon after. He didn't stay to finish the bottle. Perhaps he didn't want to wait to be dismissed. As he left, he bent over and kissed her lightly on the top of her head, in the familiar, affectionate way that she remembered as the best of him. When he had gone, she finished the wine on her own, which was far more than she would usually allow herself. She drank it curled up on the sofa, the tears rolling down her face.

When the last drop was gone she pulled herself together. She tried to steady her mind by reading a chapter of *Dumb Woman's Lane* – it was high time, she told herself, that she tackled this project of writing a life of Grandma Evelyn – but the words swam before her eyes, and she had to give up. Instead, she hauled herself off the sofa and ran a bath. She was expecting Solly, and it was part of their deal that they never presented themselves to each other as tear-stained, moody, preoccupied, fallible, or anything other than – well, animal.

And yet 'animal' wasn't the right word, either, thought Hester, because between them there was emotion, there was game-playing, there was an exploration of one another that went beyond the purely physical. But what was not allowed to intrude was the rest of their lives. So when Hester had finished her bath she put on a short red dress that Solly particularly liked and that she had, in fact, bought solely for his benefit. She applied more make-up than usual to mask the blotchiness, and brewed a pot of expresso in an attempt to feel less drunk. She should have eaten, but she couldn't, not even salad, not even a sliver of cheese. Her insides felt like a twisted handkerchief. Even the thought of eating was impossible.

Solly arrived with the reek of the garage still on him. He looked Hester and her red dress up and down, and chuckled. Then he said, 'There's an old woman hanging about outside, like she's looking for someone. Maybe you. She was looking at your doorbell.'

'You could have asked her.'

'A guy like me can't say nothing to a woman after dark.

I'd scare her senseless. She's a funny-looking old biddy. Looks like she's wearing a wig. If you want to go down and check her out, I'll come with you.'

She slipped his leather jacket off his shoulders. 'Oh, no,' she said. 'There's always funny people about.' And then Solly forgot about it, because it didn't take him long to discover that under her thin red dress she was wearing nothing at all.

'There's not a lot on,' said Guy over the telephone. 'Late August isn't a great time for theatres. There's a *Hedda Gabler* that's had good reviews, but it's a bit heavy, isn't it?'

'I'd like to see *Hedda Gabler*. I don't think I've seen one since Cambridge – do you remember, when Robin was the young man? The poetical one?'

'Yeah, I remember,' said Guy, with a laugh in his voice. 'Hopelessly miscast. OK, I'll try for *Hedda Gabler*, if you like. Or there's something at the Royal Court, some kind of post-punk thing based on *Romeo and Juliet*. Or maybe it's *Midsummer Night's Dream*, I can't remember. Set in twenty-first-century Manhattan. It might be a laugh.'

'Or it might be excruciating.'

'Or there's an Alan Ayckbourn at –'

'No, no. I'd rather have the punks. *Hedda* first choice, though, please.'

'Okey-doke. *Hedda*, and then the Royal Court if she lets us down.'

She did let them down, and if Hester was the sort of person who believed in such things, she would have read her fate in the fact that when Guy rang the box office for tickets he was told, 'I'm terribly sorry, we've just sold the last two.' So the Royal Court it was, and Hester met him in a bar in Sloane Square that Saturday evening for a drink before the post-punk Dream. It was called *PUCK*, in capital letters, and she didn't see how Guy could have thought it was *Romeo and Juliet*, even for a second.

She'd made a different kind of effort with her appearance this time. Demure would no longer do. Things were on the move, and her attire needed to point them in the right direction, so she'd gone out and bought something new that very morning. Hester was not a keen shopper. She usually set off with good intentions, but grew bored after half an hour. She tended to stick to labels she trusted; most of her clothes were variations on a theme – tailored, plain, but with well-executed detail, colours moving from cream to grey to mushroom, and lots of black. She rarely wore patterns or fabrics that floated, and she never wore yellow or pink – not much pure colour at all, which was why the red dress she wore for Solly had a special meaning. But on this particular morning she shopped differently. She wandered through Chelsea with a scrubbed face and flat pumps, and no hand-bag, just a credit card in her pocket. And her eye was caught by the swirly Rococo shopfront of a little boutique that she'd never visited before, but which she'd read about in magazines. Each garment was unique, and could be altered to suit the customer's whims. The designers used feathers, sequins, bows and lace – fussiness that Hester had no time for in her real life. But that morning she had a dreamy feeling, as if she'd stepped out of her real life. So she went into the shop, and there was the dress.

When Hester saw that dress, she felt a stab of recognition. The colour was hard to describe – like a skinned peach, but with more colour in it. It was a colour you might see in a sunset, she thought, not in the core of the sunset, but in the shiny sky above, for the little purple clouds to swim in. Or else it was the colour of a just-risen moon, a colour you might see only once a year. Most people, she supposed, would have called it orange, and in theory orange shouldn't suit fair-skinned blondes. But she put it on, and it made her come alive. It fitted closely; it was sleeveless, but it came with a bolero jacket that was hardly more than a shrug. It had tiny self-covered buttons all the way down from the deep neckline to the hem. When the sales girl folded it, it seemed scarcely heavier than its tissue-paper wrapping. Hester knew that if she wore it to the theatre, it meant that she would sleep with Guy. Not straight away, necessarily, but she was aware that it was a garment that would make her decisions for her. And wear it she did.

She caught the bus back to Victoria, the Number 11, her childhood bus, and then walked home through the back streets of Pimlico, whistling, and swinging her shiny carrier bag. She stopped at the market in Strutton Ground and bought a big bag of plums; she wanted to pile their royal purple high on her pewter plate. It was her day for colour. At the far end of Strutton Ground she caught sight of a thin woman with a quick, nervous walk, and for a moment she thought it was her mother. She even called, and waved, and felt a little flush of foolishness at the sight of the woman's retreating back. Of course it wasn't her mother. The woman had thick, dark hair, and must have been significantly younger. Perhaps it was taking that bus that had brought her mother into her mind. Hester realized with a jolt that Verity hadn't been in touch since going to stay with whichever of those not desperately exciting friends had offered to take her in until the work on the cottage drains was finished. Hester was a little ashamed that she could never quite keep her mother's old friends in focus; she couldn't really see the point of those women who ruffled no feathers and exchanged National Trust tea towels and photographs of their grandchildren at Christmas. She was pretty sure it was Gillian her mother was visiting, though whether it was Gillian's daughter who'd made a good recovery from breast cancer, Gillian's husband who was obsessed with steam trains, or whether these people belonged to Erica, she wasn't certain.

It would be Verity's birthday soon, and Hester had given it no thought. Back at her flat, she rang to see if Verity had returned, but the habit of ages caused her to ring Knighton instead of the new cottage, and the telephone was answered by Rosie. The surprise prompted Hester to ask the question she'd suppressed during previous conversations. 'Rosie, why did you invite Guy to your party without warning me?'

Rosie laughed. 'I didn't. Is that what he told you? No, he tagged along with Steve and Rach – they'd had him over for something or other. Typical of Guy to twist it round.'

'Yes, isn't it? And there was me thinking you were plotting to get us back together.'

'Hettie, I wouldn't do that to you. Or, if I did, I'd tell you first. What's the situation, anyway? Is he still sniffing around?'

'He is, yes.'

'And are you going to?'

'No. I'm not. He's still the same old Guy.'

But when she'd finished talking to Rosie, and called her mother's cottage but received no reply, she sat at her desk and wrote the date in red on a piece of paper, and then she wrote OPTIONS. She liked to think that options were what she had.

1. Remarry Guy → have baby → spend life with Guy.
2. Get pregnant by Guy → ditch Guy → single mother.
3. Ignore Guy → get pregnant by someone else without consulting them (e.g. Solly) → single mother.

4. Ignore Guy → never have children → successful career and affluent retirement.

She paused and stared at what she'd written. Then underneath she wrote, in capitals, FIND SEBASTIAN. And then she folded the paper and tore it into tiny scraps. She put the scraps into the kitchen bin, with the coffee grounds and lemon halves and shiny, ectoplasmic lettuce.

She hung up the new dress and arranged the plums on her pewter plate. She knew that Guy wouldn't keep his offer open indefinitely. He was still an attractive man, and presentable single men with no dependants were hot property in London. How would she feel if she left it too late and Guy was snapped up by some sharp-suited City type who wanted to slip her hand through the arm of a man who was going places, or who at least looked as if he was? Worse, it might be a sweet girl, none too bright, who would cook for him and fuss over his shirts and overlook his misdemeanours in return for flowers on her birthday and a nestful of blond babies. If Hester made no move, if she let fate take its course, then something like this would happen, and though common sense declared that it would be the best thing all round, she knew she would be chagrined, and she disliked that bitter taste. But Guy for the rest of her life? What would he become? An aging roué, slipping off to massage parlours? A drunken bore at a party, patting pretty girls on the bottom, leaving Hester granite-faced then and waspish on the journey home? She remembered an occasion, some time during her marriage, when she and Rosie had been discussing those little cards that had begun to proliferate in London telephone boxes, cards selling girls who offered every imaginable variation on a theme. She remembered Rosie saying, 'What kind of man would actually ring those numbers?' and Hester didn't reply for a minute because it hit her with some force that the sort of man who would ring those numbers was Guy.

But perhaps fatherhood would redirect him, give him the sense of purpose he'd always lacked. Rosie was right; everybody deserved a second chance. It was perfectly possible that he would be a good father. He was an affectionate person, that was one of his saving graces. He had loved lying in bed with her just for the sake of it. He loved sharing baths, being tickled, breaking up food into little bits and popping them into her mouth. With every year that passed she'd found this more and more irritating, but for a child . . . As parents they could provide a good balance. Guy would be warm and energetic, he'd run round the garden with them, squirting water. She'd be organized, she'd feed them properly, she'd read them the right books, she'd put the right musical instruments into their little hands.

Aloud, she said, 'You're talking nonsense!' And she went to run herself a bath.

Hester arrived at the bar in Sloane Square a studied ten minutes late. Guy didn't immediately comment on the dress, but she knew he was looking. When she went to fetch drinks from the bar, which she insisted on doing, she knew his eyes were travelling over her body, over her long thighs, her smooth haunches, her taut stomach that, unlike the stomachs of her contemporaries, had not billowed out to accommodate babies. When she brought the drinks back to their table he took her hand and said with a kind of smirk, 'Do we have to go to this play?' and she pulled her hand away and said, 'I'm looking forward to it, actually,' but she softened it with a smile. On the walk to the theatre and as they took their seats he lost no opportunity to press or stroke or brush against her, which made her think, well, I'll sleep with you one day, mate, but it's not going to be tonight.

He bought only one programme, so that by sharing they'd have to lean closer together. He made a to-do of turning the pages, because that involved passing his arm almost across her lap. 'I've never heard of any of these people,' he said, scanning the cast list. 'Oh, look, Hets, there's another Oakes.'

And indeed there was. Sebastian Oakes. One of the lovers was played by Sebastian Oakes.

'Oh, yes,' said Hester, hoping her voice didn't squeak. 'So there is.' She sat as still as she could, willing the house lights to dim, willing away the great gap of time before she could be face to face with her lost brother across that chasm of darkness.

Guy's interest in an unfamous actor who happened to share Hester's surname flickered and was gone. 'Michael Cook,' he read. 'Wasn't he in that sitcom, the one set on the canal boat? Yeah – it says here –'

'I think you're right,' said Hester, automatically. If a fire had broken out at that moment Guy would have had to carry her from the burning theatre, because her legs had turned to candyfloss, and the blood was drumming in her ears. Then the lights dimmed, and they were off.

Their seats weren't particularly good ones. The figures on the stage looked very far away. The set involved a lot of steel girders, which Hester supposed were meant as the equivalent of the trees in the forest; long shadows were cast, and the stripes of light were a harsh aluminium white, which made it even harder to see what the actors looked like. But when Sebastian came on stage, the recognition shot through her to her nerve endings. Once, when she was driving, a bee that must have blundered drowsily through the open window stung her on the tip of her finger and she had to make an emergency stop. The pain, which was almost too pure a feeling to be called pain, ran up through her hand as far as her shoulder with the precision of coloured capillaries in a biological drawing. That was like the feeling that seeing Sebastian gave her. This was her brother, all right. That was her father's walk. Her father as a young man, the young man she had never known. But she knew him now. Because here he was.

Sebastian was much darker than Simeon – she could tell that, despite the costume and the make-up. Thinner, too – a narrower frame. He was – she knew so well – thirty years old, but he still had the build of a boy, the boy with the bare midriff whose photograph she had studied until she knew it by heart. Though she couldn't see the details of his face, she knew from the photographs that his features were his mother's. But in his movements, the forward thrust of his shoulders, the long limbs attached to the torso with a cable-like tension, she saw her – their – father. Sebastian was playing what would have been the part of Lysander, except that because they were doing their Dreaming in twenty-first-century New York, he was called simply Ly. She could see why they hadn't cast him as Puck, despite his boyish grace. He was dominant, a space-filler; her brother was not ethereal. Under her golden dress, her skin was prickly, a raised pelt.

Beside her, Guy fidgeted. His hand reached out for her arm or hand or knee from time to time, but she gave up noticing. At the interval he said, with disappointment, 'You're really enjoying this, aren't you?' and she said, 'I'm absolutely enthralled.'

'Damn,' said Guy, 'I thought we could go and eat.'

'I'm not hungry.'

'That's not exactly what I meant.'

'Go if you like,' said Hester. 'But there's no way I'm leaving before the end. This is the most interesting theatrical experience I've had for a long time.'

He flumped back down beside her with a sigh.

She took in very little about the rest of the play. She had a feeling that it was a fairly outrageous interpretation – well, it would be, wouldn't it? – but this feeling was something she absorbed from the reactions of the audience, not something she registered with her conscious brain. All she saw was her brother, weaving in and out of the steel girders; light and shadow, brother and then no brother.

She couldn't hang about at the end. 'I'm sorry,' she said to Guy, 'all that concentrating has given me a terrible headache. I need to go straight home. Alone.' She gave him a kiss, the kind that would put him on hold. 'I'll ring. I promise.'

She remembered nothing of the journey home. All she took in was a slight female figure slipping away from the flats as she approached. She noticed, because it was odd to see a female, not young, not a derelict, out on the streets alone at midnight. Perhaps it's that funny old woman Solly saw, she thought. Perhaps she's a stalker. It wouldn't be surprising, given the nature of my radio programme, that my first stalker would be a nervous old lady.

But she wasn't very interested. She put the kettle on, and forgot to use it. She started to make a sandwich, and abandoned it. She opened the doors and, stalker or no stalker, she stood on her balcony in her moonrise dress, staring out into the dark street.

15

Stalking and spying tainted everything for a while. Verity should have been busy, setting the new cottage to rights. That was the kind of activity her old self would have enjoyed, but now she seemed to look at everything with corrupted eyes. The cottage seemed characterless, or what character it had displeased her. The uneven floorboards and low ceilings were inconvenient, not quaint. She resented the brown rings somebody else's misplaced frying pans had left on the wooden work surfaces. The garden was full of those miniature conifers, some vertical, some horizontal, that according to the gardening books add 'sculptural interest', but to Verity they just looked stunted, deformed. And there was a little tinkling water feature — either she'd forgotten about it, or she'd hoped they'd take it with them. Her old self would have arranged for its instant removal, but her new self said, why bother? What gives you the right to think that you can improve on anything? She looked at the cardboard boxes of books and let them lie. She hung up the Royal Horticultural Society calendar Erica had given her last Christmas, and took it down again. She slept fitfully. Waking to a new morning was like opening the door of a fridge and encountering the same bad smell. The first thing she caught sight of was her wig, which she'd hung over her dressing-table mirror as a memorial to her own folly.

The spying itself had been absorbing; even, at moments, exhilarating. She turned over her findings endlessly. What did Guy Harrison's reappearance mean? Would smoky, leather-jacketed Sol be enough to see him off? She fervently hoped so. For years she'd suppressed her instinctive distrust of her son-in-law. Now that the bottle of poison was uncorked, she was surprised at its potency.

Her ruminations were full of anxiety mixed with excitement, and more than a little disappointment. Why did Hester seem to be taking no particular steps to find Sebastian? Verity feared the upheaval that Hester's putative pursuit of her unknown brother would entail, feared revelation and embarrassment, misplaced financial gestures, the raking of embers. But, still, Sebastian's was an uncompleted story, and it left her restless. The sour taste in her mouth on her return from London was the taste of ennui as well as shame. She thought she'd set something in motion, but it seemed to have come to an inconclusive stop.

Not long after her return to Sussex came Verity's birthday. Hester rang and left a message; should she come down and take her out to dinner? No, my dear, thought Verity, most emphatically not. She rang back, at a time when she knew Hester would be out; because she'd come to prefer leaving messages to speaking to people directly. She said how kind, but not to worry, Beryl Barber had suggested the Old Clock House in Chiddingbourne, newly converted into a rather superior organic café. Then she rang Beryl, and suggested the Old Clock House, and mercifully Beryl was going to a whist drive. Verity was surprised to learn that whist drives still existed, but, she thought, if they do, it's absolutely the Beryl Barbers of this world who would frequent them. Beryl said, would Verity like to come with her, and Verity said no, thanks awfully, and put the telephone down, pleased at having fulfilled two personal obligations and still being left to spend her birthday alone, which was all she felt good for.

She sat in her new garden on her birthday morning, drinking Nescafé and scowling at the awful sculptural conifers. Her early September birthday often brought the brightest, freshest weather of the whole year, but this one was sticky and overcast. The telephone rang. Why had she brought it outside with her? She felt obliged to answer it.

'Verity? It's Rosie. Look, I know it's awfully short notice, but could you come and have lunch with us? I've just been talking to Hester and she reminded me about your birthday.'

'My dear, it's terribly kind, but I –'

'Oh, please come. We haven't seen you for ages. And I've got something I simply must tell you.'

And so Verity found herself once more sitting on the brick terrace at Knighton, drinking in the milky translucence of the autumn crocuses and listening to the shrieks of the Wilkinson children as they road-tested their new trampoline. Rosie apologized for the noise. 'School starts next Tuesday,' she said. 'I can't wait. But at least that trampoline's keeping them busy, so we can talk.' She scraped the remains of Spanish omelette and salad off the children's plates. 'I'm longing to get chickens, so that all these scraps won't go to waste. We saw some beauties at the rare breeds farm the other day. I adored the Buff Orpingtons. They're so big you could almost put a little saddle and bridle on them.'

Verity smiled. 'My mother kept poultry. I loved collecting the eggs, but Simeon didn't like the noise and mess they made, so when my mother left, so did the birds.'

'Oh dear,' said Rosie. 'I was just going to go ahead and buy a few – it's Becky's birthday soon, and I know she'd love them. But I never thought to consult Robin. What a terrible wife I am!'

'Hardly that, Rosie dear. I'd say Robin has very little to complain about. And besides' – she stirred her coffee –

'giving in to someone else's foibles isn't the best way to conduct a marriage. I should know.'

Rosie gave her a direct look, inquiry in her hazel eyes. 'Do you miss him?'

'Not in the least.' Verity was taken aback by the alacrity of her own response. She clapped her hand over her mouth. 'My goodness, what a terrible thing to say. May I modify that? Let me see, do I miss Simeon? Yes, I missed him at first, but now, even though it's only five months, I hardly think about him from one day to the next. To an extra-ordinary extent, I seem to have cleared out the attics of my mind.'

Rosie was a little shocked. 'But he was such a powerful man. And you were with him for – how many years? Can he really have made so little impact? That's scary.'

'I know, I know. I'm astonished at myself. Perhaps I've just submerged him. Perhaps he'll come bobbing back up to the surface one day. But in the meantime – well, so much has happened. I suppose I'm feeling . . .'

'Free?'

'Free? Not quite. But at least I'm learning a little bit about what freedom might be.'

'That kind of freedom would frighten me,' said Rosie slowly.

'But you don't need it! I don't wish to intrude, my dear, but it seems to me that you've achieved freedom within your marriage – you don't need to look outside. What you have with Robin – that's what love is, or ought to be. But not many people manage it. I know I never have. For a long time, I didn't believe it could exist.'

Rosie smiled, a broad, twinkling smile of pure content-ment. 'It's true. Somehow, we've managed it, Robin and I. It's hard not to sound smug, but . . . well, I do know it's rare. I only wish Hester could find something comparable.'

Verity cleared her throat. 'Rosie, you know I can't have these sort of conversations with Hester. But do you think . . . I just wondered . . . is there the smallest possibility that Guy could be making a reappearance?'

Rosie looked up sharply. 'What makes you think that?'

'I don't know. Just a feeling in my bones . . . something Hester almost said. My goodness, I do hope not.'

Rosie sipped water, considering the matter. She ran a hand absently over her stomach. 'I don't know very much more than you do. I think Guy might be after some kind of reconciliation, but I'm not sure. Would that definitely be a bad thing?'

'It most certainly would. There aren't many subjects on which I feel qualified to pass judgement, but yes, Guy Harrison is most definitely bad news.'

'But surely, people can change. Shouldn't we give him a chance? And Hester's forty. If she wants a baby . . .'

'Not everyone has to have babies. I can't expect you to agree about this, Rosie, but life can be worth living without babies.'

'But Guy would be a good father. For all his faults, he's very –'

'Rosie, think of the timing! If Guy has decided to come back into her life – if that's what's happened – why do you think he's done it just after Simeon's death? That man is motivated entirely by self-interest. He imagines Simeon's left her a fortune, and he wants to climb on the gravy train. He's lazy and deceitful. Don't fool yourself that he'll ever be any different.'

'I know. I think you're right, really. Leopards don't often change their spots, more's the pity. But if she wants him back –'

'Does she?'

'I don't think Hester knows what she wants.'

'That's the first time anyone's ever said that about my daughter.'

'But it's true, don't you think? Hester's got her flat and her job and her friends – she thinks she's got her life the way she wants it. But where's she going? What's her direction? What's her future?'

They both fell silent. I can't say more, thought Verity, without revealing things that aren't meant to be revealed. There was no indication that Rosie knew anything about Sebastian. And surely the possibility of Sebastian provided Hester with a direction, if only an uncertain one.

And then, in a flash, she saw it. How to get rid of Guy. He was after Hester's money – or rather, her money, which would one day be Hester's. What should she do with that money? It was blindingly obvious.

Give it to Sebastian.

Rosie shifted in her wicker seat. 'I admit, I'm blinkered when it comes to babies. Verity, you know when I rang, I said I had something to tell you? Well – I expect you can guess –'

'There's another on the way? Oh, my dear, how absolutely wonderful! A baby at Knighton! That's just what the old place needs.'

'It's very early days. You're the first to know – except for Robin, of course. I shouldn't be saying anything yet – it's tempting fate. And I don't want the children to know for at least another month. But I had to tell you on your birthday. It just felt so right.'

'Oh, my dear, I do feel honoured.' Verity reached out and took Rosie's small freckled hands in hers. She squeezed them with affection, then withdrew as Paddy and Bud bounded across the garden and draped their arms round their mother's neck. 'Is it time for you-know-what?' asked Bud in a stage whisper.

'I think it must be. Paddy, you go and get the things, and Bud, call the others.' Within seconds, a cake – chocolate, lopsided, with some hieroglyphic picked out in Smarties – had appeared, along with Angus, and Becky with a posy.

'Happy birthday,' she said, holding it out to Verity. 'It seems a bit funny giving it to you, because they're really your flowers, but Mum said you wouldn't mind.'

'Of course I don't mind. I'm delighted, darling. Chocolate cosmos – and those lovely rusty achilleas – and that wonderful blue salvia – Cambridge blue, isn't it? What a marvellous combination. You've quite an eye for colour, my dear.'

'She has, hasn't she?' said Rosie, pleased. 'Now, boys, give Verity the cards you made. And Bud really helped with this cake. I hardly had to do a thing.'

'It looks very – chocolatey. How delicious. What do the Smarties say? I haven't got my reading glasses.'

'Sixty-question mark. Because Mum knew you were sixty-something but she wasn't sure exactly.'

'How tactful of her not to ask! My dears, I'm quite overwhelmed. Just a little piece for me – that's perfect.'

'Oh, and there's one more thing,' said Rosie, getting up.

'Not a present, I hope, Rosie dear?'

'No, I know you said no presents. Flowers don't count. No, this is just something I found when I was turning out the cupboard in the boys' room. You know, that cupboard that's set into the panelling. I don't know what it is, but it's got your names on it.' From the dark of the house, Rosie fetched a large brown padded envelope, and handed it to Verity. The children crowded round to peer.

'For Verity and Hester. To be opened after my death,'

read Becky. 'How exciting! It's like something in a novel.'

'It's my mother's handwriting,' said Verity, feeling the edges. 'A book of some sort. I can't imagine what.'

'Open it, open it!' chorused the children. But Verity knew that she would not open it, not then, maybe never.

'It's got Hester's name on it, too,' she pointed out. 'We'll open it together. Don't worry, we'll tell you all about it.'

'Run off to play, now,' said Rosie. 'You've only got half an hour before we get ready to go to the riding stables. So scoot, all of you!'

16

15th September 1980

Today feels like the first day of autumn. It's wet, and I'm glad. For the last fortnight we've had a glorious Indian summer, and the hips and the haws warming the hedgerows would gladden anyone's heart, but the soil is baked and cracked. I don't want my garden to die before I do, so I welcome the rain.

I welcome the rain, and I'm thrilled by the wind. It's not like a summer wind, even though there's still warmth in it. It's a wind that sings of change. The big ash tree at the bottom of my garden should have gone ages ago, but I'm glad I never got round to asking young Apps to take it down, because the way it's dancing in the wind today fills my old heart with – if not joy, then energy, which is akin to joy. It reminds me that I have a heart. Hester, when you read this, after I'm gone, I hope you'll resolve to make better use of your heart than I've made of mine.

I think you'll be reading this quite soon, Hester dear. I intend to die this winter. I feel everything inside me slowing, rusting, grinding to a halt. I'm pretty sure that my body will make the decision for me, but if it lets me down, will I have the courage to take matters into my own hands? I'm sitting in my narrow kitchen, looking out at the garden. The tool-shed is all but hidden under swags of hops. My goodness, hops do grow like the blazes! I rescued these plants from Knighton Farm, when the last of the hop gardens were ploughed up. I grew them over the arbour in the kitchen garden at Knighton, and then I bought some of them with me when I moved here. I wonder why gardeners don't make more use of them. I love that Pre-Raphaelite detail, the broad, ridged leaves, the layered lime-coloured flowers, that yeasty smell they leave behind on one's fingers. I can see the last of the sweetpeas, too, still waving their pretty fondant flags, but short-stemmed now, and with mildew on their leaves. And I can see the sunflowers, a row of jolly story-book giants against the east-facing wall, hanging their heads today because of the gloom and the rain.

When one reaches my age, everything feels like a little piece of history. I look at the hops and I think of the two world wars, ploughing up the old rural way of life. No farmers brew their own beer any more. That hasn't happened for years. The big breweries have taken over, and the beer, I'm told, is sour gassy stuff, the same in name only as the rich brown pre-war brew. Well, my life was comprehensively ploughed up by the wars, too, as perhaps was true for all my generation. Ploughed up, churned up, our inner landscapes so altered as to be virtually unrecognizable.

The sweetpeas – always a favourite of mine, but aren't they everyone's favourite flower? There's nothing controversial about a sweetpea. One of the first flowers to make an impact on both Verity and Hester. I remember one hot summer's night, Hester; you were staying with me at Knighton so that your parents could have a couple of nights alone together, though I wasn't convinced that that was exactly what Verity wanted. I looked after you for them, and my goodness you were hard work. No worse than any other baby, I don't suppose, but I'd forgotten what hard work babies could be. It was so hot that I stripped you down to your nappy, and laid a damp muslin square over you, and still you couldn't sleep. So I brought you down-stairs, out into the moonlit garden, and held your little pointed face up to the sweetpeas, and you crowed with delight and reached out to grab them with both your fists.

The planting of the sweetpeas, using the seeds from the year before, became an annual ritual. I don't believe I ever missed a year. And the obligation to pick them again and again, to encourage new flowers, was part of the charm. But now I want to abdicate even that gentle responsibility. The sweetpeas shaking in the wind out there are the last I'll ever pick.

And as for the sunflowers – I think of Blake's sunflower, 'weary of time'. That's me, all right. How does it go?

> Ah Sun-flower! weary of time,
> Who countest the steps of the Sun:
> Seeking after that sweet golden clime
> Where the traveller's journey is done . . .

Well, my journey's done, my course is run. And now I turn my slow old head towards the sweet golden clime where I shall once more set my eyes upon Jack's face. Or so I tell myself, in my softer-headed moments.

There was a wind like this one, the first night I spent with Jack. I can remember all the nights I spent with him, because there were only a handful – it was wartime, he was at the Front, he was engaged to somebody else. I made my decision the day I met him; I would go to bed with him, if that's what he wanted. Almost every week brought news of the death of friends, acquaintances, distant relatives. I couldn't bear to let something like this go to waste. And it wasn't long before I told him so.

Jack returned on leave. It was his first night on English

soil. He told Dora his leave began two days later than it did. He got off the train at some little place in Kent. I met him at the station. I'd borrowed a cottage from a friend. How did we reach it? I seem to remember bicycles. Perhaps we hired them.

It was October. The cottage was hidden amid swaying, sighing trees. Sweet chestnuts thudded at our feet. The spiky cases split open on impact, the glossy nuts tumbled out. We filled our pockets to roast them on the kitchen range.

A neighbouring farmer's wife looked after the cottage for my friend. She'd left out supplies for us – bread, sausages wrapped in waxy paper, eggs in a china bowl. She'd stuck a few rusty mopheaded chrysanthemums in a blue-and-white jug and put a note underneath – 'To Mr and Mrs Albery. Welcom. Hoping your's is a plesent stay.' My friend had described us as newlyweds snatching a little time alone together. We'd given her my name, because we weren't so very far from where Dora lived.

I remember sitting by the range, shelling chestnuts. I remember burning the sausages but eating them anyway. I remember holding his hands in mine, and loving the line of his jaw and the arch of his eyebrow. I remember the high brass bed, the patchwork counterpane, the monolithic bolster we ditched by mutual consent. But I don't remember the transition from kitchen to bedroom, from clothes to nakedness. How did all that come about?

There was a small fire in the bedroom; it cast long shadows. The wind howled in the chimney, and the small-paned window rattled as if it would break. Jack twitched and muttered in his sleep. That made me feel so tender towards him; I wanted to soothe his dreams. I pressed my face against his naked back as he slept. I couldn't sleep at all, not a wink. The door of the woodshed was banging in the wind.

I dreaded that it would wake Jack, but going to fasten it meant leaving him, and I couldn't bear to leave him, not for a minute.

One bang was sudden and loud as gunshot. Jack jumped right out of bed. I could see his naked body in the last of the firelight, long and lean and beautiful. That night was the first time I'd ever looked properly at a naked man. And the fear that made Jack jump out of bed like that intensified the nakedness.

'It's only the woodshed door,' I said. 'Come back to bed, my darling.'

'I'll shut it. I'll not be long,' said Jack. He lit a candle, pulled on some clothes, stooped to kiss first my breasts, then my mouth. I sat up, bolt upright, and saw myself in the tarnished mirror, my face blurred in candlelight, my eyes dark pools. The uncurtained window was a square of stars. The wind pulled purple clouds away from a quarter moon. I got out of bed, pushed the window open, leaned on the sill, my skin tightening in the autumn air.

The banging stopped. He came back to me. He pulled off his clothes, blew out the candle, and took me in his arms again. So you see, Hester dear, when I hear a wind like this one, I remember that surge of joy, that sheer delight, the strongest, purest feeling that I've ever known.

Much of my life has been lived out of joint. Some things have felt three-quarters right; that's had to be good enough. It's the same for you, Verity, I suspect, and that may be at least partly my fault. I don't have the power to put that right. But, Hester, my dear, you're young. I can't give you much in the way of pearls of wisdom, but I will say this – when you know something to be right, and true, then seize it with both hands.

I shan't write in this book again.

17

How could it have been so easy? One day she was Hester alone, childless spinster, last of her line. And the next – almost the next – she had – well, ramifications.

But how was she to avoid scaring Sebastian off? It occurred to her that he might well know who she was. It was unlikely that he could have reached the age of thirty without having had some conversation with one or the other of his parents about his half-sister, and her name had been well known among the English middle classes for at least five years. She had to assume, then, that Sebastian had chosen not to contact her. It was possible, even likely, that he would feel sickened at the prospect of anything to do with his father. It would be easy to reach him, via the theatre. The difficult part would be establishing some kind of dialogue with him, making the kind of contact that would assuage whatever it was in her that needed assuaging, what-ever kind of loneliness, or loss.

She couldn't just march up to him and say, 'Hey, I'm your sister.' She had to get some sense of his character first, to prepare the ground a little, and to do that she needed to remain unknown. The research she'd begun into Grandma Evelyn's life gave her the idea for her alias. She would pose as a freelance journalist, investigating the life of Simeon Oakes. There'd already been a little flurry of retrospective interest in her father since his death. In the mid 1970s Simeon, then a QC, had defended a cabinet minister accused of conspiracy to murder a call-girl. No murder had taken place, though there was evidence of one bungled attempt. The minister was a Tory, of course – not a very important minister, something like fisheries or junior trade and industry. Most people believed in his guilt, but he was acquitted in a blaze of publicity because of Simeon's skill in exposing the unreliability of the prosecution witnesses and the mercenary motives of Babette de Mount, the improbably named call-girl who, it turned out, was one of a stable of such fillies ridden regularly by the minister and his chums.

Yes, there was reason enough for researching the life of His Honour Judge Oakes. To give herself more gravitas, Hester emphasized Simeon's Viennese background. She claimed to be particularly interested in Jewish refugees who'd made their way to the top of the British Establishment. She explained all this on the telephone to Sebastian's agent. And the message was not from the agent but from Sebastian himself. Yes, he'd talk. Of course he would, thought Hester. Sebastian was in work, but he was hardly a superstar. All publicity was good publicity as far as an actor like Sebastian was concerned.

Hester hardly paused to wonder what her brother would think of her when her disguise was removed, either when he saw through it or when she chose to reveal herself to him. The whole business was so wrapped in deception that telling lies didn't feel like being dishonest; it just felt like acting in the spirit of the thing. And it meant that if Sebastian turned out to be truly awful, she could retreat without ever revealing herself. But she didn't believe he would be truly awful.

'Come to my flat,' he'd said, in a voice that had a vibration in it, like her father's, but without that middle-European harshness. 'Saturday, about eleven? Is that OK? That way I don't have to get up too early. I'm not good at mornings.'

The flat was 84B Allington Grove, one of those leafy,

highly sought-after crescents between Westbourne Grove and Notting Hill Gate. The leaves of the cherry trees were just beginning to show that lovely purple-pink that by mid October makes them glow like stained glass. The little front garden of 84B was unkempt, just two big mops of Michaelmas daisies and some dank hart's-tongue ferns to show that someone had once paid it some attention.

Hester paused before ringing Sebastian's doorbell. She could see him through the uncurtained windows. She stood out of sight, watching. He stood in front of a big mirror; he yawned, flexed his arms, then ran his hands through his thick dark hair. Hester rang, mentally rehearsing her new name. Helen O'Toole. She'd kept her real initials. It was easier to remember that way.

Her rumpled brother opened the door. Eleven on a Saturday morning looked as though it was crack of dawn for him. He wore floppy white drawstring trousers, a black T-shirt with a white oval on it, like a flattened halo, and nothing on his feet. He had an earring, silver, vaguely Celtic. He was sinewy where her father had been solid, but the way his limbs joined his torso, the strong neck jutting up from the square shoulders – that felt so terribly familiar. Her father's stance – no, not *her* father, *their* father, Who art-not in Heaven, Hester would have thought, but somewhere in this room, here, between them.

'Helen O'Toole,' she said. They shook hands; the first touch of shared flesh. His grasp was warm and firm, confident. 'I'll put the kettle on,' he said. 'Sorry about the mess.' The big room he showed her into reached from the front to the back of the house, kitchen at one end, living area at the other. It was indeed a mess. The kitchen was tatty pine units and an old-fashioned gas cooker. Sebastian prised open a knobless cupboard door with a fish slice. 'Coffee?'

'Absolutely.' Hester looked round. The flat was sunny, for a basement, because there were large windows at both ends. At the garden end the sunlight filtered through unchecked Virginia creeper; the dancing shadows were pleasing. Two half-collapsed sofas were covered with batik throws. There were unwashed glasses on a blond wood coffee table, books and magazines on the floor, a CD rack with more discs scattered round it than in it. Sebastian set down the coffee and waved his hand at the clutter. 'I'm afraid it gets like this when I'm working. I'll have a good go at it when the show's over.'

Hester had been wondering about a girlfriend. She looked for signs of a female presence, but saw none – no discarded scarves or glossy magazines. The magazines on the floor were those that come with the weekend papers. And yet it didn't quite feel like the flat of someone who lived alone. Perhaps he had lots of friends round. The dirty glasses and half-full ashtray suggested that.

'What else will you do once the show's over? Apart from tidy up?'

'I'll be off to Scotland like a shot. There's a cottage there, on the West Coast. No one there except red deer and seabirds. It's the perfect antidote to this London madness.'

'Is it your cottage?'

'Yes, my father gave it to my mother, and she gave it to me. As you're here to talk about my father, I suppose it's relevant. It was their little bolt-hole, love-nest, whatever. It's stunning – you can see Ireland. It's my favourite place in the world, I think.'

Nothing in the desk drawers had suggested the existence of this cottage. Hester felt almost physically choked by the knowledge that her father had spent a large part of his life in places and with people about which she knew nothing.

'Did your mother live in Scotland all the time?' she asked, though she knew the answer.

'God, no. They only got up there a couple of times a year. She lived here, in this flat. He bought this for her, as well, when she was pregnant with me. Salving his conscience, I suppose. Of course, you know that my father was married to someone else?'

'Yes, I know all about that. So you were born here?'

'Not literally. I was born in St Mary's, Paddington. But we lived here until Mum moved in with my stepfather, when I was eight.'

'And then?'

'And then she rented it out, for years. Every time there was a property boom Ralph wanted her to sell it, but she never would.'

'Sentimental attachment?'

'I guess so.'

'And you moved back in . . . ?'

'Last year. She left it to me.' He gave Hester a direct look, as if being matter-of-fact was the only way of dealing with it. 'Lung cancer. She was only fifty-six.'

So Verity's strange, spiteful guess had been right. Hester gave a small mew of concern, but expressed no further sympathy. She asked, 'Did your father ever live here with you?'

'He was here one or two nights a week, before he and Mum split up. But I wouldn't call it living here. There were a couple of his suits in Mum's wardrobe, but that was about it. He used to arrive late, often after I was in bed.'

'Did he come in to see you? Did he – take an interest?' Hester thought of her own nightly interrogations. She thought back, too, to an earlier time, when they lived in the mews house in Chelsea. His big hands lifting her up, out of bed, throwing her in the air, making her squeal. Then he'd toss her down on to the bed again, and her nightie would flap up over her face. Did Sebastian know that feeling, of laughter knotted with dread?

'Did he take an interest? Not much. Well, some, I suppose – let's be fair about this. I wasn't allowed to come out of my room if he arrived after bedtime, but he used to come in and read to me. I had a book of Robin Hood stories – I remember him reading those. And he used to take the change out of his pockets and let me count it, and if I got it right I could keep it.'

'And if you got it wrong?'

'He twisted my ear and put it back in his pocket.' Sebastian looked suddenly self-conscious. 'I haven't thought about that for ages, the ear-twisting. It hurt. Don't put that in whatever it is you're writing.'

'I won't.' That was the truth. Hester was an experienced interviewer. She knew that she had Sebastian, now. She'd be able to ask him anything she wanted, almost.

'And weekends? Was he ever there?'

'No. Maybe once or twice. I remember once playing football with him in the park, how weird it felt.'

'Did you ever ask why he couldn't stay?'

'Nope. Don't think so. I was only a kid, and kids just take things for granted, don't they?'

'Would you have wanted him to stay?'

Sebastian thought for a moment. 'I don't think so. I used to resent it when he turned up.'

'What did you resent?'

Sebastian shifted his position, rearranged his long legs. He didn't answer immediately. Then he said, 'He made Mum act differently. I mean, I had her all to myself, and then it would be one of Dad's days, and she'd look different, she'd smell different. She'd be absent-minded, try to put me to bed earlier, that kind of thing. Once she was making up her bed. Their bed – I never thought of it as their bed, but I bet she did. She'd bought new sheets, it was a big deal. And I got into it – I often did – and pretended I was in a wigwam or something, and she really lost it with me. Everything had to be perfect for Dad. She was a mistress, my mother. A real old-fashioned kept woman. That's her, behind you.'

Hester started; Sebastian laughed. 'Sorry, I didn't mean to spook you. I meant that photo. The black-and-white one.'

The photograph was extraordinarily good. Paulina lay on her stomach on a white fur rug, ankles crossed in the air, pointed chin resting on her folded hands, a string of pearls dangling from her fingers. Her black hair was coiled on top of her head, save for two ringlets just in front of each ear. Her eyes were immense, the brows and lashes almost architectural. 'She was very beautiful,' Hester said, with sincerity. Sebastian looked pleased.

'Bailey took that picture. Mum was a model, before me. She wasn't tall enough for catwalk, but she worked for cosmetic companies – Lancôme or something. And hand-modelling. She always looked after her hands.'

Hester thought of her own mother's hands, thin, red-knuckled, the fingertips purpled by her furtive, never-cured nail-biting. She imagined Paulina's smooth fingers, almond-tipped. She imagined them gliding the length of her father's back, raking through the springy golden hair. But it was Verity who held on to him. How had she managed that?

She turned a page of her notebook. 'How did your parents meet?' she asked. This was something she knew nothing about.

'He was knocking off a friend of hers. He was a complete bastard, my father, but I expect you've already found that out for yourself. Her friend – I think she was called Melanie, I don't know what happened to her, except that they didn't stay friends – anyway, she worked in a casino, and she'd met him there.'

'He was a gambler?'

'Oh, yeah. But under control. I never heard he got into serious money trouble. You'd know more about that than I would.'

It took a moment for Hester to remember that Sebastian attributed her knowledge of Simeon to her role as researcher, not as daughter. 'I'm at the early stages,' she said. 'Still talking to lots of people. But I think you're right about the money. Go on.'

'About Mum? Well, one night Melanie had to work an extra shift at the casino, which meant standing Dad up, and she couldn't get in touch with him, so like a fool she sent Mum along to tell him she couldn't make it. And that was that. Dad fell for Mum straight away. She had that effect on people. He chased her for a month before she gave in. She told him she'd had enough of married men, she wanted to settle down. But he filled her flat with lilies, day after day. Heart-shaped boxes of chocolates, jewellery, perfume, messages in the newspaper. Mum loved telling me about all that.'

'And did you like hearing about it?'

'Oh, yes. When I was little, it was part of the bedtime-story repertoire. My mother the princess. It was heady stuff. But when she used to harp on about it, towards the end of her life – well, that was just a bit sad.'

Hester longed to ask more about jilted Melanie. Of course, if she'd thought about it, she'd have realized that Paulina would be only one of a series, given artificial prominence perhaps, because she'd had Sebastian. But she found she hadn't imagined this. And the pain she felt for her mother grew.

'So it took a month. And then?'

'And then he booked the flights to Paris. Best hotel, separate rooms. No pressure. The taxi arrived at her door with two suitcases for her, already packed. New everything – beautiful stuff. He'd worked out her clothes size, shoes, everything. She was only twenty-one – I mean, was she expected to resist? She hopped into the taxi and off she went.'

Hester tried to suppress an image of her mother in her blue towelling dressing gown, her hair in a plastic bath hat, her feet reddened by hot water. 'And your mother told you all this?'

'When Dad wasn't around, she didn't have much else besides me.'

Hester knew she ought to switch the subject back to His Honour Judge Oakes, but she wanted more of Sebastian and Paulina. She wanted some of her flavour, the black-coffee-and-cigarette flavour of his boyhood. 'That must have put a lot of pressure on you,' she said, 'to be treated as a substitute for your father?'

'I didn't see it like that at the time, but yes, I suppose that's true. She used to like me to come and sleep in her bed sometimes, when she felt lonely. And she liked taking me out to eat in restaurants. Even when I was quite little. She'd get me to choose the wine. It was a kind of game.'

'So, from acting your father's role, you became an actor. Any connection?'

Sebastian smiled, but not with ease. 'Hey, this is getting heavy!'

Hester changed tack. 'So they went to Paris, and his wife knew nothing –?'

'Have you talked to his wife? Verity, isn't it?'

236

Hester's heart somersaulted. Had she talked to her mother? She replied, 'Yes, but not about this,' which was little more than the truth.

'Do you think she knows? It's something that's always bothered me.'

It was nice of him to be bothered. She prevaricated. 'She's quite a – quite a reserved woman. Quite hard to read. Did your mother ever mention her?'

'She never met her, as far as I know, but she used to make a few little references to her. She was scornful of her. I remember Mum and Lucia, my aunt, having a conversation, and Mum saying something that implied Dad's wife was no good in bed. That she didn't know how to make a man happy, or something. I should have been too young to understand, but I wasn't.'

Even at forty, one does not want to be forced to acknowledge the sexual life of one's parents. Hester felt a flare of not wholly reasonable rage against the luscious Paulina for daring to discuss Verity in such terms. To Sebastian she said, 'But your father stayed with her. The frigid wife. Why do you think that was?'

Sebastian looked surprised that she'd asked. 'Well, she was the business, wasn't she? House and home. She was the stability. My father may have been the love of Mum's life, but she was never more than his bit on the side. She tried to kid herself, but she knew it, really. That's why she married Ralph.'

'So Verity was the love of his life, all along?'

'No. My father didn't like women. He needed them; they kept him on track. But I don't reckon that anyone was the love of his life, unless it was his daughter.'

'You knew about his daughter? Your half-sister. Did you ever try to meet her?'

'I've thought about it. Since my father's death, I've thought about it a lot. But I'm worried about how I'd react to her. You see, I think I kind of hate her.'

Hester began to shiver. She couldn't control it, could only hope Sebastian wouldn't notice. 'Why should you hate her?' she asked, and she knew her voice sounded squeaky and cracked.

'It's not rational. That's why I hang back from meeting her, because it wouldn't be fair on her. But I hate Dad's wife, you see, because my mother taught me to despise her. But just despising her wasn't enough, because she hung on in there. She won. My mother lost. So I have to hate her. I think you tend to hate people you can't defeat. I do, anyway.'

'Why would hating the wife mean hating the daughter? Surely, if anyone's innocent –'

'Oh, sure, she's innocent. But guilt and innocence don't really come into it. I always hated the idea of the daughter, as soon as I knew about her, because she and her mother got everything and I got nothing. That's how I saw it – it was childish, but then I was a child.'

Hester put down her notebook. Her hands were shaking too much to pretend to write.

'My goodness,' she said, 'is that really the time? So sorry – I've got to be the other side of town in half an hour.'

Sebastian looked startled, even disappointed. 'Is that it?' he asked, with a lopsided smile. 'Are you done with me?'

'No – oh, no. By no means. I mean – if you don't mind, I'd love to see you again.'

'That's good,' said her brother, taking her hand, 'because I'd like to carry on, too. It feels right, somehow. Same time next week?'

'Perfect.' Was it just her imagination, or his actorish show of sincerity, or did he truly hold on to her hand more tightly and for longer than the rules of normal courtesy demanded?

The telephone rang almost as soon as she'd opened the door of her flat. It'll be him, she thought. He's changed his mind. He wants me to leave him alone.

It was Rosie. 'Hets? Where've you been? I've been trying to get hold of you all morning. Listen, I haven't got long. We're all off to the rare breeds farm to buy some chickens. Isn't that great? But I've got something to tell you. Can you guess?'

'You're pregnant!'

'Got it in one! I didn't mean to tell you for another month, but I was overcome with this irresistible urge –'

'Oh, Rosie, that's fantastic. A baby at Knighton – that's just what it needs. Do the others know?'

'I haven't told the kids yet, but I think they'll be fine about it. It's Angus who's been talking about babies the most, funnily enough. He's a nurturing kind of boy – like his father, really.'

'And Robin's delighted?'

'Oh, yes. Thrilled to bits. He loves to know he's not firing blanks.'

'I'd have thought he'd already had plenty of evidence that he isn't.'

'Well, I suppose so, but he enjoys a bit of reassurance. You know what men are like.'

'Do I? I wish I did. I think I've forgotten.'

'Oh, Hets, I do wish – no, I mustn't say it. But I can't help thinking it.'

Hester knew full well what Rosie was thinking. A joint pregnancy; the two old friends, sitting together on the terrace at Knighton, warming their huge bellies in the spring sunshine. 'Sorry, Rosie. No chance.'

'Oh dear. What about – no, I won't ask. Robin's tooting the horn – I must go. Oh, but one other thing. I told your ma. I told her on her birthday. Hope you don't mind?'

'Mind? Why should I mind?' But Hester found she did mind.

'Well, that I told her first. But it just felt appropriate. Oh, God, Robin's going mad. They're all waiting for me. Bye for now.' And she went.

No chance, repeated Hester, aloud to herself. No chance, no way, not on your life. She paced the flat, opened the balcony windows, stretched her long limbs in the gentle September air. 'On the other hand,' she said to the plane tree, 'I could just do it.'

Guy, or Solly. She had only to choose. Or –

Because I'd like to carry on, too. It feels right, somehow. She recalled Sebastian's voice as clearly as if he were standing there beside her. She thought of his skin, smooth above the drawstring of his trousers, somewhere between golden and olive. She thought of her hand in his, that prolonged, firm grasp.

That way, madness lay. 'Don't even think about it,' she told the quiet street.

She rang Guy first, and suggested lunch. She didn't want him in her flat again. They walked in Regent's Park; they sat on a bench and held hands. 'I'm sorry about that night at the theatre,' she said, 'and I'm even sorrier about Rosie's party. Please be patient with me, Guy. I think I'm getting there.'

He was tender and solicitous, and stroked her arm, but attempted nothing more. He called her attention to the beauties of the season, to light effects and cloud formations and the activity of squirrels. When they parted, Hester said, 'Guy, you know I've never seen your flat.'

He missed a beat. What didn't he want her to see? Evidence of debt, or of other women? 'Well,' he said, caressing her cheek with his forefinger, 'we must put that right. Of course we must. Come to dinner. I cook now, you know. Er – how's next Wednesday?'

Hester had studied her reproductive cycle as if revising for Biology O-level. Peak fertility should be this weekend. Next Wednesday would be a little late.

'I'll ring you,' she said, kissing him lightly on the mouth.

Back at work, she pondered. She was going to deal with it all at once. Solly, Friday night. Solly would have no objections. She would simply fail to insert her cap. He wouldn't know, he'd never taken the slightest interest in that side of things. And if she did become pregnant – well, would she even tell him?

Guy, Saturday night. Forget about his flat if it was going to create problems. She'd take control. She'd book a smart London hotel for Saturday night, one of those town-house hotels with Japanese food on room service and underwater flower arrangements and every coffee spoon designed to within an inch of useful life. Guy would love all that. He'd love it even more if she was paying.

So. Solly Friday night, Guy Saturday night. And an interview with Sebastian in between.

'How's the research on your grandmother going, Hester?' asked Jean, the iron-haired research assistant, as she shuffled past Hester's desk to reach the coffee machine.

Hester jumped. For how long had she been staring into space?

'Not as quickly as I'd hoped, actually. I thought I'd hole

up somewhere in a remote cottage and just crack on with it.'

'That sounds sensible. You don't want to let the idea grow cold. It would be a pity to waste such an interesting grandmother.' Jean poured coffee for herself without asking whether Hester wanted any. Penny always asked. Hester was never sure which was the more irritating.

The idea of this working holiday hadn't occurred to her until this moment, but now it struck her as a good one. She would take herself off and think about her grandmother and let a baby grow inside her. She'd go somewhere far away, where Solly and Guy would be unable to find her. She had some holiday owing to her. She reckoned she could manage a fortnight. She looked at her work diary and highlighted some dates.

That evening, she rang Solly. 'Friday night?' she said. 'My gaff?' She knew that using words like 'gaff' didn't suit her, but when she talked to Solly they just seemed to slip out.

18

The parcel sat in the middle of the small round breakfast table. Verity could leave it there for as long as she chose. There was nobody else to open it, touch it, even glance at it. On its own, it had no power to arouse curiosity; its power was under Verity's control. She had to remind herself that this was the case. Even now, five months after Simeon's death, she had not fully comprehended the limitlessness of her solitude.

She left the parcel untouched for three days. She shopped a little, gardened a little, did a little housework – Mrs Davidge she'd bequeathed to Rosie with, she discovered, only faint regret. The contents of the parcel would be in some way revelatory, that was obvious. It was a boobytrap, laid for her by her mother twenty years ago. Verity took her emotional temperature at intervals. She watched for the moment when opening it would be the right thing to do.

'For Verity and Hester. To be opened after my death.' How typical of a novelist to attempt to control outcomes! How typical, too, of Evelyn Albery to attach such importance to whatever it was she had to reveal! Verity, emptying the sweepings of the kitchen floor, banged the bin lid down with uncharacteristic force. In the quiet cottage the sound startled like a drum. Why couldn't Evelyn just have said whatever it was she wanted to say, straight out, while she was alive?

Verity thought about those final months, of her twice-weekly duty visits to the Ewes Green cottage. She liked to have a pretext for her calls, like bringing something from the kitchen garden, or a letter from Hester. She'd asked her mother, many times, to be allowed to do her shopping for her, because that would have killed several birds of duty with one stone, but her offer was usually rejected. Evelyn liked stumping along Ewes Green High Street with a tartan shopping bag on wheels. She seemed to take to playing the part of a shabby old woman with relish; she wore short boots, sheepskin lined with zips up the front, and a plastic rain hat that tied under the chin and folded away like a fan.

The visits became easier towards the end. Evelyn did not display the usual wanderings of old age, did not become muddled or forgetful, or even querulous. Rather, she seemed increasingly remote. Her interest in Verity's activities dwindled to almost nothing – a relief, as this interest had only ever manifested itself in the form of interference and unsolicited advice. She seemed gentler, or a little vague – no, not vague, but detached, as if her living was being done elsewhere, in some mental space that had little to do with this cottage, this shapeless octogenarian body, this walking stick looped over the arm of the chair.

What had they talked about in those last months? Nothing, apparently, of any great significance. Unlike many old people, Evelyn had not particularly wanted to harp on about the past. She hadn't seemed much concerned, either, with passing on pearls of wisdom to her only child and grandchild, though Verity did remember that at times her mother would strive to impress on Hester the importance of certain historical events – the suffragette movement, for instance, came in for quite a lot of emphasis. A waste of a resource, thought Verity now. Evelyn had had an interesting life, even a remarkable one; questions should have been asked. But Verity's pride and Hester's youth had prevented that from happening.

If Verity had taken her mother's remoteness for indifference, she'd been wrong, she thought now. There was something in the parcel Rosie had found that had been carefully prepared. Why had Verity not come across it before? If the parcel had transferred itself from the Ewes Green cottage to Knighton, how had she not noticed? It was not as if she'd been blinded with grief.

She considered the circumstances of her mother's death. It had been Simeon who found her, oddly enough. It was a Saturday in October, the weather had turned chilly and Verity wanted to check that her mother's heating was in good working order, but she had a cold which she didn't want to pass on. Simeon volunteered to go. He rang the cottage; no reply. 'She's probably out shopping,' said Verity. 'Try later.' An hour later there was still no reply. 'I'll go and check,' said Simeon. 'You never know.' He took the spare keys to the cottage with him.

He'd found Evelyn sitting in her armchair looking out on to the street, except that she wasn't looking at anything any more, and never would again. The doctor said she'd been dead a while, probably since the night before. 'Do you mean hours?' questioned Verity. 'You do mean hours, not days?' 'No, no, not days. And it would have been instant. Her heart just stopped. Old age, nothing more.'

Evelyn was fully clothed. Remains of supper were on the kitchen table – a boiled-egg shell, a banana skin – but there was no evidence that she had started to get ready for bed. It was some time before Simeon called Verity. He called the doctor first, and then, he said, he did some tidying up. He carried the body to the bedroom, laid it on the bed and covered it. It seemed disrespectful, he said, to leave her sitting in the chair like that, her mouth and her eyes open.

Now, it occurred to Verity, Simeon must have found that

parcel. She and Mrs Davidge between them had cleared out the cottage in the course of the following week, and she didn't see how they could have overlooked a thing like that. Had Simeon brought it to Knighton, hidden it in the cupboard? She could think of no other explanation. There was no end, it seemed, to the amount of control other people had seen fit to exercise over her life.

She picked up the parcel and examined it. The padded envelope was self-adhesive, but a strip of Sellotape had been used for extra security. That didn't necessarily mean that Simeon had opened it. Evelyn might well have stuck on the Sellotape herself.

Verity could see no obvious tamper marks. She opened the envelope and drew out a notebook, A4 size, black with a red binding. An ordinary notebook, the sort that could have been bought at the newsagent's in Ewes Green. Verity opened it.

'1st January 1980.' It was a diary. That was all she needed to know. She closed it, put it back into the envelope, sealed it with fresh Sellotape. She'd had enough of other people's affairs. Whatever it was her mother wanted to tell her, she wasn't going to listen.

But it was addressed to Hester too. She had no right to destroy or withhold it. She would summon Hester, exercise a little control of her own. She'd tell her of the decision she'd made about Sebastian and the money. She'd hand over the book, on the condition that Hester keep its contents to herself. And after that, perhaps she would be free.

She set the parcel back in the middle of the breakfast-room table, where it would be safe from anyone, herself included. And then she reached for the telephone.

19

Hester slipped her body, still alive from the shower, into Solly's red dress. This could be the last time she ever put it on. She wanted Solly to sire her child, not father it. If a baby happened – and somehow she hadn't got round to thinking that it might not – then her life would change, and Solly would belong to the past. Would she miss her late-night adventures south of the river? Would she yearn for the creak of his leather jacket, his smoky kisses, the calluses on the palms of his hands? Perhaps. But it had never been meant to last for ever.

Guy, though. If there was to be a baby, then Guy couldn't be quite so easily dismissed. She had to accept that a baby would mean Guy in her life for the foreseeable future. But the problem with the future was that it wasn't foreseeable at all. The future was murky – swirling mists in a tarnished crystal ball. What if the baby was Solly's? Would she know? What would she do about Guy then? She pushed it out of her mind. The future could wait. It was the present she had to deal with.

She dabbed Opium on her neck and wrists – Solly's favourite, not hers. She usually went barefoot in the flat, but she'd bought some absurdly high strappy red shoes – a goodbye present to Solly, though he wouldn't know it. They'd cost an incredible amount, but she wanted to give him a good send-off. He'd said he'd arrive early tonight, because there was something he had to go on to. That was unusual, but she wouldn't question him. She never did.

He rang the bell at seven. It still made her heart jump, every time. She would have to be strong, to leave it all behind.

He looked different – a clean, open-necked shirt, pale suede jacket, narrow boots; he looked like George Best, spruced up between benders. She'd often thought he looked like George Best, he had that same dimple in his chin. But he kept his face averted. He was closed to her, though she did not know why. To the sight of her in her mile-high red shoes he reacted not at all.

He came in, but he didn't sit down. His stance was awkward, reverent, like a policeman come to break bad news. She brought out a bottle of beer, dewy from the fridge, but he waved it away.

'Solly,' she said, 'is everything OK?'

'You and me,' he said, 'you know, we've always – well, we've had good times. We've had great times, don't get me wrong. I'm not being funny, but –' he sighed, immensely. 'Hester, I've got to tell you something. May as well get on with it.'

He never used her name. If he called her anything, he called her doll. The inappropriateness of it had always amused her. Now, she knew that he would never call her that again. She moved out of the doorway, suddenly conscious that the light from the kitchen would reveal the absence of underwear beneath her dress. Not that he was looking.

'Just tell me, Sol. What's her name?'

'Jody. She's . . . she's great. She's fantastic. I think she's the one. I never thought that about no one before, but – she's a lady, you know? I mean, she's not any kind of tart.'

'I think you'd better go now,' said Hester.

Solly nodded, and made for the door. 'I didn't mean it

to sound that way,' he mumbled, 'but I just needed to tell you that – you know – things have got to be different.' He stretched out a hand as if to touch her. She stepped aside.

'Yes, I know. You don't need to say any more. Goodbye, Solly.'

When he'd gone, she put the chain across the door.

She was not alone with her chagrin for long. Almost the moment Solly had gone, the telephone rang. She let it go on to message, because she couldn't imagine there was anyone in the world she'd want to speak to, just at that moment. But she was wrong.

Sebastian's voice. 'Helen? Seb Oakes here. My understudy's on tonight, the director wants to give him a go. So I'm ringing on the off chance that you're free and that you'd like to meet for a drink or whatever. But you're out, so – well, see you tomorrow morning, I guess.'

There was disappointment in his voice, she was sure of it. She rang back, straight away. 'No, I'm not out. Just missed the phone. I'd love to meet. Where, do you think?'

'Have you eaten yet?'

Had she eaten? She honestly couldn't remember. She looked at the clock and thought, I probably haven't. 'Not really. Have you?'

'No, unless you count a tube of Pringles. Do you know the Risen Moon, on the corner of – you do? Shall we meet there? Half past – does that give you enough time?'

'Plenty. See you there.'

Hester pulled off the short red dress, folded it neatly, out of force of habit, and stowed it in a carrier bag together with the ridiculous shoes. Dustbin or Oxfam; she could decide in the morning. But meanwhile there was tonight, a balmy September evening, and a date in a Notting Hill gastro pub with her secret brother.

She stood in front of her long mirror, scrutinizing her nakedness. Was she deluding herself, to think her forty-year-old body could pass for ten years younger? She carried no excess weight. A little cellulite dimpled the tops of her thighs – hardly any, though, compared to the almost geological formations she noticed and winced at on strugglers at the gym and swimming pool. She could still get away with going bra-less, if she felt like it, just. She had observed her post-breastfeeding friends with pity, their sad empty sacks, striated with stretch marks. Her stomach, too; the skin taut across her hips, no bulge, no wrinkles. Yes, there were dusky creases she didn't care for in the folds of her armpits, and the pads of skin on the points of her elbows were like elephants' knees in miniature, but weren't everybody's? It was a good body, tall and slim and straight. It was a body that could still do her work for her.

She opened her wardrobe. The dress hung there, that dress the colour of a skinned peach. Its shimmer seemed to light up the dark interior. The dress she wore to the theatre, the night she found Sebastian. Her lucky dress.

She drew it out and held it at arm's length. Could she really wear such a thing to a pub, albeit a fashionable West London pub that would probably be full of aspiring actors and models? Well, why not? She could dress it down, with leather flip flops and a denim jacket. She was tall and slender enough to get away with that. Sebastian's telephone call had been one piece of luck. She needed this dress to extend her luck still further.

He was already there when she arrived. He rose to greet her, out of the smoky shadows. His linen shirt was rumpled and only half tucked into his jeans, but he was freshly shaven and his dark curls were still damp from the shower.

A bottle of wine and two glasses waited on the table. 'I hope you like rosé,' he said. 'It's kind of my flavour of the month.'

The room was warm; there was no reason not to slip off her jacket. 'Hey,' said Sebastian, 'that's quite a dress. Does the wine match it?' He held his glass against her, pressed it lightly into the space between her breasts. 'Nearly. Anyway, it looks pretty.'

Hester smiled. To her, the colour of the rosé was nothing like the colour of the dress. 'Something I've always thought,' she said, 'is that men and women see colours differently. But of course everyone thinks that the way they see a colour is the right way. I mean, your shirt. What colour is that?'

'Blue,' said Sebastian. 'Right?'

'Wrong! It's green – jade green. That's not blue, by any stretch of the imagination.'

'It's the lighting in here. I swear it's blue. It was blue when I put it on.'

'I'm afraid not. Jade green. But it's a nice shirt. It suits you.' She looked him full in the face, and smiled her warmest smile.

He raised his glass, tapped hers with it. 'So, what other differences are there between men and women, apart from the fact that we tend to be right about colour?'

'Hmm. There are several. There's the fact that, however long a couple's been together, it's always the woman who remembers to send *his* auntie a birthday card, and she goes on doing it even after they've split up. And then there's the obvious one, about reading maps –'

'I can't read a map to save my life.'

'And I'm rather good at it. So that won't do. Well, men

laugh at different things. There isn't a woman alive who thinks Mr Bean is funny. Men think it's amusing to watch someone falling over, but I've never met a woman who enjoyed slapstick. Stuff like Charlie Chaplin –'

'Leaves you cold?' put in Sebastian. 'Well, me, too, actually. But finding Charlie Chaplin embarrassingly unfunny's a generation thing, don't you think? I think what you find funny's got much more to do with the age you are and the times you were brought up in than with whether you're male or female.'

'You mean, like Shakespeare's jokes?'

'Yeah, just like that. Don't get me wrong, I love Shakespeare, he's God as far as I'm concerned, but his jokes are Not Funny.'

'Nor are God's.'

'Does He make any?'

'It depends how you look at life, but – yes, all the time.'

Sebastian looked at her full in the face, held her gaze. 'I suppose God's main joke is fate, coincidence, whatever. He's a corny scriptwriter.'

'Did your father have a sense of humour? Talking of God . . .'

He groaned. 'You're not far wrong, you know. I'm sure that's how he liked to see himself. You know, being a judge and all that . . . But to answer your question – yes, he would have said he had a sense of humour, but it used to make me cringe. He loved wordplay – there was always some thumping great pun or double meaning. I can't stand that sort of thing.'

'Shakespeare again.'

'You got it. Any joke that needs a footnote to explain itself is dead in the water as far as I'm concerned.'

'Do you think your father liked that sort of thing because

English was his second language? Would that have made him more aware of the meanings of words, perhaps?'

'It hadn't occurred to me, but you could have a point.'

'Did he ever use German? I mean, that was his first language – maybe his only language – until he was, what, fourteen?' As she spoke, Hester realized that she had never properly registered before that, no, her father had never spoken a word of German in her hearing.

'I never really thought about it. I don't think I ever heard him speak German. It was an option, for me to do it at school, but I chose Russian and I seem to remember that Dad was pleased. I don't know whether he kept his German up. It's shocking, how little I know about him. Hurry up and write your book, so I can find out.' He smiled and winked.

'My book – oh, yes. Well – preliminary stages and all that. Did he ever talk to you about his early life? About when he lived in Vienna?'

'Never. Anything I know comes from Mum, and that's not much. I know his family were killed, or they disappeared, but I don't even know their names.'

'Eichenbaum. Josef and Anna were the parents. And there was a sister too, Elisabeta.'

'Hey, thanks for researching my family tree for me. My grandparents and my aunt, and I never even knew what they were called! They don't sound very Jewish, do they? I thought –'

'They're kind of cross-cultural, aren't they, those names? I expect that was deliberate. I don't think the family had practised Judaism for quite some time. They believed themselves to be thoroughly assimilated. I suppose that's why they didn't see disaster coming.'

'I'm half Jewish,' said Sebastian, thinking aloud. 'Half Austrian Jewish, and a quarter Italian, on my mother's side.

I'm hardly English at all, and yet it rarely occurs to me that I'm anything but. Time I found out more about my heritage. Somehow, it becomes more interesting as you get older.' He swirled his wine round his glass. 'God, I'd love a cigarette. But I said I'd quit when I turned thirty, and I'm sticking to it. What about you, Helen O'Toole?'

The false name startled her. 'Me? I've never smoked.'

'No, no. I mean, what's your background?'

'I'm – well, I'm a mixture, like you. Really quite similar to you.'

'With a name like O'Toole, you should be Irish, but you don't look Irish.'

'What does it involve, looking Irish?'

'You know – freckles, red hair, flat faces. Or little wizened pointy ones, like jockeys. But you look too elegant to be Irish. There are Irish beauties, too, of course, with long dark hair and pale skin and green eyes. But I don't associate them with being – well, poised. You're poised, Helen O'Toole.'

Hester laughed, and shifted a little, to make her dress shimmer. She picked up the bottle and refilled both their glasses. 'That's enough about me. I'm supposed to be asking the questions. Your father – what did he look like?'

'Surely you know what he looked like?'

'I want to know what he looked like to *you*. I want you to describe him.'

'All right. Well. Um. Where do I begin? When I was a child, he looked very big. Broad, and tall. His face seemed a long way off. But that's not very interesting, because I guess that's how adults always look to children. Let's see if I can do better.' He took a gulp of wine. 'My father had blue eyes, light blue, and they were quite protuberant. They used to get watery when he laughed and that scared me a bit because it made me unsure whether he was laughing or crying, and the idea that he might be crying was horrendous. He had a big nose with a bump in it, and thick wiry eyebrows that were almost ginger. The rest of his hair was springy and a sort of tawny colour, with some silver in it. He had very hairy hands – the hair kind of curled out from under his cuffs, like smoke. His hands made me think of a lion's paws. He was probably quite hairy all over, though I wouldn't know. I never saw him naked.'

'Never?'

'Does that surprise you? I suppose sons do usually see their fathers naked, don't they? But he just didn't feature in my life that much. And I was under strict instructions never to go into their bedroom when he was around. I hated that. I used to wake up early and sit in my bedroom playing with my soldiers for what seemed like hours.'

'I can't imagine you playing with soldiers. You don't strike me as the warlike type.'

'Oh, I wasn't particularly interested in making them fight. They were characters, acting little dramas. I was an actor-in-waiting, even then. I didn't have any girly toys, not having a sister, so I used those coloured plastic clothes pegs and pretended they were women. Dad gave me those soldiers, come to think of it. They arrived in a great big box one Christmas. That was pretty exciting.'

'Was he ever there at Christmas?' Hester knew the answer.

'Nope. Not once. Christmas we always spent at my Aunt Lucia's. It must have been grim for Mum. No wonder she jumped at the chance when Ralph proposed.'

'Tell me about Ralph.'

'There's not a lot to tell. He was dreadful. Shortie raincoat, grey plastic shoes, sideburns. That sort of thing. Homophobic, racist, a real bigot. He was an estate agent. He couldn't stand me.'

'How did your mother meet him?'

'She got a job with his company. Just a little secretarial job. I think she was trying to wean herself off Dad. She must have twigged by then that he was never going to leave his wife, so she thought she'd better carve out a bit of independence for herself. But Mum didn't do independence, bless her. She hadn't been there long before Ralph slipped a ring on her finger. Platinum – dead vulgar.'

They both laughed. 'Wasn't it a bit of a comedown, from modelling for Lancôme to typing in an estate agent's office?' Hester asked.

'Mum had to get used to comedowns. They were the story of her life. For women who've based their careers round being beautiful, they usually are.'

'But she must have still been good-looking' – Hester didn't feel quite generous enough to use the world 'beautiful' – 'when she married Ralph. Still young, too. Young enough to have more children.'

'They didn't, thank God. Ralph didn't want children. He had two grown-up daughters of his own. Linda and Beverly. They moved to Canada with their mother. I only met them a couple of times, but that was plenty, thank you very much.' He pulled a tragicomic face and waved to a passing waitress for a second bottle. 'Hey, where's your notebook? Shouldn't you be writing things down? Or are you recording me?'

Hester could think of no way of pretending, so she said, 'Neither. I'm just enjoying listening to you. And I've got a good memory.' She leaned a little closer, folded her arms under her breasts. She wanted to reach out and touch his jawbone with her forefinger. 'Sebastian. When was the last time you saw Simeon Oakes?'

'Not that long before he died. I hardly ever saw him after

he and Mum split up, for the first four years. Once in a blue moon he'd swoop down on me at my boarding school, watch a play or a match if I was in it, and take me out to dinner. I dropped out of school before A-levels – did I tell you that before? – and he was pretty pissed off with me – all that money down the drain, as he saw it. He didn't make any attempt to see me for at least a couple of years after that, and I was certainly in no hurry to contact him. Then when I began to make it in a small way, when my acting began to take off, he started turning up to my shows. I remember I was doing some Pinter thing at the Bush, and there he was in the front row; it really put me off my stride. I don't usually take in people in the audience, but Dad always gave off – I don't know – "aura"'s the wrong word, too spiritual – but you could always sense when he was there, like a kestrel, hovering. But it seemed he was after some kind of reconciliation, and I thought, well, I can manage an expensive dinner once in a while. So that's what started happening, and he'd order a grand wine and try to get me interested in it, and hold forth about things he thought I ought to know about. He didn't take much interest in what was going on in my life, but that suited me, as I'm sure you can imagine.'

'Did he ever mention his own private life – his marriage or –' Hester's scalp prickled as she asked.

'Never. The meetings I had with him were kind of sealed off. We had an unspoken understanding about where the boundaries were. He hardly ever mentioned Mum, either, or only in the most superficial way. But when I realized – when it got so bad' – Hester was startled to see that he was struggling against tears – 'Sorry. When she was dying, and there was no mistaking it, I thought he ought to know. So I arranged to meet him one lunchtime, which was unusual, because normally he made the arrangements. He agreed to meet, but he was abrupt about it. I didn't mess about. I told him everything he needed to know – what state she was in, where she was, how long the doctors thought it would take. He took it all in, took it seriously. He said, "If I went to visit her, do you think that would be the right thing to do?" It was the only time he'd ever asked for my opinion about anything at all.'

'And you said?'

'I said I couldn't make that decision for him. I said, "I'll just have to leave you to make up your own mind about that." And he nodded, and called for the bill, though we hadn't finished eating. He left the restaurant in a hurry. We said goodbye – he always shook my hand, rather too hard – and I set off in the opposite direction, but then on a whim I turned and followed him at a distance. He stood on a street corner and made a phone call. This woman came out of a café opposite and went over to where he was standing. He put his arms round her and off they went. And I just thought, you bastard, I never want to see you again.'

'Was it his wife, do you think?' Hester was sure it was not.

Her brother's laugh was short and bitter. 'Shoulder-length blonde hair, about thirty-five years old? I think not.'

'And did he visit your mother?'

'No. Well, if he did, she didn't mention it. And I think she would have told me. It would have been a big deal for her.'

'Did she talk about him, during her . . . when she was in hospital?'

'Not much. I think she wanted to, because quite often she'd say, "Your father gave me this" or "Have you still got that – whatever – he gave you?" So I guess she was trying to open the subject, but I always shied away from it. I never could stand people trying to probe my feelings, trying to make me feel something in a particular way.'

'Same here. I can't stand that either. I'm surprised you don't object to talking to me.'

'But you're not directing me, you're just asking. That's different. It's quite therapeutic, actually.' Sebastian refilled their glasses. 'One thing Mum did talk about a lot, and that was the cottage in Scotland. It had been let for years – holiday lets. She and Ralph hardly ever went there. I don't think Ralph could see the point of it, except to bring in a bit of extra income. But she flatly refused to sell it, and she really, really wanted me to keep it and use it. I think all the associations she had with it were happy. It was a sort of cocoon, where nothing bad could touch her.'

'Had so many bad things touched her?'

Sebastian shrugged. 'You couldn't call it a happy life.'

There was a pause. Hester traced patterns in the condensation on the side of the wine chiller. 'It must have been difficult for you,' she said at last, 'having no one to share the burdens, I mean – stepsisters you didn't want to know, and a half-sister you'd never seen but hated anyway.'

'Did I say I hated my half-sister? Oh, I did, didn't I? Well, yes, I hated her in one way, but I had a strong sense of her, too. She was a real person to me, much more so than the dreadful Linda and Beverly. She still is real to me, in a way, because I know who she is. She's on the radio. You must have listened to her – Hester Oakes.'

Hester swallowed and nodded. 'But you never contacted her.'

'No. I could have done, easily. But I never have. And funnily enough, I've never told my friends that she's my sister, either. I really don't think I've mentioned it to anyone before tonight. I suppose I'd need a shrink to help me figure out why.'

'Do you know what she looks like?' Hester's heart pounded. 'Would you recognize her in the street?'

'I don't think so. I don't think she's ever on TV, or if she is, I've missed it. Dad had a photo of her in his wallet. He never took it out and showed me, but he sometimes left the wallet lying around.'

Hester held his gaze. 'What did she look like?'

'Fair hair, thin nose. A sort of thoroughbred look – very English. It was one of those passport photos. You couldn't see much. And she'll have changed a lot since then.'

Hester knew which picture it was. One of the spares from the set she'd had done when she'd needed her own passport for the first time, to go and stay with her German exchange family. She would have been fourteen. 'Do you think' – she began, pushing a drop of wine along the table top with the tip of her forefinger – 'have you ever thought that having a child would help? Are you ever tempted to create some kind of family of your own? To fill in the gaps, or – sorry, I shouldn't ask. It's a bit too personal.'

Sebastian was frowning. 'No, no, it's not. It's a perfectly fair question. It's supposed to be what we all want, isn't it, to pass on your genes, but I don't know that I'm so very enamoured of mine. I mean, my parents – that wasn't a good set-up. I was a mistake. My father was totally screwed up by what happened to him – not his fault, you could argue, but he did a lot of damage to the people in his life. Mum, me, probably his wife and daughter, too. I always thought it was ironic that his job was judging other people. No, I'm quite happy to dump his genes in the dustbin of history, and serve him right. I want to move on.'

'A lot of people see having a child as a way of moving forward, of putting things right.'

'Sounds like the triumph of hope over experience to me. Anyway, it's not an option for me, so, no, I don't think about it.'

'Why is it not an option?' Oh God, should she have asked that?

'Dylan wouldn't want to. I mean, I know it's perfectly possible these days, and people pay surrogate mothers and give the babies silly names like Cinnamon and, oh, I don't know, Sugarplum, and dress them in designer outfits, but Dylan wouldn't be into any of that. He lives in the present, and I guess I do too. That's probably why we're so close.'

'Dylan?'

'Don't say I haven't told you about him! My partner, Dylan. He's Australian – he's a stuntman. I met him on the set of the one and only Hollywood movie I had a part in. Six lines – I was the token posh Englishman. Dylan had to abseil down the side of Caesar's Palace in Las Vegas. The movie was a complete turkey, but at least I met Dylan. That was four years ago, we've been together ever since.'

Of course, of course. Straight men didn't talk like that. Something spun round, fast, inside Hester's head. For a moment she thought she was going to black out.

Sebastian carried on, with the satisfied obliviousness that insulates happy couples, which to the listener seems either sweet and touching or irritating and smug. Talking about Dylan was clearly a favourite pastime. He provided Hester with a kind of verbal CV of the beloved, including a list of his especial virtues and graces. While Hester nodded and smiled, she felt a decision gathering inside her.

And then she was listening again, with closer attention.

'What you said about being alone, about carrying burdens – that bothers Dylan,' Sebastian was saying. 'He's from a great big happy family – they're scattered all over the world, but they speak to each other the whole time. He's a bit sad that I've got so little family. He'd love it if there was more of me.'

Hester cleared her throat. 'Sebastian, I've got news for you. There *is* more of you, and it's here in front of you, if you want to take it.' She opened her bag and took out the identity card she used at work to get through the security barrier. 'I'm not sure that this is the best way of telling you, but I'm not sure of anything right now. I've been deceiving you. I'm not a journalist, and my name's not Helen O'Toole. And I'm not writing a book about your father, who is actually *our* father.' She pushed the card across the table to him. 'You've already said you hated me. Now you've got reason to. Even more reason.'

She'd imagined this moment in all sorts of ways, and some of them made her blush. But whichever way she'd imagined it, she'd been wrong. Sebastian stared, open-mouthed with astonishment, and then he reached over and took her hand. He fanned her fingers out, turned her hand palm upwards, examined it closely. Then he ran the tip of his forefinger along the lifeline that curved through the centre of her palm.

'My flesh and blood,' he said. Then he looked at her face. 'Hey, why are you crying?'

20

October 2000

This is Sebastian's cottage; this is where I am. Alone for a fortnight – alone with a suitcase full of my grandmother's books and papers. My mobile doesn't work here on the ragged west coast of Scotland, and I'm eleven miles from the nearest pint of milk. So, no excuses; I'm going to begin.

'Drive slowly once you're past the lion gate,' Sebastian had said. 'It's very easy to miss.' I collected a hire car at Glasgow airport and let his directions draw me over grey stone bridges, past steep white rivulets smashing through bracken the colour of foxes, along the shores of flat pewter-sheened lochs, through wind and rain and mist. Any sense of where I'd come from fell away behind me; everything narrowed to a focal point, as it must have done for my father and Paulina all those years ago.

The lion gate I was to look out for was the wrought-iron entrance to a large estate. A long drive led up to the house; all I could see were grey Victorian turrets pointing up out of a battalion of beech trees. The turrets would have looked grand if the hills hadn't looked so much grander. The beech trunks shone dull like armour in the gleam of an afternoon sun that pushed down shafts through swells of cloud. Two stone lions crouched on top of the gateposts, their ferocity smoothed by time. A red deer tiptoed out by the side of the gate, lifted its head, and pulled away.

'Don't turn down the drive,' Sebastian had told me, 'carry

straight on.' The cottage, once part of the estate, was right down by the sea. Once, it had housed farm labourers; you'd have needed hundreds of acres of this thin-skinned rocky ground to pull together any kind of living, and the sheep still wander right down to the shore, grazing on whatever's there. Other low, white-walled cottages stand along the sea road with gaping roofs and rafters blackened by fire. What had made Simeon single out this one for salvation?

Dark was falling when I arrived – though 'falling' is the wrong word. Dusk was seeping across the hills; behind the tangled thorn trees the light thickened, grey and soft, but out to sea there was still a band of colour, a strip of orange bandaging the horizon beneath a mass of purple cloud. I parked in the shelter of a stone wall and began to unload. As I lugged my first two fistfuls of carrier bags – I'd bought food for the whole fortnight in Safeway in Dumbarton, an interesting exercise in itself – a heavy shape flopped across the stony path in front of me. A baby seal! Beyond the white fluffy stage, but too young, surely, to manage on its own. The rolling of the sea had lessened now, but earlier the day had been squally. The seal must have been hurled over the beach by a powerful wave, and not had the sense to find its way back again. I looked about – no one in sight, of course. The seal lay beating on the sharp stones, exposed, like an organ ripped from a living body. It had the slippery density of a pig; I didn't think I'd be able to pick it up. I stood behind it and clapped my hands, startling myself with my own human noise, then flapped tentatively at its tail. It started to move away from me. I followed, stamping to make the ground vibrate, to encourage its forward movement. At last it had humped its way to the sea's edge. 'You're on your own now,' I said aloud. 'I can't do any more to help you.' I zipped my fleece up to my chin and sat on a flat boulder, watching the seal turn dark and graceful in the water. It was gone in a moment, but I gazed out to sea until the strip of orange on the horizon had burned itself out.

Back at the cottage, it was all but dark. One of the carrier bags I'd left propped against the stone wall had toppled over, and even with a torch I wasn't sure I'd retrieved everything that had spilled out. I unlocked the door – 'Give it a kick, near the bottom,' Sebastian had said – and stepped over the threshold, imagining my father. Their first time, had he carried Paulina in?

I propped the front door open, to let the sea wind disperse the long-locked-up smell of a holiday house. The caretaker had laid a fire. I held a match to the twists of newspaper and was glad to have a source of sound in the place that wasn't either me or the wind. The double bed was made up, the top sheet folded down. I set up camp, as I always do – hung my clothes, lined up my shoes, stowed food in the appropriate places. In the middle of the sitting room was a low table with a few magazines fanned out on it with titles like *Scotland Today*. I moved these to a half-filled bookcase, and on the table I placed the package my mother had given me – the package she'd summoned me to collect, via a message on my answer-phone that I'd found waiting for me when I reeled in, drunk and exhilarated, after that first evening with Sebastian. 'Darling' – my mother's voice had filled the flat, unusually high and resonant – 'could you ring me back, as soon as you can? I've made a decision, and it's rather important.'

I rang her the next morning, once I'd shaken off the tatters of the night. I'd slept, as one might have expected, badly. At dawn I woke for good, jolted out of sleep by a dream in which I was lying in a hospital bed being given an ultrasound scan and there, looming out of the dark swirling vapours inside me, was Sebastian's face.

My mother and I hadn't spoken of Sebastian since that day in June when she'd laid out the contents of my father's desk like a minefield through which I had to pick my way. I'd retreated to London with a briefcase full of photographs and school reports and she'd never said another word about him. She must have wondered. She must have wanted to know, quite badly, whether I was taking steps to find my unknown brother. But I never thought about it, because I've never been in the habit of bearing my mother's feelings in mind. That's not a good thing, it's just a fact. So when I rang her that Saturday morning, I should have been surprised to hear that the decision she'd made was something to do with Sebastian, but somehow I wasn't.

For once, I didn't hang fire. I said, 'It sounds as if I ought to come to see you,' and she said, 'That would certainly make things easier.'

My mother was waiting for me in the garden of her new cottage. It was my first visit since she moved in, and I could see why it had attracted her. Everything was small and neat and orderly – no dark corners, nowhere to stow a secret. Very little character, really, and it struck me that she would find that restful. Standing at her garden gate in a floral blouse and brown corduroy skirt with useful pockets, her faded hair short and neatly set, she looked the epitome of middle-class respectability.

'There are two things,' she said, leading me into the breakfast room. 'One to tell you, and one to give you.' She'd laid out a tray for coffee with her usual precision-folded napkins, milk in a jug. I looked about me while the kettle boiled. She'd hung some quiet watercolours, scenes of lakes and not very mountainous mountains. I recognized them from a spare bedroom at Knighton. They were painted in the 1880s by my great-grandmother, Lionel

266

Conway's mother, she'd had a gentle talent for these things.

My mother brought in the coffee pot and sat down. 'Hester,' she said, 'I'll come straight to the point. I've been thinking about your father's money and what you said about it, and I've come to agree with you. It doesn't seem right that we should have it all. There must be reasons why Simeon left his . . . his other child out of his will, but he left no indication of what those reasons were, so I feel we're free to act as we see fit.'

I nodded, impressed.

'If he hoped to spare our feelings by leaving out any mention of his son,' my mother continued, '– and I hardly need remind you that sparing people's feelings wasn't Simeon's forte – but if he did, why leave the evidence untouched? He knew he was growing old, he knew his heart was bad. He mentioned death quite often. If he'd wanted to keep the boy's existence from you, then he should have taken more radical steps.'

'Did he know you knew?'

'He must have done. It was never discussed, but he wasn't a fool. So his will as it stands is the coward's way out. And I want to be brave where Simeon failed.' I dreaded a wobble in her voice, but there was none. 'I want to transfer half the money to Sebastian Oakes, if you agree. Interesting that he was given our surname, not his mother's. Do you know, I don't even know what her surname was? Not that it matters, now. What matters is to trace the boy and set the legal process in motion. And, Hester, I want you to do that for me.'

I could have told her, then, that it was barely twelve hours since I'd been hugged goodnight by my father's son, under a lamp post in Notting Hill, but I didn't. My lifelong habit of reticence was strong. Instead I said, 'Yes, I'll do my best. I don't think it will be too hard to find him.'

My mother seemed relieved, if anything, by the flatness of my response. 'Good,' she said, 'that's decided, then. Let me know how you get on.'

I said that I would.

We drank our coffee in silence. Then to speed things up a little I asked, 'There was something else, too?'

There was a Jiffy bag lying on the table between us. I'd barely taken it in. My mother pushed it across to me. I read the inscription. 'For Verity and Hester. To be opened after my death.'

I said, 'I'd know that handwriting anywhere.'

My mother spoke quickly. 'I don't want it, Hester. It's yours; do what you like with it. I can see it's some kind of diary, but I haven't read it and I don't intend to. If you're still interested in researching Grandma's life, then perhaps it'll be of use to you. But I'd rather you didn't open it in front of me. I just feel as if I want to be rid of all that.'

I was startled, but I didn't argue. I slipped it, un-opened, into my bag. 'Fine. Yes. I do still mean to do some research into Grandma. I just feel that someone's going to some time, and I'd rather it was me. I'm going to take a couple of weeks off work soon, and hide myself away somewhere and just get on with it. Have you got those boxes of letters, by the way? I'd like to have a look at those.'

'They're all at Knighton still, in the attic. Dear Rosie said it was quite all right to leave them there, for you to collect whenever you want. I told you, didn't I, that Rosie suggested we call in for lunch? What do you think?'

The thought of Rosie was like an open window. 'I think that would be a very good idea.'

So we had a salady lunch at Knighton, and with Becky's help I brought some shoeboxes full of old letters down from the attic and stowed them in the boot of my car. We talked about the coming baby; the children all knew about it now, because Rosie and Robin don't keep secrets for long. Rosie said that if it was a girl she'd like to call it Evelyn. Angus pulled a face and said that sounded like a granny's name, and I said, well, yes, that's absolutely right. Rosie said it could be shortened to Eve, or Evie, and Angus said that would be better but it still wouldn't be his first choice. 'What would you choose, then, Ang?' asked Robin, and Angus said firmly, 'Jade.'

'You could call it Evelyn whether it was a boy or a girl,' pointed out Becky, who had *Decline and Fall* on her school reading list. I told her about Evelyn Waugh's first wife also being an Evelyn, and how they had called each other 'He-Evelyn' and 'She-Evelyn'. That led to a conversation about the Bright Young Things, and I thought, for by no means the first time, how lucky I was to have such an intelligent and interested goddaughter. I looked at Rosie, at her small, stubby, capable hands serving food and wiping up spillages and reaching out to pat whichever human or animal came within her orbit; and I thought, yes, hers is the baby that should be born. And suddenly I thought, Guy. Oh shit. Guy. When I got into the car to drive back to London, Rosie came up close and murmured, 'Guy?' and I said, 'No. Absolutely not.'

They all stood at the door, waving me off, but as soon as I came to the first lay-by I pulled in and reached for my mobile. As I scrolled down for Guy's number I had a sudden sharp vision of him sprawled naked across a hotel bed with a half-smile of anticipation, and I shuddered.

His answering voice was gruff, early-morning-ish, although it was late afternoon. 'Guy? It's Hester. I'm really sorry, but –'

'Don't tell me,' he said, 'you've got a headache. I've heard that so many times before.'

'Yes,' I said, 'yes, I have got a headache. And it isn't one that's going to go away.'

There would be repercussions, I knew, but not for long. His campaign to woo me back had already lasted longer than most of his enterprises; he'd soon be diverted on to something else. The unfairness couldn't be helped; at least I was saving him from a greater unfairness. I'd had a plan. I'd booked a room in an outrageously priced London hotel so that I could have sex with my ex-husband in an attempt to impregnate myself. I had planned to create a child with a man I didn't love, didn't even respect, simply because a child was the one thing I didn't have, and you couldn't just buy one in a shop. Yesterday this plan had made perfect sense to me; today it made me giddy with shame.

That was all about a month ago. I still haven't told any of them about Sebastian, but I will. I want it all to be sorted, all the stuff about the money, and it very nearly is. This fortnight in Scotland is some kind of turning point. When I return, everything will be made clear.

I've told Sebastian about the money, but only recently. I wanted to get to know him first, and for him to get to know me. I wanted to be sure that there was some foundation for our – friendship? Kinship? I don't know what to call it – that wasn't overshadowed by money. Sitting here staring at the fire, I realize that it's been years since I truly wanted anybody to get to know me. We've spent a fair bit of time together in the last few weeks, sometimes with Dylan, sometimes without. Dylan's blond, crop-headed, tanned arms bulging out of a white T-shirt, with a wide Australian smile that's almost as white. He and I went to see Sebastian in the play again, and Sebastian and I have had meals in and meals out and walks in the park. I don't know whether it feels as if I've truly got a brother, because I don't suppose I've any way of knowing what that feels like, but I do know that this feels – exhilarating. Set apart from anything else I've ever felt. Pure, almost. Free.

Sebastian gave me the use of this cottage before I told him about the money. He gave me a set of keys, and told me they were mine to keep. He said he was hoping not to have to let it again, just lend it to friends – 'Friends – and family,' he said smiling. He said he wanted to make more use of it himself; he'd like to spend time there with Dylan, make their mark on it, make it feel personal. This was the plan, but he wasn't sure he could manage it without the rental income. And that's when I stepped in and told him about the money. It took a while to sink in. We talked about it a lot, and we've got more talking to do. I still don't think I've quite persuaded him that we're both in earnest, my mother and I. He said, 'I think I ought to meet your mother,' and I agreed that would be the right thing to do, but not quite yet.

So here I am, alone in the cottage with the words that Grandma Evelyn left behind her. I'm sitting on the sofa with her diary on the table in front of me. My surroundings don't give much away. The furnishings are simple and functional, displaying neither taste nor the lack of it. Carpets and curtains are the texture and colour of oatmeal, the walls a uniform cream. The framed black-and-white photographs of rock formations I attribute to Sebastian or Dylan, or both. As far as I can see, there's nothing to conjure up Simeon-and-Paulina. At Knighton, even now that the Wilkinsons have overrun the place, and the front hall is filled with bicycles and wellington boots are strewn round the back door like the stumps of a fossilized forest — even now, one would only have to scratch the surface to uncover evidence of my parents' marriage. In spite of my mother's startling decision to throw so much away, her union with my father has, if you like, a solid historical framework. It happened. There are witnesses. But my father and Paulina — it all melts away. The ripples spread and vanish.

Grandma Evelyn — she's still to be found at Knighton, too, even though she removed herself thirty years ago. And she left all these words for me to sift through, so she clearly didn't seek her own erasure. I want to write her life — I don't need to, but I do want to. I thought I needed a baby, but curiously enough I find I don't. Somehow, I've managed to liberate myself from thinking about my life in terms of need.

I didn't sleep much last night — my first in the cottage. I'd meant to start reading Grandma's diary, but in the end I let it wait. I gazed into the fire until it had died right down, and then I lay in bed, thinking, examining the quality of this new aloneness, listening to the rattle of the wind and the distant thud of the sea. And after a while I could no longer deny to myself that there was another sound, a sound that was neither wind nor sea. An irregular, sniffling, scratching sound, much closer to the house; a living, breathing sound.

My heart did a thump, I have to admit, and my limbs felt heavy and weak — why is this paralysis a useful response to fear? I've never understood that. But I've always thought I'd rather face an assailant on my own two feet than be stabbed or strangled in my bed. So I persuaded my shaking body that it had to get up. I pulled a sweater on over my pyjamas, crept into the kitchen for a bread knife, and drew back the blind, just a little.

I didn't need a torch; a white three-quarters moon had

bounced clear of the clouds. I heard a scalp-prickling squeal, and then my eyes made out the two lithe, dark shapes squabbling over something in the courtyard. Weasels or stoats, or even pine-martens – I'm no expert on those narrow snaky mammals, but I could see what they were fighting over. I recognized the paper wrapping of the kipper I'd bought for myself when I stopped for lunch at Loch Fyne on the way down. It must have been one of the things that fell out of my carrier bag when I was busy with the seal. It had looked like a particularly magnificent kipper, tarnished gold, like an Etruscan artefact. I'd been looking forward to grilling it for my breakfast, with tomatoes.

I laughed out loud. I watched the tussle for a while, but when I twitched the blind to get a better view, the creatures looked up, listened, and undulated away into the darkness.

When I woke, the wind had dropped, the day was still and grey, almost warm. A good day for getting on with reading, for reacquainting myself with my grandmother. After breakfast – toast and grapefruit, and I regretted the loss of the kipper – I went outside to clear away the scraps of fishy paper the weasels had left behind.

There was hardly a garden at all – no need of one, with the shore and the hills stretching away for ever, and no one to tend to it, in any case. There was the stone wall, and a paved area for an outside table and chairs, and a curved stone seat set into an inlet in the wall that I hadn't noticed the night before. The seat was positioned to face west; one could sit and watch the sunset. I went in to fetch some coffee and my grandmother's diary, and took them out with me to that seat. What better way to spend a morning?

Then I noticed that the seat had a back. It was a single, large, smooth stone, grey with white speckles like a seal, and it was heart-shaped. It looked as if it had already been that shape, and a stonemason had worked on it to make it more so. There were initials chiselled into it, expertly, in a faintly Gaelic script. S.O. and P.O. And a date.

Had Paulina taken my father's name, then, or had her own surname, coincidentally, also begun with an O? I would remember to ask Sebastian, but there was no hurry. I leaned my back against the heart-shaped stone and drew my grand-mother's diary out of its bag. The past stretched behind me, the future before me, and both were as wide as the horizon.